A TWIST OF FAE

THE SECOND BOOK IN THE FINDING FAE TRILOGY

Also by
EL HOLLY

Finding Fae
Fate of the Fae

PHANTASMIC WARS
The Book of Imagination
The Quest for the Artifacts
The Waking of the Nightmares
The Hunt for the Five
The Return to Phantasmagoria

Praise for *Finding Fae*

"YA fantasy fans will be delighted by this coming-of-age story about identity, friendship, and love. Un-put-downable."
~The Prairies Book Review

"A page turner- once I started I didn't want to set it down."
~Amazon Review

"Despite the light tone of the prose, the novel deals with weighty topics, including identity issues, questions of adoption and identity, self-doubt, determination, courage, and perseverance…Sure to please fans of the YA fantasy genre."
~BookView Review

Praise for *A Twist of Fae*

"Themes of adoption, adventure, courage, and magic are expertly developed in this book. There is an addictive simplicity in prose that augments the beauty of the narrative and Eevee's voice…You'll find it irresistible."
~Christina Prescott, The Book Commentary

"A deft blend of a coming-of-age tale and fairy-tale quest."
~The Prairies Book Review

"The engrossing narrative is full of shocking revelations and unexpected twists as all the disparate plot threads come together, creating a highly engrossing story…"
~BookView Review

EL HOLLY

A Twist of Fae
Book Two in the Finding Fae Trilogy
By El Holly

Contents

Visions from a Cantankerous Cat

6 Days Until the Winter Solstice

I'm adopted. And as far as adoptions go, I lucked out. My mom and dad are pretty great, even if they tend toward the stereotypical Midwestern parent vibe most days.

They don't talk about the fact that their oldest adopted daughter is fae, though. (Not for lack of trying to broach the topic since I told them the first time, I might add.)

Honestly, I'm still trying to understand what being fae means for me, for who I am.

Who am I? Evelyn Gray Acker. Eevee. E.

A fae raised by humans.

For seventeen years I'd lived with humans, believing I was one. Yes, my hearing was abnormally acute, but I never thought I was too out-of-the-ordinary. I had a few friends, did okay in school, and could hear whispers from a couple rooms away. No big deal.

I grin ruefully down at my red, soapy hands, which are immersed in the sink. Now I'm an eighteen-year-old fae with fists that can burst into flames (unreliably) and an ability to sense animals, who works at a diner just outside Duluth, Minnesota while attending the local high school. It sounds like something out of a sitcom.

The dishwater is tepid to the touch, but at least it's warmer than the weather outside today. An almost uncontrollable urge grips me to leave these stacks of dishes. Step outside in the snow and take my next step in the fae realm, somewhere in the Seelie territory where it's always summer.

But thoughts of the Seelie territory in the fae realm bring up memories I'd rather not relive. Terror grips me, freezing me in place in front of the dishwasher in Gramp's Diner, solidly in the human realm. My breathing quickens and I count by twos in my head, trying to dispel the images of that night–Homecoming night.

Since that night, I've avoided going anywhere in the Seelie territory, and instead spend most of my time in Elfaeme in one place, which is as cold and frozen as it is in Minnesota today.

A server drops off another pile of dishes and bustles away, looking exhausted. When I clocked in earlier today, punching my time card beneath the employee clock decorated with twinkling Christmas lights and shiny green tinsel, I was immediately swamped with piles of dishes and cutlery needing to be sent through the machine or scrubbed by hand. Though I've been at it a few hours now and the brunch rush is over, the dishes aren't. A little snow isn't enough to keep Minnesotans from their Saturday plans.

Back here in the kitchen, the chattering of the guests is drowned out by the 80s music pumping through the speakers. I pull my cell phone out of my back pocket with soapy, gloved hands. Checking to make sure Mike, the head chef, isn't paying attention to me, I scrub my palm on my jeans to rid it of some of the soap scum and swipe up. My phone glows. The background picture is of me and my best friends, Cam and Maggie, at our usual table at the Java Jive. It's my new favorite picture of us, taken just last week, when we couldn't do one more minute of homework. My stomach clenches uncomfortably when I see the picture, though, as much as I love it. Pictures can't capture all the secrets I've been keeping from my best friends lately.

With my light brown hair still short since I chopped it in August, it's been hard to hide the fact that as the winter solstice nears, my ears have been growing into little points at the top. In the picture, my ears are mostly hidden. I made sure of that, deleting any that showed the pointy tips peeking out of my hair.

The ears are new, at least in this realm. They've always been pointed in the fae realm, which I've only started visiting in the last few months, since that's about as long as I've known I'm fae and not human. Recently, though, the points have become permanent, part of who I am in both realms. I raise the hand not holding the phone and rub a finger on the tip of my left ear. At least they're easier to hide than my wings would be, even with short hair.

In the picture, Cam sits between me and Maggie, their hair short-cropped on the left and chin-length on the right. Their longer hair is dyed an electric blue, which brings out the blue of their eyes. Maggie's laughing, her head tilted forward into her hand, showing the bright pink barrettes dotting her Afro.

As much as I love the picture, it's not why I opened my phone. I check my messages. Nothing. Quince was going to try and message me today, since the winter solstice is officially less than a week away and we are in major planning mode, but he didn't make any promises. If my heart could sink any lower it would, but it's taken up permanent residence in my stomach for a while now. Ever since–

"Better put that away before the boss sees you," Mike says over my shoulder. He's holding a steaming plate of hash browns and scrambled eggs. His expression is stern. The weekend brunch rush makes him cranky, and not even Cyndi Lauper belting through the kitchen speakers puts a smile on his face today.

"You know Harriet's been on a 'no phones on the clock' kick," he adds, setting the plate on the warming table and bustling back to the grill to flip some sausage patties.

I no sooner slide my phone into my pocket when Harriet herself pokes her head into the kitchen. "Big group just arrived, 80th birthday party. Eevee, can you stay a little longer?"

I shrug. "Sure." Why not? It's not like I can see Quince "maybe-would-be-my-boyfriend-if-he-could-live-in-the-same-realm-as-me" Florentz, since he's somewhere in the fae realm with his parents, thus out of cell phone range until we can meet again. Though I had hoped maybe he'd be able to sneak away for a bit.

Besides, my friends, Cam and Maggie, are both busy today; Cam is at home completing an art project, and Maggie's working a double shift at the Java Jive.

Back at my house, my little brothers, Greg and Charlie, are no doubt in the living room jumping on the couch cushions (their current favorite Saturday activity), and Amelia hasn't been home much now that she and Trent are "official." Watching a movie with my other little sister, Jess, would be fun, but Jess is at a friend's house for the weekend, so I'd otherwise spend my afternoon alone in my room, avoiding my homework, and bugging Cam via text while they draw. Might as well make some extra money.

"Thanks," Harriet says, brushing back her frizzy bangs. She flashes me a grateful grin. "I know you probably have better things to do on a Saturday."

I plunge my hands into the warm water, grabbing a coffee cup with a lipstick-stained rim. If only my social life were as exciting as Harriet assumes it is.

The next hour and a half flies by, thanks to the copious amounts of dishes the servers keep bringing me. At the same moment I set the last warm plate on the clean dishes rack, a sensation of urgency grips my brain so hard I stumble, knocking the tower of plates with enough force it sways dangerously, like a miniature Leaning Tower of Piza.

Mike shakes his head at me as I stabilize the stack with trembling hands.

I recognize the presence in my mind, though it's been over a month since I'd felt it. With the temperatures dropping and snow covering the ground, I'd given up Scamp, the cat who haunts the alleys around Gramp's Diner, as a lost cause.

Yanking on my winter coat, I rush out the back door, then run back in to grab my purse and clock out. On my way past the dishwasher, I scoop some leftover eggs and sausage from a dirty plate into a napkin.

Exiting the kitchen a second time, I look around the alleyway, my breath puffing up in clouds in front of my face.

"Scamp?" I whisper. I hold out the sausage and eggs. "Here, kitty, kitty!"

His proud disdain is a palpable presence in my mind, but I can't see him.

"'Thou crusty batch of nature,'" I grumble. In *Troilus and Cressida,* this phrase may have been used in a joking context, but I'm only half-joking now. I've been worried sick about Scamp, and now he shows up out of nowhere and has the gall to act all high and mighty.

My phone dings, so I set the food on the ground. It's a message from my little sister, Amelia.

A: *omg i NEED a gramps muffin. banana nut. plz???!!!*

Her message is followed by about fifty hearts and heart-eye emojis.

I text her that I can grab it, slip my phone into my purse, and turn around to head back in. The next second, my palms slam into the icy cold ground, Scamp's scruffy body tangled around my feet.

"Scamp, what the heck?" I complain as he yowls at me. His presence in my mind is full of righteous indignation, as if I should be ashamed of myself for tripping over him when he was winding himself around my feet.

Then the cantankerous cat does something I don't expect. As I push myself up off the snowy ground, he bumps his one-eared head against my bare hand, like he's trying to nuzzle me.

I can't help but laugh. "Scamp, this isn't like you! I missed you too, buddy. It's—"

I pull my hand back, but not before the vision hits me.

A meadow floods my vision, full of long grasses, and flowers of all colors dancing in a balmy breeze. Laughter tickles my ears, from many voices.

Then, a hush. A woman singing, her voice sweet and ageless, full of longing.

> "Come to the meadow,
> pick a flower or two.
> Save one for me
> and the other for you.
>
> Dance in the meadow
> 'til your feet soak with dew,
> then look for the fairies.
> We'll be looking for you."

Scamp blinks his bright green eyes up at me, all innocence, as I eye him suspiciously.

"You're not just a cat, are you?" I ask.

In response, he picks the bite of sausage up off the napkin, leaving the egg, and zooms away, his skinny, dusty-colored body disappearing around the corner of the building.

The vision he'd given me is seared in my memory, the words of the song playing on repeat in my head. I crouch in the snow, trying to make sense of it.

I need to talk to Quince, or Cam, or Maggie about what just happened. Talking to Quince is out of the question until we can meet up again, so I send Cam and Maggie a quick text.

E: *saw Scamp just now. something weird happened. txt me ASAP!*

Hopefully they get back to me soon. My phone buzzes as I'm about to put it away, and for a moment I think maybe I've caught Maggie on break, but it's another message from Amelia: *Trent is bringing me home right now. can't wait 4 my muffin!* <3

My mind is a swirling mess, but I re-enter Gramp's, dusting the snow off my jacket, and buy Amelia her banana nut muffin, plus a double chocolate chip one for me.

By the time I sit down in the car, my muffin is gone, but the vision remains.

My skin prickles with goosebumps.

Whatever that song might mean, whoever sang it, one thing is clear: someone in Elfaeme wants to meet me.

Fae Magic

Amelia's doelike eyes light up when I deposit the muffin bag in her lap.

"Thanks, Eevee! You're the best!"

With one hand, she digs in the bag and pulls out the muffin, her eyes on her phone's screen as she finishes up a text (most likely to "shoulders guy," aka Trent, though there's a strong possibility she's messaging her friend Phoebe, too).

Text complete, she sets down her phone, and devotes all her attention to the muffin. "I've been craving a Gramps muffin so bad, you have NO idea." She tears the top off the muffin and tosses the bottom back in the bag.

I've long given up trying to convince Amelia to eat any other part of the muffin aside from its top. But I still frown at her.

"Your guilt trip won't work on me," she says through a mouthful of banana nut. "If you think it's such a waste, why don't you eat it?"

I grimace. "You know I don't think nuts should be in muffins. Or any baked goods."

She shrugs. "See if Greg or Charlie want it then."

It doesn't take long to find them. The living room is an absolute disaster, pillows and couch cushions acting as safe islands across the lava floor.

"Don't step there!" Charlie, my youngest brother, warns me. His sandy blonde hair sticks up on the back of his head.

"The floor is lava," Greg informs me gravely. "You'll burn your feet."

I jump from pillow to couch cushion until I reach the coffee table, thinking how fun it would be if I could use my fairy wings. But in the human realm, I look human (enough, minus my ears), and my wings are nowhere to be found as I perch precariously on a square throw pillow. Besides, none of my siblings know I'm a fairy. I would love to tell them; dad always says how we're the Ackers and "we'll stick together through it all," but if I'm being honest, I'm afraid. Not of what my siblings will think of me being fae. I'd earn automatic cool points if my little brothers knew I once punched an ice troll with fists of fire.

No, I'm afraid of them knowing too much and drawing the attention of Nightglade, the Unseelie King.

"Here," I say, depositing the bottom half of the banana nut muffin onto the table. "First one to the muffin gets the bigger half." I split it and grin, then hop away as they let out bloodcurdling yells and jump from their safe zones toward the coffee table, making sure to avoid the floor lest they get burned by lava.

"Eevee, honey, is that you?" mom asks. Her voice is muffled, distracted. I wander downstairs to the basement and find her sitting at the desk in her home office. Her round, cheerful face creases with concentration as she frowns at the screen.

"It's Saturday, mom," I point out. "You said you wanted to be better about leaving work at work, remember?"

I'm not sure she's heard me. Her eyes have gone unfocused as she gazes at her computer.

"Mom?"

"Sorry." She blinks and looks at me, her face drawn and tired. The dark smudges under her eyes and the messier-than-usual bun on her head saying more than she ever will to me about how well she's been sleeping lately. About as well as me, I think.

My stomach tightens with guilt. When Quince was unconscious in my yard, I thought telling my parents the truth about me being fae was the right decision.

But ever since, it's been this awkward, unspoken tension between us, a rift I don't know how to bridge. They don't bring it up, and when I bring it up they don't say anything, so instead it sits there, the elephant-sized fae truth in the room.

"What did you want to talk about, Eevee?" she asks, leaning back in her ergonomic office chair and yawning.

I hesitate, concerned. "You're the one who called me in here?"

"Oh, right." She rubs her temples, chuckling at herself. "It's absolutely nuts at work right now. We're on a deadline to get our reports in, with the new year coming up in a few weeks, and..."

The vision from Scamp still dances at the edge of my consciousness, beckoning me as she talks. I don't mean to zone out, but I do, and it's only when she's staring at me that I've realized she's asked me a question.

"Sorry, what?"

She sighs and my cheeks flush with embarrassment. I don't mean to zone out when people talk, it just happens. A lot (thanks, ADHD).

"I was asking about your friend, Quince. How is his arm doing? And does he have any winter break plans?"

"He probably has plans," I answer quickly.

"Ah, too bad." Her voice is vague, her pale eyes flicking toward her computer screen, which just dinged with a new email. "And his arm? I've been worried about him since…" She trails off. The confessions I'd made that night about my other life, my fae life, hang between us, and I long to break this wall and talk about it, actually have a conversation about it, but I don't know how. Any time I hint at it, my hints are thoroughly ignored. And it's been months now. The longer we go without saying anything about me being fae, the harder it is to bring it up.

Instead, I say, "His arm is better. He got his cast off and has a sling to use if he needs it."

"That's nice," she murmurs, scanning the email she'd just opened.

"Mom," I say, steeling myself and placing my hands on her desk. She stops reading and looks up at me, her kind face with its round cheeks and faint worry lines tense with annoyance and concern.

"What?"

Come on, Eevee. Just tell her. Tell her you got a vision from the stray cat behind Gramp's Diner. Tell her you think someone in Elfaeme wants to see you. Ask her what she would do if she were you.

Okay, even though she knows I'm fae, I think I might lose her at "vision from a cat."

The words crowd in my mouth. I swallow them down and force a watery smile on my face. "Just, you know, wanted to remind you to stop working so much."

I lean over the desk and give her a quick peck on the cheek, but the tension in my voice has caught her attention.

"There's something else, isn't there?" She crosses her arms across her chest, and I know she's not going to back down until I tell her what's going on.

I lower my voice to a whisper, in case anyone passes by in the hall. "It's–something happened today. I think someone wants to see me in Elfaeme, in the fae realm. I don't know who, or why, but…" I hesitate, then add, "I think it might be connected to my birth parents."

I watch as the worry lines on her face even out. The concern seeps from her features, leaving her eyes blank.

Eerily blank, like two tiny, pale blue slates which have been wiped cleaned.

She blinks, and the weariness returns to her face. "Is that all?" With a shrug, she turns back to her computer screen. "Do you have homework, Eevee? You should get some done before dinner."

I stare at her, at a loss for words. Where is the Penny Acker with the inner mama bear ready to come out swinging if her kids are in trouble? Her calm face and relaxed shoulders are exactly the opposite of how I thought she'd react when I brought up Elfaeme.

Now the hints I'd dropped in front of her and dad, all those hints which went ignored and made me feel like I was talking but someone had hit the mute button, take on a new meaning.

I chew the hangnail on my thumb as I study my mom's unnaturally relaxed features. The question, now, isn't *if* there's some kind of fae magic at work on my parents. No, the question is *whose* magic is making it so my parents treat any mention of me being fae as unimportant and utterly forgettable.

Disturbed, I exit mom's office and run right into Amelia. Her whole body is buzzing with energy, from her curly brown hair down to her pink, fuzzy socks.

"What?" I ask her, an eyebrow raising.

She looks like she's about to ask me something, but then stops herself. She gives me a sly, secretive smile. "Nothing," she says innocently.

"Okay." I shake my head and turn toward the stairs.

"You can trust me, you know," she calls after me.

I swear internally. Did she somehow hear what I'd told mom?

Nerves on edge, I try and play it cool, turning around casually. "What do you mean?"

"I'm your sister. If you ever want to talk, you know where to find me." My suspicion must be obvious, because her smile drops and she adds, "Something's been bugging you for, like, months now."

I open my mouth to deny it, but I can't. I might have come into my full fae powers when I turned eighteen in September, but I'm also bound by the rules that govern the fae, including the big one: fae can't lie.

"Just...you can talk to me, Eevee. If you want," she adds in the silence. Her cheeks redden, and she adds, "You know, now that I have a boyfriend, too, I might be able to help."

Warmth and guilt fill my chest. Amelia is so

sweet, always looking out for others. Her friend Phoebe calls her the mom of their group, for good reason. And lately, in the last few months, I've been avoiding Amelia, even sometimes pretending to sleep when she knocks at my door late at night.

"Thanks, Ames," I say, and I mean it. "I appreciate it."

I wish my problems were boy-related.

I feel my phone buzz in my pocket. Taking the stairs two at a time, I pull my phone out to see a chain of messages from Maggie.

M: *sup, E?*

M: *?*

M: *???*

M: *dont leave me hangin!*

r u done w/ work? I text her, meandering to the kitchen to grab a snack. Smells of the butternut squash lasagna dad's making for dinner make my mouth water. Ever since I told my parents I couldn't stomach meat anymore, my dad has spent hours online finding vegetarian recipes for me, for which I'm grateful. Quince told me not all fae are vegetarian by nature. His father isn't. But my taste buds and stomach are in agreement: meat is not for me anymore.

The apple I bite into is tart and juicy. I grab a paper towel to wipe my chin and crunch into it as I climb the stairs to my room, closing the door. Maggie's already sent follow-up messages.

M: *just finished up. y?*
M: *is it something 2 do w/ …?*

yeah, I text. Three dots pop up on my screen and a text from Cam appears.

C: *whats going on with Scamp?*

You have no idea, Cam.

E: *hang out 2nite?*
M: *i volunteer Cam's place*
C: *u do huh?*

A smile creeps across my face despite the knots in my stomach. No matter what life has thrown at me—including, but not limited to, finding out my birth parents were fae—I've always been able to count on Cam and Maggie to be there for me and cheer me up, even if they don't always see eye-to-eye with me.

My smile fades. I wonder what they'd think if they knew what I've been doing every Sunday night since Homecoming...I shake my head. No. I can't let myself think like that. I'm doing what I need to do.

Instead, I check my unread messages.

C: *i mean its fine*
M: *yay!*
C: *but my room is messy*

M: *have u seen my room? no judgment here*
M: *besides, u got a couple hours, i gotta finish up next week's
episode of the NSN podcast*
M: *7:30 work 4 u guys?*

works 4 me, I type.

C: *i have 2 wait until then for Scamp news??*
E: *u will survive*
M: *u can distract urself by cleaning… ;)*
C: *…*

Setting my phone down, I lay on my bed and close my eyes, the song from my vision playing on repeat in my head.

Always There For Me, Huh?

"You're kidding. You're not kidding. Oh. Em. Gee. Eevee! You seriously got a vision from a *cat*?!"

"Again, Scamp has proven to be not just 'a cat,'" I say, laughing. "But yeah."

Maggie shakes her head, her hair styled in two puffballs on her head, each tied with a pink ribbon. "Your life is so much more interesting than mine."

"You got free coffee today," I point out.

"I always get free coffee when I work."

"Well, I'd love free coffee," I grumble.

"You know I can't be lettin' all my friends get coffee for free! I want to keep this job."

"And the new crush on your coworker Jeff has

nothing to do with your renewed interest in being a barista?" Cam teases, a twinkle in their eyes. Their smile is thin, tentative, and Maggie forces out a laugh.

"Yeah. Nothing at all."

Cam flushes and looks down at their phone. I wonder if Jim has messaged them? Maggie took her breakup with Jim pretty well, but I know it's hurt her, seeing Jim and Cam spending time together recently. Duluth High's theater department is entering the One Act Play Festival, and Cam decided to be on the crew for set design. Jim, as usual, is doing the light design, and they've formed a theater bond, a quick friendship forged from a mutual love of their art. I'm happy for Cam, though. The way they light up when they talk about the meanings behind the colors they are using in different backdrops is fun to see, and it's getting me excited to see the show.

Maggie's less enthusiastic. She's not one to be jealous or hold a grudge, and she's admitted to me she thinks Jim and Cam would make a cute couple if either of them would ever make it official, but there's an edge to her happiness for them and their shared theater interest, a veneer of bitterness.

Maggie looks at me. "Free coffee versus mysterious visions...it's no comparison, E. Your life is a thousand times more interesting than mine."

There's no jealousy in her statement, just amusement.

"Believe me," I say, closing my eyes and relaxing onto the large Snorlax pillow on Cam's bed, "I wish my life weren't so interesting sometimes."

"No you don't." Cam's voice is unassuming, but I feel defensive anyway.

"Fae can't lie," I remind them, opening my eyes and sitting up.

They shrug, set their phone down, and look up at me. "So would you rather your birth parents were human?"

Would I? It would make things so much easier.

For example, I wouldn't be styling my hair every morning to hide my pointed ears from my family and friends and classmates.

My birth mother wouldn't have felt it necessary to create elusive clues for me to follow just to find her.

And I wouldn't have the King of the Unseelie Court interested in me, thinking I'm his daughter. Though, his tactics at bonding with me lately have been cryptic and insincere, since he's currently holding my birth parents hostage. Maybe he'd be cryptic and insincere regardless?

If my birth parents were human I'd still be living in ignorant bliss, believing the human realm to be the only realm.

As much as I want to say, "Yes, I wish my birth parents were human," the words dry up and crumble into acrid powder in my mouth.

Because if they had been human, I wouldn't know about the fae realm, which exists side by side with the human realm, accessible only by fae folk or the occasional human who happens to be in the right place at the right time.

I wouldn't have wings or fists which could burst into flames or the ability to blend into my surroundings.

I wouldn't have gotten to know Quince or his cousins Sean and Shannon, and I wouldn't be able to sense animal emotions.

I'd be, well, ordinary.

And there's nothing wrong with being ordinary. But I have to admit, I do love being fae.

"That's what I thought," Cam says when I don't answer. They pick up their sketch pad and concentrate on their drawing of a moonlit scene.

Silence settles around us until Maggie's gum pops loudly, making me jump. My fae hearing is sharp, and the pop of gum is like a gunshot, startling me out of my thoughts of flower-filled fields sparkling with dew.

We talk about the vision some more, our conversation going in circles.

"You sure you didn't recognize the voice?" Maggie asks.

I shake my head. "It's definitely female. Other than that, I don't recognize it."

Maggie doesn't ask if it's Maeve singing. We both know it can't be, not after what I'd found on Homecoming night.

"Okay, hold on. Before you go off and do something rash, think about it, Eevee. Almost every time you've gone to the fae realm, you've run into danger..." Cam trails off, their gaze falling to my right arm. Beneath my oversized blue sweater, there's a long, jagged scar which runs the length of my forearm. The fingers on my left hand trace up and down the part of the scar just above my wrist. The scar was from a wild fae I'd met in the woods near a circle of moonstones. That fae's glowing eyes and sharp talon fingers still make me jerk awake at night, drenched in cold sweat.

I definitely don't want to end up with any matching scars, or worse.

"It's not dangerous every time. When Quince and I visited on Homecoming night-" I start to say. It's an old argument between us, though, and Cam cuts me off.

"You guys were lucky the only fae you ran into was Folsom, who's too weak or too cowardly to do anything to you. Do you really want to go back to the fae realm and test your luck, when Nightglade's left you alone this whole time?"

I don't answer, because it's not entirely true. Sure, he hasn't done anything directly to me. But he has my birth parents, and he knows I know that.

"She has to go!" Maggie rushes to my defense without a second thought. She answers a text on her phone, then sits next to me on the bed, crossing her long legs beneath her. "What if whoever sent this vision did it because they know what happened to Eevee's birth parents?"

I wince. I know what's happened to them, but I've been keeping that information from Maggie and Cam, too. Quince and I promised, after some convincing arguments from Sean and Shannon, not to share what we know with anyone, not even Cam and Maggie; we don't want Nightglade thinking they have any knowledge of my fae side, or my fae birth parents. Better to let him think they're my ignorant, human friends.

Given I barely lasted a week before telling them about being fae, these last few months have been exhausting. Keeping secrets is tiring, on top of not getting enough sleep (or enough coffee). Or answers.

In short, I'm at the wanting-to-tear-my-hair-out stage of frustration at the moment.

And, yeah, I'll say it: I told them about the vision tonight because I feel guilty for not sharing all the other stuff about my birth parents with them. Plus, it is nice to talk about my crazy moment with Scamp with people who know I'm fae and don't have some kind of fae magic affecting them, like my parents.

"I'm sorry," Maggie says, seeing the pained expression on my face. "I know it's a sore subject."

I nod, willing to let her think that.

But my silence says something else to Cam, my best friend, my 'friend in invisibility' since second grade. They frown at me, and I try to shove the guilt deep down where they can't see it, but it's no use.

"You know something about them. Something you're not telling us."

"E?" Maggie's eyes narrow in suspicion. "Is that true?"

I want to tell them everything. But the promise

I'd made prevents me from saying anything. My throat burns with all I can't say.

It's for their own good, I remind myself. *The less they know, the better. Besides, you can't say anything. You're bound by the promise you made.*

I still feel like the worst friend ever, though. I don't know how Sean and Shannon can handle keeping as many secrets as they do. Is it as torturous for them as it is for me? Or have the centuries dulled this feeling in them, so their insides no longer rip in two whenever they withhold information from their loved ones?

Then again, I'm not sure who Sean and Shannon consider to be their loved ones. I've never heard them talk about their immediate family in any of my visits with them. They seem to like Quince alright, but I also don't see them having any problem keeping secrets from him.

"You're keeping something from us," Maggie says, her dark eyes narrowing.

This I can answer truthfully, if miserably. "Yes."

Cam chews at the inside of their cheek with worry.

"Are you in trouble?"

I lift my shoulders noncommittally and my heart cracks into pieces at the shuttered expression on their face.

"You've become good at hiding over the last few months." Cam's voice is flat. "I had no idea you've been keeping something from me and Maggie until now. I'm usually always able to tell."

"Cam-"

"It's like you've forgotten who you are since finding out you're fae."

Their words sting, cutting into my already broken heart with barbed wire.

Maggie slides off the bed and reaches a protective arm across Cam's shoulders. "I think you should leave, E."

"But-"

"You obviously don't trust us," Maggie says. Cam's nodding, their eyes downcast. "And what kind of person doesn't trust their friends?"

"She's not a person, she's a fae," Cam mumbles quietly.

I now know what it feels like to have your entire body shatter to pieces yet remain standing.

"I'm doing this to protect you!" I want to shout, but I don't. Saying it would only lead to more questions I can't answer, and I suddenly have no energy. All of it is being spent trying to make it look like I'm not crumbling to dust from the inside out.

"I agree with Maggie, I think you should leave, too," Cam says.

This can't be happening. I look at my two best friends in the whole world, and think that in this moment I'd truthfully be able to say I wish my birth parents weren't fae, if I knew it would lead to secrets kept from my best friends and hurt feelings and rifts I can't fix right now.

"You don't mean that, do you?" I ask, trying to

keep the tears out of my voice. *You don't mean that I should leave, you don't mean that about me not being a person, you don't mean...*

"Go home, Eevee." Cam's tone is final.

In a daze, I pick up my purse and leave their room.

Maggie meets me at the door as I'm sliding on my winter jacket.

"You gotta understand, E," she says in a whisper, looking back to make sure Cam isn't near. "Cam and I, especially Cam, we're used to you telling us everything going on in your life. Even when you first found out you were fae, you broke down and told us almost right away." She pauses, her lips thinning as she presses them together. "You've got a right to privacy, and it's not fair of us to expect you to tell us everything-"

"No, it's not," I agree, my tone harder than I intend it to be. It's as brittle as how my heart feels right now.

"But if you're in danger, we'd want to know what's going on, because we care about you."

A dry laugh escapes me. "Mags, I'm keeping what I know from you and Cam because I care about you guys. I don't want anything to happen to you two. That night, with the tree spirit lady..."

Her normally vibrant face goes ashen. "Not gonna lie, I still have nightmares about that night."

"Same," I admit.

We're silent, staring at each other.

"Promise me you'll take care of yourself?" she asks.

"I'm doing my best."

She hugs me. "I'm sure you have your reasons, and from what you've said, it sounds like they're due to some whack sense of honor, but don't let all of this change you, E. You're great as you are."

Tears threaten to spill out of the corners of my eyes. I'm starting to regret my rushed promise not to tell them anything about saving my birth parents at the Winter Solstice Festival, but maybe I haven't totally ruined things beyond repair. Maybe Cam and I can still be best friends, even though I'm fae.

"I won't." I pause, then pull away. Considering my words carefully, I say, "There's something I need to do. Once it's done...I should be able to tell you guys all about it."

"It's got to do with that meadow and your birth parents," she says.

I meet her gaze, hoping my eyes say what my mouth can't.

"Be careful, E."

"You know I can't promise that," I reply, not meeting her gaze.

She sighs. "I know. And, I'm sorry. You came here to share with us what you could, and instead..."

"Instead Cam just sees what I can't say."

"They'll come around. They just need time."

I nod. I want to tell her how sometimes I feel like I'm going crazy, living this double life as a normal,

Minnesotan teen and the only daughter of the former Unseelie Queen. How talking about it out loud keeps me from totally losing my grip on reality.

She pats my shoulder in the silence. "I gotta get back to Cam. We still love you, E. You two have been friends forever. This'll pass. It always does."

"Yeah." My smile is more of a grimace. Will it? *"She's not a person. She's a fae."* Cam's words run on repeat. Not a person. A fae. Though they said it so quietly I don't even think Maggie could hear it, the contempt in the words was enough to make me question everything.

I clear my throat. "I know. I feel awful not sharing everything, Mags. I hope you guys understand that."

Without waiting for her to answer, I head to my car, more confused than ever about what I should do about the vision from Scamp.

As I pull onto the icy road toward home, the snow-dusted landscape reminds me of another, perpetually snowy land in the fae realm, and an ice-covered mansion with a cozy interior.

We're not supposed to rendezvous until tomorrow night, our last meeting before we infiltrate the Winter Solstice Festival next week, but maybe Sean and Shannon wouldn't mind a visit from me a day early.

Secrets, Secrets Are No Fun

"Eevee," Sean says from the crack in the doorway. His voice is mild, calm even, but the icy blue eye I can see is flinty.

"Is this a bad time?"

"Yes."

Not even a slight hesitation there. Wow. My stomach churns; ever since I left Cam's I've felt off, like the world's spinning faster than usual. Not a lot faster, but enough to make my stomach protest. I hate fighting with Cam. *Not a person. A fae.*

I push those thoughts aside and force a grin on my face. "Okay, sorry to bother you."

"No, it isn't a bad time, not at all!" Shannon's

voice is muffled, yet cheerful. Sean's scowl deepens when Shannon adds, "Come in, come in!"

With reluctance, Sean opens the door just enough to let me inside.

I slip my jacket off, letting out a breath and loosening my shoulders like Quince taught me. I've become quite skilled at making my orange butterfly wings non-corporeal, or "non-corp," in order to take jackets and coats on and off, especially with so many trips to Sean and Shannon's. Their icy fortress—which they affectionately call their winter cottage, though it bears more resemblance to a mansion than any cottage I've seen—is right in the middle of the Unseelie lands in the fae realm, and is surrounded by an everlasting winter wonderland.

It's beautiful, but cold.

As soon as my jacket is on the coat rack, Sean takes my elbow and guides me to the sitting room. His entire body is even more tense than usual, and I wonder if all our preparation for the winter solstice is draining him. By this time next week, maybe he can relax. If all goes according to plan.

We find Shannon already in the sitting room, lounging on a plush red couch with an air of someone who is innocently relaxing.

His chest, rapidly rising and falling, and hastily thrown on robe betray him, though.

I flutter my wings, settling on the arm of the couch closest to him.

Close up, I can see his cheeks are flushed and

his hands are covered in bandages.

He catches me looking and plunges his hands in the pockets of his silk robe, hiding them from view.

The smile on his face widens. "So lovely of you to drop by. It has been…" he cocks his head, the lock of black hair on the left side of his face flopping over his eyes. "Eevee-less, this evening."

I notice he doesn't say uneventful or boring. But I am familiar enough with Sean and Shannon by now to know it's pointless to ask.

From somewhere in their labyrinthine interior I hear what sounds like a keening cry.

"Is there someone else here?" I ask.

Sean, who had been about to sit in the rocking chair next to the fire, freezes.

They exchange a look, Sean's face as stormy as Shannon's is sunny.

"Some*one*?" Shannon finally answers. "Why, no, my dear, there isn't someone else here."

Sean lowers himself into the chair, but his eyes dart between his brother and the direction of the cry we heard.

"So it's just us?" I press.

Neither of them answer, which is a bit worrisome, if I'm to be honest. I don't know what made that pitiful crying sound, but it can't be good if they're trying to hide it.

"Why did you come tonight?" Sean asks shortly, rocking back and forth in the rocking chair so hard the wood squeaks. "We didn't expect to see you until tomorrow."

"Is there news?" Shannon asks, clapping his hands together. He winces and stuffs them back in his pockets, then adds, "It's been so long since we've had any new leads, and there is only so much left for us to do to prepare for our little rescue project next week."

My wings tremble at the mention of the solstice. It's less than a week away, but even if it were a year away, I don't think I'd be ready for it.

"There might be news…" I say, trailing off when the words of the vision come back to me. "I had a weird moment with a cat today and it might mean something?"

They both lean forward, and the squeak of the rocking chair stops.

Having their undivided attention is unnerving. I wish Quince were here to take some of the tension out of the moment. I'll see him for a bit tomorrow, but tonight he's at some event at the Unseelie Court, as he is most days now.

"I promise I'll share it in a minute, but," I gnaw at a hangnail on my thumb. It's not often I'm with Sean and Shannon without Quince. "What have you heard from your contacts at the Unseelie Court?" I ask them. "How's Quince doing? Really?"

Sean resumes rocking in the chair, his thin lips pressed together.

"He's doing as well as can be hoped," Shannon says with a sigh when Sean says nothing. I grind my teeth at the non-answer. "It's never bothered me or

Sean, of course, his mother being from the Seelie Court, but there are many who hold such silly prejudices still, you know."

I do know. It's why, though part of me would like to give up our crazy plans for the Winter Solstice Festival, I don't. Instead, I'm at Sean and Shannon's house, every Sunday night. Preparing.

It's one hundred percent a trap, we know that much. But it's also the best opportunity we have to reach my birth parents.

Because to Quince, they're not just my birth parents. My birth mother, Maeve, is a symbol of hope to him and others like him. If we can save her, we may be able to convince her to overthrow Nightglade's reign and take over the Unseelie Court, ending the rift between the Seelie and Unseelie Courts. The reasons why she left her position as Queen of the Unseelie Court are murky and mostly riddled with rumor, but there's enough to hint that she's sympathetic to the cause of uniting the courts, something which hasn't happened in centuries.

I know next to nothing about my birth mother outside of those rumors, only what little she's shared with me, blood clues left across the fae realm, but I do know Nightglade is not my birth father, even though he thinks he is. The medical records my mom and dad gave me clearly listed my birth father's physical characteristics—blonde hair, green eyes—and Nightglade's gray eyes and dark hair are proof enough.

Nightglade is convinced I'm his daughter,

though, and I hope he continues to think so. It's what is keeping me alive.

We know nothing about my birth father, really. Except that whatever he and my birth mother are saying to Nightglade as his captives is obviously enough to keep Nightglade convinced that he is my father.

My true birth father is a mystery to me, a shadowy shape of a man. I have no idea what kind of fae he is, but from what we learned about the members of the Unseelie Court from Sean and Shannon, we know my birth father was not one of them. It's the main reason Quince hopes that Maeve may be sympathetic to people like his parents, who found love outside their own court.

Really, though, I don't know how anyone could hate Quince after getting to know him, even if his parents are from opposing courts bogged down by centuries-old conflicts. He's full of infectious energy, one of those people who you can't help but go along with whatever crazy adventure they pull you into.

But I've seen firsthand how some fae act toward him when they know of his parents. Our encounter with Folsom, a demoted member of the Unseelie Court, stands out in my mind. Even with months to reflect, I can't figure out Folsom's intentions, and I'm not sure what he meant in his last words to me before he disappeared: "I never told him. Remember that."

His feelings about Quince were pretty clear, though. Anytime I see Quince's enthusiasm dim, every time he talks about his difficulties fitting in at the Unseelie Court, where he and his family are staying full time, I think about the venom in Folsom's voice when he called Quince a "bastard son of an Unseelie traitor."

The rift between the courts is wide and I'm not sure even Maeve can unite them.

But I'm going to rescue her, if it can give Quince even the littlest bit of hope.

"Why have you come, Eevee?" Sean asks. He's lounging in the rocking chair with the grace and energy of a cat ready to pounce at the slightest provocation.

"Yes, you can't mention weird moments with cats and not elaborate," Shannon chides me.

I stop gnawing on my fingernails and mentally push my worry for Quince aside for the time being. Their undivided attention still unnerves me, but I tell them about the vision I'd had only hours before, after touching Scamp outside Gramp's Diner.

In the middle of reciting the song, there's a knock at the door, interrupting me from my storytelling,

"Hide her," Sean hisses to Shannon, taking long strides out of the sitting room.

Before I can react, Shannon pulls me onto the couch and throws a large woolen blanket over my head.

"Stay still," he commands me cheerfully.

I listen to his humming as he exits.

Under the thick blanket, my cheeks flush with the heat. The scratchy wool presses uncomfortably on my wings, which are not used to any kind of pressure on them.

Snatches of conversation drift from the hall toward where I huddle under the blanket in the sitting room.

"—could use your influence at court—"

"—busy, you know how it is—"

"—he's insisted, we have no choice in the matter—"

"—protect him as best we can, Myska, that's all we can promise—"

Myska! My breath catches and I clap my hands over my mouth to stifle the sound of my gasp.

What is Quince's mother doing here, so late at night? Could they be talking about Quince?

I strain to hear more, but they're far enough away, and either Sean or Shannon must have asked Myska to lower her voice, because now I can only catch a word here or there.

I struggle with the impulse to sneak closer to them. If Myska were to see me here, she'd forbid Quince to visit his cousins, and our weekly visits, even with Sean and Shannon as strange chaperones, have been one of the bright spots for me.

Instead, I flatten myself beneath the blanket as much as I can with my wings and hold my breath, then lift a corner of the blanket and press my ear to the small opening.

"—our connections—"

"—are not as secure as you may think!"

Some muffled words I can't hear, then: "—court

has changed! Nightglade...unpredictable–solstice–"

A door closes, followed by silence.

I risk swiveling my head and peeking out of the edge of the blanket.

Sean and Shannon both have worry creases between their eyebrows. By the way they are gesturing at each other in the doorway to the sitting room, I'm guessing they're carrying on their conversation telepathically, a gift they share as twin fae.

Still gesturing with one hand and staring at his brother, Shannon rips the blanket off me.

I let their silent conversation go on a minute longer, then clear my throat.

They turn their identical blue gazes toward me in surprise, as if they had forgotten I was there, watching their silent conversation.

"Not to interrupt, but it's already late, and–"

"You should go," Sean cuts in.

I try not to feel insulted, but given this is the second time I'm being kicked out of someone's house in the same evening, it's hard not to let that get to me.

"Okay," I say in a choked voice, edging toward the door.

"He means to the meadow," Shannon explains, giving Sean a reproving look. "From what you told us, before…" he pauses, then glances at Sean and says, "ah, before we were interrupted, it sounds like that vision could be a message for you."

"From who, though?" I ask.

They both shrug at me, their expressions

impassive.

"Someone who knows who you are," Shannon finally answers. "Who knows?" He flips his hair over his shoulders with both hands. "They may want to help you."

"Or kill me," I say, rubbing the scar on my arm.

"Or that," Sean agrees. "But you won't know until you respond to the message and go to the meadow."

"I don't know the meadow." I frown. "I've never been there before."

"It's a matter of following the vision," Shannon explains, as if this is common sense. Which it may be, for a fae who has lived in Elfaeme for centuries. But as a fae raised by humans who only visits the fae realm sporadically, these aspects of fae magic don't come naturally to me.

"And when you do," Sean adds, "make sure you have enough magic in reserve to return to the human realm quickly. In case it's a trap."

I shift my gaze from Sean, who looks cryptic as ever, his blue eyes cold and closed off, to Shannon, who bounces on his heels, humming a nonsense song to himself.

Fear tangles with excitement in my chest. A part of me knows I was always going to go to the meadow, no matter what anyone advised. I knew it the moment Scamp gave me the vision. But having Sean agree with me that I should go? That gives me hope. He is one of the most cautious fae I know, preferring shadows to sunlight, and his two centuries of living in the fae realm has to mean something.

Then again, the smile he gives me is more unnerving than reassuring, like the gleam of a knife in the dark.

"I'll...I'll follow the vision then, I guess." I check my watch. "Just, not now."

"Well, then," Sean guides me to the door, but I dig in my heels.

"What did Myska want?"

Sean's grip on my arm tightens.

"Whatever do you mean?" Shannon asks lightly. He's no longer bouncing on his heels, but standing unnaturally still. The lock of black hair framing the left side of his face falls in front of his eye, which is cast downward, avoiding my stare.

"She came here to ask you guys a favor," I persist in the uncomfortable silence. Sean's fingers dig into the flesh of my upper arm like icy claws. "I couldn't hear a lot from under the blanket, but that much was obvious. What did she ask you guys to do?"

Finger by finger, Sean releases my arm. When he turns to me, his face is devoid of emotion. "You know we can't tell you that, Eevee."

I want to wipe the mask off his face and reveal the secrets tangled beneath, but I ball my hands into fists instead. Another secret for Sean and Shannon. They collect secrets like some people collect stamps.

Both of them appear wholly undisturbed keeping the secret, too. I guess centuries of secret-keeping really does harden the heart.

"It had something to do with Quince," I say quietly. "I'm not stupid. He's my—I lo—he means a lot to me," I finish, flustered. "I just want to know that he's okay. Ever since he's been forced to stay at the Unseelie Court, he's changed. He's tired all the time, it's like what makes Quince *Quince* is fading."

They don't answer, but Shannon's gaze twitching toward his brother gives it away: I'm on the right track, even if they won't say anything explicitly.

I relax, releasing my fists, then shaking them. I hadn't even noticed they had burst into flames at my sides.

When the last lick of fire on my pinky knuckle dissipates, Sean says, "Well done. I think that's the quickest I've seen you extinguish your fiery fists."

I'm not sure if he means it as a true compliment or not; his tone is as bland as the expression on his face. But I find myself bristling at his words anyway.

"It's not as easy as it looks. I've been trying to do what you guys taught me, but fire is unpredictable!"

"And ice is a slippery thing." Shannon conjures a ball of ice in his hands, which both glow white with magic, illuminating the ice like a crystal ball.

It doesn't take a big stretch of the imagination to picture Shannon wearing a sweeping purple cape with stars, standing on stage and dazzling a crowd with his magic, then meeting one-on-one with well-paying patrons (in a tent matching his cape) to read their futures in his glowing ball of ice.

Think of all the secrets he'd have learned!

For all I know, he has done that, or something like it. There's much about Sean and Shannon's lives I don't know.

Shannon's powers of telepathy don't extend beyond his brother, but I don't like the conspiratorial grin he's giving me, like he can picture the flowing purple robe and crystal ball along with me.

Another keening cry pierces the silence between us, exactly like the one we heard earlier. I frown, looking at the ceiling. It's definitely coming from upstairs. But what is it?

Returning my gaze to Sean and Shannon, I open my mouth to ask them again, but stop when I see Shannon's cheerful veneer slip, revealing the panic in his eyes, but only for an instant.

"Well, it's late," he says, all signs of panic gone, a smile plastered on his face. "Time to turn in for the night." He stretches his long arms above his head, the ice ball disappearing with a fluid flick of his wrists, and yawns.

"Wait." I plant my feet into the dark red carpet which lines the hall in the entryway.

But as much as I will my feet to grow roots, my months of learning how to use magic are nothing next to Sean and Shannon's almost five hundred years (combined), and they're not exactly weak.

Frost sparkles around me as a chilling wind hits my skin, and the force of the gale pushes me out the door as easily as if I were a leaf.

"How do I find the meadow? What does it mean, to follow the vision? How do I do that?" I stick my foot in the doorway, grunting in pain as it's crushed between the heavy wooden door and the ice-crusted frame.

"Here's an idea: ask the cat," Sean says shortly.

Shannon splays his hands out, then flattens them toward the ground beneath my feet. The foot I'd been leaning on slips on the magicked ice and I flail.

While I struggle to remain upright, out of the corner of my eye, I catch sight of my jacket sailing through the air a split second before it hits me in the face. *How graceful*, I think. The front door closes with a thunk and I hear the click of a lock.

I pick up my jacket and rub my throbbing foot, thinking.

I could always realm-hop. All fae have the ability to move between the fae and human realms with no more than a step—and no more side effects than a little disorientation and dizziness.

But realm-hopping comes with a price: a drain on your magic.

I saw this firsthand, less than two months ago, when I left Quince trapped in the fae realm with a group of malicious fae who apparently had nothing better to do than prey on young fae like us. Luckily I still had enough magic to go back and get him. I shudder to think what would've happened if he'd been left there on his own.

Fae magic isn't endless. It's kind of like weight

lifting: the heavier weights you lift, the fewer reps you can do. And realm-hopping is the equivalent of a heavy weight; it takes a lot out of you, which is why rest is so important.

Like I've been getting a lot of that lately.

So, yes, I could travel back home, then return to Elfaeme, appearing right next to the crackling fire in Sean and Shannon's sitting room.

However, not only would popping into another fae's house uninvited be the epitome of bad manners, but then I might be stuck in Elfaeme with two pissed off fae, and no way to get home until I've rested and regained some of my magic.

I'm about to leave the fae realm and return to my bed to grab a couple hours' sleep before, inevitably, either Greg or Charlie (or both of them) wakes me up with a dinosaur roar, when a glimmering on the snowy ground catches my eye. I look up to see a light on in one of the second story windows. Shadows pass in front of it, bustling back and forth.

A little peek at what they're hiding couldn't hurt, right?

I crouch and flap my wings a couple times, feeling the familiar thrill rush through me right before a flight. Flying, by far, is one of the best parts about being fae.

Before I can talk myself out of it, I launch myself into the air and fly up to the second story window, stopping and hovering out of sight just below it.

Flapping my wings to stay aloft, I grip onto the icy sill and peer over it into the room. Like all the windows on their mansion, this one is obstructed by thick icicles, giving the impression of prison bars. Sean or Shannon's shadowy outline darkens the curtain in front of the window, batlike wings extending as if he were going to take off into the air. For a moment, I think the shadowy figure is coming my way, but then the wings retract and it walks out of sight of the window.

I strain my ears to hear anything, but the ice covering the exterior of the mansion muffles their words.

I'm not sure how long I stay here, my fingers slowly losing feeling as the cold seeps into them from the icy sill, my wings flapping just enough to keep me aloft, but I'm finally starting to shiver when I realize their conversation has stopped.

The curtain is yanked to the side, and I squeak, forcing my frozen fingers to let go. In my surprise I forget about my wings, dropping through the air, and, fearing I'm already caught, think wildly of my bed as I plummet toward the ground, bracing for impact.

My body thumps into the lumpy mass of pillows and blankets on my bed at home, and for a few minutes I lay there, letting my heart rate settle and my breathing return to normal.

When I'm able to breathe without gasping, I sit up. The house sleeps around me, dark and dreamy. Outside my window, I can see our neighbor's

Christmas lights twinkling on their bushes and rafters.

I tuck my knees up to my chin. What are Sean and Shannon hiding in that room? And why didn't they want me to see?

Feet Soaked With Dew

5 Days Until the Winter Solstice

It feels weird being at Gramp's Diner without my usual plastic apron on. I wait at the front counter, pretending to decide between caramel apple or pecan pie. (No contest, really. Caramel apple all the way.) I'd told my parents I wanted to check the updated schedule, but then mom made a comment about how it would be nice to have a pie for dessert tonight, so here I am, perusing pies.

I steal a look out the glass front door, trying to see into the shadowy places beneath cars and bushes in the parking lot, searching for any sign of the one-eared, vision-sharing cat—the true reason for my visit. And yes,

I'm going to check the schedule, too, like I said I would, since fae can't lie. I just didn't tell my parents the whole truth about why I wanted to come in today.

"So what'll it be, honey?" asks Laverne, the wife of the late Gramps. Her voice always sounds rough, like she smokes, but anyone who knows Laverne knows she hates cigarettes with a passion. "Awful-smelling addiction sticks," she calls them. Her voice is naturally like that–low and rough. I personally think it's from how much she talks. I've been waiting in line for what seems like forever, and not because the line is long.

"The caramel apple," I say, pointing to it.

"Good choice."

Whatever anyone decides to buy is a "good choice" to Laverne. If you decide to buy nothing, then it's "Ya sure? My baker's the best in the Duluth area, you won't regret it..." followed by a guilt trip two weeks long.

She packages up the pie and hands the box to me.

"Thanks for comin' in, honey," she says as I hand her the money mom gave me for the pie. "Always good to see ya."

"You too," I say. Before she gets distracted by the next person in line, I add, "Hey, Laverne? I'm going to head out through the back so I can check the schedule."

She nods at me with a distracted air, her eyes already on the older couple behind me. "Kay and Bob! Am I happy to see you two! It's been a few weeks…Yes, I know, that weather out there sure makes the roads icy this time of year. Do you want your usual table? No, Bob, I can't allow customers to adjust the volume of the music, you know that…"

I zip away, darting between tables and slipping into the kitchen. Out of obligation, I scan the staff schedule as I walk by it. My schedule doesn't change much, really, so no surprises for this week. Not wanting to get caught up in any conversations, I scurry past Mike, who is dancing while scrambling eggs in a bowl.

He nods to me, apparently not in a chatty mood either, which is a relief. I was not looking forward to explaining why I am running through the kitchens with a pie on my day off.

On my way out, I swing by the pile of dirty dishes and nab a half-eaten sausage off a plate. Steve, the dishwasher today, is another Duluth High kid. All I know about him is he's a junior and plays trumpet in the marching band. We never really cross paths at school.

"Gross, you're not gonna eat that, are you?" he asks, wrinkling his blackhead-covered nose at me.

"Nope, vegetarian," I explain over my shoulder, leaving Steve scratching his head as I exit into the back of Gramp's Diner.

The weather today is warm for mid-December, in the thirties, but it feels cold after the heat of the kitchen.

Come on, Scamp. I hold out the sausage like an offering. "Here, kitty, kitty!" I call, turning this way and that, looking for any sign of the feline.

What if he doesn't appear? And I'm just standing here in the snow holding a partially masticated sausage in one hand and a box of pie in the other? The image is ridiculous, even to me.

Ask the cat, I think in disgust. What am I thinking, following Sean and Shannon's advice? I don't even know what it means to "follow the vision."

I could be at home right now, snuggled under the blankets in my bed, drifting back to sleep after Greg's incredibly loud T-Rex roar this morning, and instead I'm freezing, holding half-eaten food, and hoping a cat shows up with more magical visions.

I drop the sausage on the ground near the dumpster where I've seen Scamp appear from many times before. Hopefully he finds it before something else does.

Turning toward the parking lot, I pause. Did I hear something over the sound of my boots crunching in the snow?

There it is again! A familiar "Meow?"

Whirling around, I scan the shadows–there! Behind the dumpster, his two green eyes gleam at me.

Ask the cat. Follow the vision.

Picking up the sausage I'd discarded, I hold it out to him. "Hey, Scamp," I say coaxingly, waving the sausage back and forth. His eyes follow it hungrily. "Look what I've got for you!"

He pads out from behind the dumpster and meows again. His presence in my mind has always been clearer than other animals, like a video in better focus. I feel his question in my head. Not with words, I can't understand animals like that. But he's full of confusion, and accusation.

I take a deep breath. Ask the cat. "So, Scamp…" I check to make sure no one else is behind the diner with us.

Seeing nothing except a few squirrels–I always feel them as a chattering, hungry presence, easy to ignore–I step closer to Scamp. His body stiffens, the dusty-colored hairs on his back standing up, so I stop.

"It's okay," I whisper. I break the sausage link into four bite-sized pieces and scatter them on the ground in front of me.

His eyes gleam and his wariness dissipates. He pounces on the sausage pieces, and as he gobbles them up, I ask him quietly, "Where was that meadow you showed me, Scamp?"

He swallows his last bite and sits on his haunches, licking his lips with a contented air. If he's hiding something, he's doing it well. Or maybe he's a normal cat and yesterday was a fluke.

All the extra sleep I could be getting right now taunts me. *You could be sleeping, Eevee, but instead you're hanging out by the dumpster behind your work, in winter, on your day off. With a stray cat.*

And then I feel it–Scamp's presence in my mind sharpens, his eyes intent on my face.

I try again. Because I'm here, and I already look crazy talking to a cat.

"The meadow from the vision, Scamp," I say, staring into his green eyes. "I don't know where it is. Can you show me?"

He cocks his head as if listening to something far-off, then dashes toward me.

I can't sense any real thoughts, but his feelings in my mind are filled with a desire for back scratches.

But Scamp hardly ever lets me pet him, and when he does, it's with an air of heroic suffering.

He stops at my feet and meows.

"You want me to touch you again, like when you showed me the vision."

I don't know why, but I scramble backward, away from his scrawny body.

Usually he gets skittish and runs at any kind of spastic movement, but now he's striding toward me, unperturbed.

This is what I wanted, I remind myself. Ask the cat. Well, I asked him, and now…

I reach out a hand, petting the coarse fur on his back.

At first, nothing happens.

No sensations, aside from Scamp's back vibrating as he purrs, no clear feelings from that part of my brain that can sense him.

And then Scamp's barreling away and I'm rushing after him.

"It didn't work!" I call as I run. "I didn't get any visions this time. Scamp!"

We hurtle through the snow, and I zero in on

his swishing tail, ignoring my surroundings.

Because I don't know what Shannon meant about following the vision, but I know how to chase a cat. Poor Slinky. Our family cat is old, now, but when he and I were both younger, I would track him down and chase him anytime I needed kitty snuggles.

I reach out my fingers to grab Scamp, leaning forward to snatch him before he can escape into the woods.

The woods.

I stumble in my pursuit and clutch my head with one hand and the pie box with the other, suddenly unsteady on my feet, my vision blurry.

"Whoa." I fall back, my butt landing on moss-covered ground. Not a flake of snow in sight, except what is stuck to my boots.

"Scamp, how?" I ask weakly.

He sits at the base of an aspen tree, looking pleased with himself.

"Not on his own, that's certain," says an ancient, amused voice, like the laughing, dusty pages of a book. "He did it because I instructed him to bring you here, and gave him the power to do so."

The speaker materializes from behind a tree, chuckling, and I have to force my jaw to remain shut.

She's as ancient as her voice. In fact, I don't think I've ever seen a fae so old. Her wrinkles have wrinkles. Laugh lines all over her face give her a pleasant appearance, like an old grandmother who always has cookies in the oven for you when you arrive.

But she doesn't look like any human grandmother I've seen, aside from the wrinkles, and the age spots which dot her face and hands.

Her shoulders are broad, her upper body built like a barrel. Not only that, but the human grandmothers I know don't have curly ram horns on their heads or furry legs. She kneels, her knees cracking with the movement, and pats Scamp on the head with a wrinkled, gnarled hand. "Scamp, is it?"

He meows up at her, his tone full of mumbling embarrassment.

"Oh, no, we're not going to forget that anytime soon, *Scamp*," she says with another chuckle.

"And—and who's we?" I manage to ask, gripping my knees and meeting the old fae's gaze.

Her eyes, like two clear pools, soften. "We are the fae of the forests and the streams, of meadows and dew. We love all things wild and untamed. We are your father's people, and we have been watching you for a while now, Evelyn Gray."

Beyond her, in the meadow, I see shapes appearing. Heads covered in wildflowers, and fae with skin as waxy and green as leaves in summer. They're hesitant, at first, when they see me, but at a nod from the old fae standing by me, there's a burst of shouts and laughter and song. So much singing! Their voices mingle in harmonies, their bodies swaying to the beat. More fae join them, and the meadow is soon full of wild fae, all dancing and singing.

"What are they doing?" I ask the old fae.

"Celebrating your arrival. They are overjoyed you have returned to us. Can't you hear it?" she responds, tilting her head and gazing at me, neither judgmental nor concerned, just waiting.

So I listen.

> "Daughter of trees and sweet berries
> comes home to us at last.
> Out of the realm of children lost
> our daughter returns at last.
>
> Gone so long, a friend we found
> to aid her in this task.
> Daughter of the forest streams
> returns to us at last.
>
> But where is her father,
> prince of the faerie wild?
> Where is he to welcome she
> with a carefree smile?
>
> In a cage he waits his doom,
> his days are numbered few.
> But his daughter heard our call and came
> our hopes are renewed.
>
> Daughter of trees and sweet berries
> comes home to us at last.
> Out of the realm of children lost
> our daughter returns at last."

"What do they mean, prince of the faerie wild?" I ask, turning to the old fae.

"Oh, that." She shakes her head. "Poetic nonsense. Aspen is no more royal than I am. But we wild fae, we all inherit the land. Any wild place, here or on earth, we claim as ours. Flowers bloom in welcome when we come, and brooks babble their greetings."

Aspen. My birth father's name is Aspen. I hold both of their names on my tongue, experimenting with how they sound: Aspen and Maeve. Maeve and Aspen. My birth parents. It's sweet, knowing both of their names, but the taste soon turns sour. Poetic nonsense aside, the song isn't wrong about one thing: Aspen and Maeve have been captured and are waiting for their doom to come on the winter solstice.

Unless I can stop it.

"Do you know him then?" I ask. The winter solstice is five days away. I have five days to prepare, to figure out how to save him. But right now, I'm with his people–my people. The wild fae. They called me here for some reason, but while I'm here I may be able to fill in some of the holes about my birth father. Aspen.

The old fae doesn't answer, but I think I see tears welling in her eyes. "Come!" She pulls me off the ground with more strength than I'd expect from someone as old as she looks, even with her barrel-chested frame. She looks like she could be as old as the dirt, or the hills.

I'm shoved out into the meadow. "Dance!" she instructs from the sidelines.

At first, I'm all awkward elbows and left feet, surrounded by a swaying, singing crowd of fae, humming along because I don't know the words to the new song they're singing.

But then, I start to get into it a little. I'm not graceful by any means, but I do my best, getting into the beat, stomping my feet and swirling with abandon. Soon, my winter gear becomes too warm and my socks all bunch at the toes of my boots from my goofy dance moves. I make my way to the edge of the meadow, dancing the whole time. If I stop, there's always a fae to yell at me to "pick up my feet," and "feel the earth laugh at our revels." As quickly as I can, I relax my shoulders, making my wings go non-corp, and shed my jacket, then kick my boots off, socks and all.

Afraid it might get squashed beneath the stamping feet, I pick up the box of pie and bring it back with me into the meadow. The earth is warm against my bare feet, and the grasses, bent from so much movement, tickle my toes. As I rejoin the throng, a fae takes the box out of my hands and opens it.

"She has brought us a gift! A baked good, made by one of the lost children!" The fae calls above the singing in a voice as clear as a cold spring on a summer day.

"How quaint!" one replies.

"Actually, that's for someone else–" I interject, grabbing at the box.

The fae who took it from me is oblivious to my protests.

He lifts the pie, box and all, to his face and takes a bite.

"My mom wanted that–"

Another fae snatches it from his hands. It's passed from one to the other, each pausing their song and dance to take a bite of Gramp's caramel apple pie until the box, empty, is discarded.

"You can get another pie, Eevee," I mumble to myself. "It's not the end of the world."

"The baked good was delicious!" exclaims a fae, the one I saw earlier with wildflowers covering her head like hair. She laughs, and her laugh is like sunshine sparkling on a lake. "For human food, that is!"

My disgruntled feelings don't last long with so much joy around me. For a time, all I care about is the feel of the dance and losing myself in each new song the fae sing. My legs burn and my feet turn wet with dew, just like the song said in my vision, and I go hoarse from singing and humming. I lose track of time, but I don't care.

Though I'm the only fae wearing leggings and a sweatshirt (one of my favorites; it has a profile of a bear and is captioned with the infamous stage direction from *The Winter's Tale*, "Exit, pursued by a bear"), I feel more at home here than I have anywhere else in Elfaeme, or with anyone else, except Quince.

My dancing slows, and like waking up from out of a dream, I blink blearily around me. The sun is now high in the sky, and many of the fae have left the meadow without me noticing until now, leaving me dancing with only a few stragglers.

The old fae woman and Scamp look on from the shadows of the trees. Her gaze is enough to wake me fully from my dancing delirium—cold and calculating, as if she's assessing my qualities and finds them lacking.

I gather my boots and jacket, leaving the last couple wild fae to dance and sing in the meadow. Their dancing has lost its exuberance, but their voices are still clear and unbroken as they sing, smiles on their faces.

"Daughter of the trees and sweet berries
comes home to us at last.
She who's from the winter breeze
is home at last, at last."

I extract my bunched up socks from my boots and pull them onto my wet feet. My toes are numb from the chill of the dew and from hours of dancing barefoot in a meadow. How many hours, though? I lift my hand, shading my eyes, and squint at the sun. Back home, where there's snow and icy roads, are my mom and dad worrying what's taking me so long to get pie at Gramp's?

"I'm sure you have a lot of questions," the old fae says. Scamp, who's trailing after her, sits down at her feet. He meows and licks his paw before rubbing at his lone ear.

"A few," I admit, trying to push down my worries about my mom and dad. This is why I came, after all. To figure out why that vision was sent to me, and learn more about these wild fae who know my birth father.

To the side of the meadow I see the discarded pie box and, draping my coat over one arm, go over and pick it up. I'd hate to be accused of littering this beautiful place.

The old fae follows me. When I turn around, she's nodding thoughtfully. "I thought you'd have a question or two for me." As if coming to a decision, she snaps her fingers. "Better come with me, then."

Without waiting for me, she strides into the forest, her furry legs surefooted and strong despite her age.

I hurry to catch up. The green canopy above us sighs as a balmy breeze blows through it, and as sunlight peeks through it dapples the mossy floor with afternoon light.

I don't have to wonder where we're going for long, because when Scamp zooms ahead of us, my attention is drawn to where he's heading.

Barely visible through the trees is a little log cabin.

When we reach it, the old fae hobbles to the door, which opens at her approach.

She turns to me.

"Boots off at the door," she commands. "And leave that electronic pocket distraction you call a phone outside as well. I can't stand the things, and they don't work in Elfaeme anyway."

With that, she enters the cabin.

"No dawdling!" she calls from within.

I kick off my boots and zip my phone in my coat pocket, leaving it all in a pile next to the overgrown flower garden out front, then step through the door.

Waxing and Waning

Inside the cottage it's an explosion of colors. Wildflowers are stuffed to bursting in simple clay vases on every surface. The walls are hand-painted with murals of the four seasons—one season for each wall.

At what looks like a wood stove from the 1800s, the old fae busies herself, humming.

I sit in a chair at a small table and absentmindedly play with the wildflower arrangement in front of me, moving a red flower to the center, where its vivid color stands out more against the yellows and whites, and fiddle with some of the sprays of greenery.

When I look up, the old fae is watching me, a

peculiar expression on her ancient face, which is framed by her curled rams-horns.

Afraid I've offended her by touching her flowers, I pull my hands back.

She sits in the chair opposite me.

"Aspen has a gift for that, too," she says after a long pause.

My eyes dart to the flowers, then back to her.

"Are you his grandmother or something?" I blurt out, unable to contain my curiosity any longer.

She laughs a long, dusty laugh. "Or something. I suppose it is time I introduce myself. My name is Olearia, and I am eldest of the wild fae who live in these woods. My children's children's children are grown and have children of their own. I've seen many ages come and go in the human realm, where they live and burn and die as quickly as fireflies."

I start in my chair. Her words remind me of Quince, who also sometimes refers to humans as fireflies.

"Olearia," I say out loud, repeating her name. It feels old, like her, but it has a smooth cadence to it: ohl-AIR-ee-uh.

Before I can ask any questions, she sucks on her teeth and then says, "There's no beating around the bush. I can guess your first questions. Why have we sent for you?"

I nod, not voicing a related question which nags at me. Why now? Why didn't they reach out before, once they knew I'd been to the fae realm? They'd obviously been keeping a close eye on me through the years.

It's a sad, bitter thought, but I think it anyway. They need something from me, that's why.

Maybe some of this thought is visible on my face, or maybe Olearia sees the flames licking at my knuckles, itching to roar to life, to punch–not Olearia, she's old. But something.

"And why now?" Like she's read my mind, she asks my unspoken question aloud, blinking down at her gnarled hands, not willing to meet my gaze.

We sit in silence, and I think she's waiting for me to answer. I move my hands below the table, shaking out the last of the flames.

But I can't put out the fiery anger burning in my heart.

"Those questions are a good starting point," I force out, trying not to let my anger show too much.

She meets my eyes, and I'm surprised to see the deep sadness in hers. It permeates her whole face, etching every line and wrinkle with grief and suffering.

"We've wanted so badly to meet you," she whispers, her voice hoarse. "But *she* wouldn't allow it."

She is said with such venom, I find myself leaning back in the chair.

"She being…"

"Aspen's biggest folly and greatest love. Your mother." Olearia spits out the words like they're dirty.

I'm not sure how I should react to this information. I haven't met my birth mother yet, and when people say mother, my first thought is of Penny Acker with her red cheeks and messy bun and warm, welcoming hugs. Maeve is a mystery to me, though I've learned a little about her through other fae.

It's strange she wouldn't allow the wild fae to contact me. And yet, in the adoption packet my parents gave me, amongst medical records and a picture of me as a baby, is a letter from Maeve to me, written using blood magic only I could read, detailing how to find her.

But by the time I tracked down the cottage in the woods where they'd been hiding, it was too late.

Like that, my mind returns to that night, standing outside my birth parents' home in the woods, my hand raised to the door to knock. To meet them.

A knock on the door can convey so much meaning, for how simple of a gesture it is.

It can say, "Hey! Listen up and pay attention to me!" or "Sorry, I didn't mean to disturb you, do you have a minute?" or "Help! Come quick!" or "Just dropping something off, thought you should know."

I wonder if my knock on this door properly conveys, "Hi, it's me, the daughter you put up for adoption. I followed the clues you left me and now I'm here?"

If it does, should I be worried there's no answer?

"Eevee?"

I've been so wrapped up in my own thoughts I almost

forgot Quince, standing on the mossy path behind me.

My shoulders do a half shrug thing as I turn to look at him. I can feel my wings, the orange butterfly-like wings I still can't believe are mine, shifting with the muscles of my shoulders as they move. Though it's been almost a month since I first visited the fae realm, the fact I have wings is still novel to me; if I wanted, I could launch myself into the sky, far away from this door and this cottage with its empty windows.

"Maybe they're deep sleepers?"

Quince crosses his arms, his dark brown eyes glittering like obsidian in the dusky light of the evening. "Maybe."

My stomach knots itself into a mess not even the best detangler could fix. Something feels off to me. The dark windows, the quiet of the forest around us. My fae hearing is exceptional, yet I can't hear any of the usual night-time sounds. No critters chittering or bugs buzzing.

And before this, back in the clearing of mage stones, the only other fae we'd met was Folsom, the frog-like creature I'd run into on my first ever visit to Elfaeme. Considering the last time I'd been in that clearing with Quince, just over a week ago…

I touch the top of my right arm, where a jagged scab runs from my wrist to my elbow. That time, we'd met resistance. But tonight, the clearing was quiet as well.

Too quiet.

The look on Quince's face is troubled. "Is it bleeding again?" he asks, taking a step closer to me.

I remove my hand from my arm. "No, I'm just thinking."

I turn back to the door and knock again. The scab isn't bleeding, but it does itch. I try to ignore it like I try to ignore the rising panic swimming in my gut.

To my ears, my knocking sounds like it's saying, "Come to the door, prove to me you're here, acknowledge my existence, damnit!"

But the windows of the secluded cottage in the Seelie woods remain unlit. I don't understand. This is where my birth mother's last clue led me. This is where my quest was meant to end, where I was supposed to...what?

Truthfully, I don't know what I expected. A big, happy reunion, full of tears and hugs? An awkward situation where the door opens and my birth parents don't know who I am? An Eevee moment of blurting out the truth, where I say how I know who my birth mother is, and how she had abandoned her life as Queen of the Unseelie Court to live in hiding with my birth father, but also decided to leave me, her only daughter, behind in the human realm to be raised with no knowledge of my true identity?

The worst part of all the confusion and panic I'm feeling is the tendrils of resentment snaking through my blood. I hate how these people I've never met have so much control over my emotions, like I'm a puppet and my strings are attached to a puppeteer I can't see.

Quince puts his hand in mine, which is still raised to the door, and slowly lowers it.

I can feel the disappointment emanating off of him. They're not his birth parents, but my mother represented hope for him and his kind, children of the Seelie and Unseelie Courts, children of estranged kingdoms in the fae realm. Queen Maeve had left the Unseelie Court willingly, despite the consequences. Out of all the kings and queens in Elfaeme, she is the one most likely to be sympathetic to the prejudice Quince and others like him face.

"They're not here," I hear myself say. I'm numb.

"No," he says, drawing me in for a hug.

I want to stay here, in his embrace. It's warm, safe. But his cousins, Sean and Shannon, can only distract his parents for so long. He isn't supposed to be with me tonight, either back at the Duluth High's Homecoming dance, or here in Seelie territory.

Maeve is my birth mother; she left the Unseelie Court against her husband's will, and King Nightglade is known for holding grudges. Understandably, Jerry and Myska want their son as far away from trouble as they can keep him.

I break away from his embrace and look up at him. More than anything, I want to pull him back to me, feel his arms encircling my waist below my wings, and breathe in his fresh smell, which reminds me of a forest stream. But instead, I hear myself saying, "You should go. I'll stay here and look around, maybe see if I can get inside the cottage."

A wrinkle forms between his eyebrows. "Eevee-"

Crap. My eyes are watering; if he keeps talking, they'll threaten to spill over. "Just go. I don't want you to get in trouble because of me. Besides, it's my birth parents' house. I want to do this alone."

I don't want to do this alone, but I try and put as much emphasis behind those words as I can.

He hesitates, then his lips form a thin, determined line. "I'm probably already going to get in trouble for tonight, no matter how well Sean and Shannon distract my parents. They'll know something's up."

The door opens. It isn't even locked. And inside...

"Eevee? I don't see eye to eye with Maeve. I'm not going to apologize for what I said, but if I've offended you–"

"No," I say, bile rising to my throat. *Don't think of that night*, I tell myself. "It's not that. I'm just confused about something."

She nods, as if this is all the explanation she needs.

Amidst the wreckage we'd found inside my birth parents' home that night, there was a note. It wasn't addressed to anyone specifically, but I knew it was meant for me.

Don't think of the note, don't think of that night, don't–

"She never told us her reasons for keeping you from us," Olearia explains. "Maybe she had a good reason, I don't know. If she did, she kept it to herself."

It is curious. Why did Maeve, the same fae who left me clues across the fae realm to follow so I could find her someday, also forbid my birth father's family to make contact with me?

"Her power wanes, though," Olearia whispers to herself in a trembling voice, wrenching me from my thoughts once and for all. Her head is in her hands, which grip the curly horns, her knuckles white. "Her power wanes when it should wax. Her power should be strongest on the winter solstice, like King Nightglade and the Unseelie fae she left behind when she renounced her throne."

She raises her head, hands still clutching her horns like someone holding onto a branch over an abyss, hoping the branch doesn't crack and send them to their doom.

"Why is it waning?" I ask, my mind racing. Internally, I'm panicking. We shouldn't have been playing Nightglade's game, we should've done what Quince originally suggested and tried to rescue Maeve and Aspen as soon as we knew Nightglade had captured them.

It's been months now. Who knows what tortures he's put them through?

Her power is waning, not waxing.

Olearia shrugs her shoulders. "I don't know. I don't know." She keeps saying it, over and over, like she's stuck on repeat.

Scamp meows, and I sense his concern as he jumps in her lap. His presence has a calming effect on her. Olearia falls silent, dropping her hands from her horns and stroking his head.

"Any guesses? You're…" ancient, I want to say, but I settle on, "obviously experienced. What could cause a fae's magic to do that?" I squint at her, suddenly suspicious. "And how do you know that, about her power?"

Maeve is hidden away, somewhere so secret in Nightglade's kingdom that no one knows where she or

Aspen are being kept.

"The wild fae may not align ourselves directly with either court, Aspen-daughter, but we have our connections, our eyes and ears." Olearia straightens her shoulders, lifting her chin proudly.

I'm impressed. "None of my connections know that," I mutter.

"What?" she asks, cupping a hand around her pointed ear.

I don't repeat myself. Last night, I saw proof that Sean and Shannon are hiding something in their house, something they haven't told me about. Or Quince either, I bet.

What if that isn't all they're hiding?

Oily unease settles in my stomach. I shake off the feeling as best I can, but sense it lurking in my gut. "Nothing. But," I hesitate. "It's not natural, right? Maeve's power waning?"

"Not natural, no." A shudder passes through Olearia, strong enough to shake Scamp from his spot on her lap. He clambers back up, growling in irritation.

I think that's all the explanation I'm going to get, but then, in a hoarse whisper, she adds, "He's invoked the curse of the revoked crown."

She stands abruptly, sending Scamp, who had just settled back down, tumbling and yowling, then plants her hands on the table. The flowers in the vase between us start wilting and turning brown. Thorns sprout up and down the stems, black and venomous.

"Which is why we need you to enlist the help of

the only fae who have the power to stop the process once it's begun–the King and Queen of the Seelie Court."

I gape at her. Her eyes burn like two pieces of coal in her ancient, wrinkled face. "Once Maeve's power is gone, so is Aspen's protection."

The cabin is so silent, I can hear my heartbeat in my ears.

Between a Rock and a Hard Fae

I stand to face Olearia and fold my arms across my chest. "I'm sorry, but that's a load of crap."

If I wasn't so angry I might have laughed at the goldfish-surprised face she has right now.

"I'm eighteen," I say, almost shouting it at her.

"I am aware of your age, Aspen-daughter."

All the frustration I've felt the last few months spews out of me. "I'm barely an adult. I don't know how things work in the fae world because I was raised by humans, and in that world, I haven't even graduated high school yet."

"Pah, humans." She spits in disgust. "You're stronger than any human your age. You're fae. You're—

"

"Aspen's daughter. Yeah. And Maeve's. But I'm also the daughter of Todd and Penny Acker. And they've taught me the importance of doing well with my studies. I am trying to do what I can to help save Maeve and Aspen at the winter solstice, but that's not my only responsibility! I need to keep up in school, and go to work to save money for college."

She purses her lips but says nothing.

The words pour from me. Now that I've started, I can't stop. "If that weren't enough, I also have been keeping secrets from my best friends."

"Best *human* friends," she mutters.

I glare at her. "To protect them. Human or not, Nightglade would be a lot more interested in them if he thought they knew about my fae identity. Somewhere in there, I've also been finding time to do things with my family because the last thing I need is my siblings getting suspicious and poking their noses into my dangerous fae life."

I don't mention my worry about my parents' memories already being affected by fae magic. They're humans, Olearia probably wouldn't care.

"And now," I finish, "on top of all of this, you're asking me to go talk to the Seelie King and Queen and get their help with this 'curse of the revoked crown?'" I scoff. "No. Get someone else. I can't."

My angry energy leaves me as quickly as it came and I'm as limp as an overcooked noodle. "I can't," I repeat weakly.

Scamp rubs along my legs as Olearia and I face off, neither of us breaking eye contact.

I can't, I tell myself. When would I go on this mission? My teachers are piling on the projects and papers for this last week of school before winter break.

Oh, and the Winter Solstice Festival is this Friday night, after all those finals and projects are due. And I'm expected at Gramp's early the next morning. Mom and dad want us to have an 'Acker family night' this week, too–just us, before our crazy relatives get here next week for the holidays.

I can't.

It's too much.

"There's no one else," Olearia says, removing her hands from the table. The thorns melt away and the flowers in the vase spring back to life, lush green and vibrant petals. Her face is impassive as she stares at me. Does she ever blink? "It has to be you. A daughter's plea holds weight at the Seelie Court."

"But–"

"We've tried," she interrupts. For the first time since I met her, she sounds impatient. She takes a breath. Scamp, who is now wandering on top of her cupboards, meows. "Yes, dear," she says to him. "I was getting to that."

I raise an eyebrow at her.

"So many fae, wild fae like Aspen, Unseelie, Seelie, have petitioned the Seelie King and Queen to help release Maeve and Aspen from Nightglade's secret prison. But to each, they say, 'We will wait for the daughter of Maeve herself to come forth and ask. No other requests will be considered.'"

"I—but—that's not fair," I splutter.

Olearia doesn't answer.

Of course not. She knows it's not fair.

I swallow. "And if I don't?"

We both jump when Scamp knocks a wooden bowl off the cabinet and it falls with a thump to the packed dirt floor.

"Out, you menace!" She chases him, waving her arms, and he hisses and streaks like a dusty bolt of lightning out the open window.

When she turns to me, her face is grim. "If you don't, Maeve's power will continue to wane, and there's no guarantee Aspen will be alive for you to save on the winter solstice."

I barely remember leaving Olearia's home. Slipping on my boots and coat, traveling back to the human realm, all happened in a blur.

"I'll think about it," I'd told her.

All my earlier protests—I can't, it's too much, it's not fair—echo in my head.

And yet.

How many times have I seen my mom smile when I know the pressure from her work was getting to her? And I can't count the number of times my dad has put down a book to help me and my siblings with homework.

These moments stick out to me now, as I'm considering whether to go to the Seelie Court, because mom and dad, my human parents, are my heroes. Every day they make sacrifices for each other and for us. They do it without complaining (at least, without complaining in front of us), and they do it out of love.

Even small sacrifices are heroic.

I know what Olearia is asking me to do is no small task, but when I think about what Todd or Penny Acker would do in my situation?

My jaw juts forward. There's no question what they would do.

I'm going to the Seelie Court to petition the King and Queen to save my birth parents.

As I trudge through the snow, mulling over what Olearia told me about the Seelie King and Queen, my coat pocket buzzes insistently.

Shit. I pull it out and see a string of missed texts and even a few calls from mom and dad.

Because Elfaeme has no cell service, it's impossible to know when the texts and calls had been made. My phone registers them all as arriving at 2:32pm, meaning I've been in the fae realm for about four hours.

I let the car heat up and read through them, starting with the one that surprises me the most, a text from Cam. After last night, I thought it'd be a while before I heard from them.

C: *u o me*

Confused, I open my text conversation with mom and dad.

M: *Where are you?*
D: *She actually wants to know where the pie is hahhahaha*
M: *Seriously, Evelyn, why aren't you answering our calls?*
D: *You okay, Eevee-bug? Harriet didn't rope you into working, did she?*
M: *Just called Cam & Maggie. Cam says you're with them and your phone's dead. Tell them they're welcome to come over for dinner and pie tonight, once you get this.*

I text mom and dad a quick reply, then stare at the message from Cam.

C: *u o me*

Gnawing my bottom lip, I finally text them, then run inside to buy a second pie. Laverne is done for the day, luckily, so it's a quick process to get the pie and run back to my car.

When I'm buckled, I notice my phone blinking. Cam's responded already! When I see their message, I grin widely.

C: *yeah ok*

Less than enthusiastic, as far as responses go, but I'll take it. To mom and dad I type, *Cam says they'll take a slice of pie but idk if they can come over 2nite. sry 4 not answering earlier*

My heart is lighter than it's been all day, except for maybe when I was dancing in the meadow. My feet ache still as I press on the gas and head toward Cam's house, mulling over what to say to them. Things may be weird between us right now, but at least I know that they're there for me, no matter what. After yesterday, I hadn't been so sure, and not believing in your best friend is probably one of the worst feelings out there.

The light-hearted sense of elation lasts up until I arrive at Cam's house.

"Thanks for the pie," they say as soon as the door opens. "Gimme a sec, I'll cut out a slice and be right back."

Pie is ripped from my hands for the second time today, and the door slams in my face.

I stand there, shocked. Then anger kindles in me. How dare they? After everything I've been doing to keep them and Maggie safe these last few months?

I don't think, I just act. In the space of no more than ten seconds, I'm in the fae realm, near the large oak in the In Between. Nostalgia floods me, and then panic. This is where I'd first appeared in the fae realm, not long after discovering I was fae. It's also where I met Folsom, someone I'd prefer not to see again anytime soon. Or ever.

I focus on my destination, gritting my teeth through the nausea and dizziness that comes with realm-hopping. Then I'm back in the human realm, in a place I've called my second home for ten years now: Cam's house. In their kitchen, specifically.

"Holy sh–" They drop the pie wedge they're holding. It clatters to the polished concrete counter top of the kitchen island.

Their words from yesterday ring in my head, a cruel echo to the clattering of the pie wedge. *She's not a person. She's a fae.*

"Okay, first, I know I shouldn't just pop in to your house uninvited."

"No kidding." They stare at me, unmoving.

"At least there's no magical fae ministry sending me a summons for arrest by owl," I joke. The fae are too disorganized and divided for any kind of organized government. They prefer their courts and intrigue, the ebb and flow of power from Seelie to Unseelie, with the wild fae existing on the edges and benefiting by being left alone from the constant inner turmoil of the courts.

"What do you want that couldn't have waited until I returned your pie?" they ask, their voice icy. They pick up the pie wedge and stab it into the pie.

"Cam–" I start, then pause, my promise to Quince, Sean, and Shannon effective at keeping me from explaining anything to Cam about the solstice coming up.

"If you're not going to tell me what's really going on, don't bother," they say in the silence. "I don't want your excuses, Eevee."

I choke on the lump of anger and frustration in my throat. "That—it's—not cool, Cam. The hell? You think I *want* to keep my best friend in the dark?"

They shrug, then hand me the pie box, with a small sliver of pie cut out. "Sure seems that way." Their eyes soften a little. "I'll always be there for you, Eevee. I thought me covering for you today proved that. It doesn't mean I'm not upset though. And scared for you."

I take the pie box, blinking back tears. "Cam, I'm scared, too, for you and Mags. You know what the fae are like—I can't risk you guys getting hurt. I—I'd never forgive myself."

My body curls around the pie box. Even thinking about Cam and Maggie getting hurt because of me makes me sick to my stomach.

"And you think we'd forgive ourselves if you got yourself into a dangerous situation and we could've done something to help but didn't?" They shake their head. "Stop thinking like a hero in a book, E. Start thinking for yourself. You promised not to tell me and Maggie about your plans in order to protect us. But who is it protecting if we get captured by a fae and have no idea why or what to do?"

They have a point. I run one of my hands through my short hair, some of it sticking up in the back. "I can't tell you what you want to hear." I hesitate, fiddling with the pie box. "But everything's going down the evening of—" the words 'winter solstice' dry in my mouth. I cough, and Cam's eyes widen with concern.

An idea occurs to me. When I'm finally able to speak, I say, "You know, our math final for Mr. Jenkins' class is this Friday."

Their brows furrow, then smooth in comprehension.

"Not here." I hope they pick up on the fact that by "not here" I mean "in the fae realm."

The hint of recognition in their blue eyes, tinged with fear, lets me know they've figured out what I'm referring to. I've seen that same fear in their eyes anytime the fae realm is mentioned, and I can't blame them. Cam's first experience there wasn't exactly sunshine and sparkles.

"Is it–is it where Nightglade lives?"

The question is too direct; I can't answer it without breaking my promise, and my whole body freezes.

"Never mind," they say quickly, noticing my abnormally motionless posture. "I can guess enough on my own. What about that vision from Scamp?"

Released from having to answer a question I can't, I relax. "You'll never believe where I was today, Cam!" I exclaim.

There's still a wound between us. But as I leave their house to finally deliver pie to my mom, I'm at peace. Because though we're a little more broken than we had been, our friendship will heal.

She's not a person. She's a fae.

I shake the words out of my head the best I can. Cam had been angry. Our friendship can survive this.
I think.

Amelia the Sleuth

"Are we gonna talk about the fact you literally disappear off the map at least once a week, sometimes more?"

My head, which had been drifting toward my chest as I read *Pride and Prejudice* for English class, snaps up. "Wait, what?"

With a smug smile on her face, like a cat who's spotted its prey, Amelia saunters into my bedroom brandishing her phone in front of her.

The door closes behind her with a soft click.

"It's this new family tracking app thing—remember mom and dad had us install it on our phones about a month ago?"

I frown. "Kind of?" The memory is vague–anything beyond a week ago is in that blurry zone of "the past," where my memories tend to blend together unless it's really important. And my brain has no specific criteria for what counts as important. I remember my first time in the fae realm clear as day, for example, but also days like when I was a kid and I swallowed gum and thought it was going to plug my stomach and kill me.

She sighs, plopping down on the bed next to me, her messy curls up in a bun on the top of her head for the night. "This app, Eevee." She tilts her phone to me, revealing the app's home page. At the top are the words *Safe Family Tracker*.

Like it had been waiting for this moment, a tiny speck of a memory rises to the surface. "Oh yeah! Didn't they have us install it because of how much time you'd been spending over at shoulder guy's house?"

She rolls her eyes. "Uh–no. That's what they told you?"

I set *Pride and Prejudice* down on the end table and cross my arms, scowling at her chuckling face. "What are you saying, Ames?"

A line appears between her eyebrows as she taps at her phone, then she shoves it in my face. I blink, leaning back into my pillows and squinting at the screen.

She's opened up to a page titled *Eevee Map Activity*.

"How come *you* can access this?" I hiss at her,

careful to keep my voice down. I snatch the phone from her, scanning it. The more I read, the more my whole body grows cold.

I scroll through, all the way back to November, when they'd installed the app.

Amelia plucks her phone out of my hands.

"You wanna know the weird thing, though?" she asks, leaning in toward me conspiratorially.

No, I don't. I'm frozen—I can't fathom any of what's happening right now.

Her lips are right by my ear when she whispers,

"Mom and dad act like they haven't noticed."

The fae magic, I think wildly. It works on them, but not on my sister. Why?

I swallow. My throat is constricted, like someone is grabbing it and slowly tightening their grip. "That's weird," I rasp out.

Thoughts race through my head. Fae can't lie. If Amelia asks me directly, I'll have to tell her the truth about where I've been. Is there any way I can talk around it, like I did when I was telling Cam about the Winter Solstice Festival?

"I want to know how you do it," she says, pinning me with her gaze. Her large eyes are steely.

"How I–how I fool the app?" I shake my head. "Nu-uh. You want to know so you can see shoulders guy more."

"Trent," she says, exasperation all over her face. "His name is Trent. And no, that's not why. I'm just sick of them invading my privacy, that's all."

When I don't answer, she switches tactics, her bottom lip jutting out and her eyes glistening with unshed tears, a perfect image of innocence wronged.

"Please, Eevee?" she pleads, pressing her hands together like in prayer. "Help me? I won't tell mom and dad, promise."

"I can't help you," I say shortly. At her crestfallen face, I nudge her shoulder with mine. "Believe me, if I could, I would. But there's something–um, different–between us which makes it–"

"It's because you're a legal adult and I'm not,

isn't it?" She pouts. "Not fair."

Lots of stuff isn't fair right now, Ames, I think. I say nothing out loud, letting her think she's come to the correct conclusion. Better than her finding out where I'm really going at those times.

As if she can hear my thoughts, Amelia frowns at me. "Where *are* you going all those 'unknown' times, Eevee?"

I swear the girl is trying to stare into my soul. If she doesn't grow up to be a badass crime-solving detective, she'll have missed her calling.

"I'm tired," I reply, evading her question. The Winter Solstice Festival looms in my mind, as does Nightglade's stony, no-mercy face. There's no question in my mind; Nightglade wouldn't hesitate to have Amelia killed if she were in the fae realm, if it meant it would hurt me.

"Huh." Amelia clicks her tongue and shrugs. "Here I thought you were wanting to kick me out so you could go to Elfaeme," she says, all casual and cool. "Every Sunday night, as far back as the app can track, anyway." She narrows her eyes at me, waiting for a response.

This time I'm not speechless out of choice. I gape at her, all words absolutely obliterated from my mind.

Even in the dark I can see her cheeks turning rosy. "At least, that's what Ilinor thinks you're doing on those nights."

My little sister knows about Elfaeme. And I

wasn't the one to tell her.

"Ilinor?" I rack my (admittedly poor) memory to dredge up anything, but it comes up blank.

"Honestly, do you even know me anymore?" Amelia asks, betrayal coloring each word.

"I don't know," I admit in a daze. Has Amelia mentioned Ilinor to me before and I'm forgetting it? Have we really not talked that much in the last few months?

And, more importantly, who is Ilinor?

"She moved here in November. She's from Elfaeme. Like you." She shakes her head. "And here I thought being adopted from Ecuador was exotic. You're from a totally different realm."

My whole body shakes and I feel both hot and clammy cold, like when I get a bad fever. How stupid of me to think Nightglade was leaving my human family alone all this time. His plan, or part of it, is suddenly crystal clear to me. He's wanted me to feel safe all this time, lulled into a false sense of security, thinking my family and friends were safe from his influence in the human realm.

Now I know that couldn't be further from the truth.

"There's something I've been wondering, though," Amelia says, chewing thoughtfully on her lower lip. "How did you find out your birth parents were fae?"

Her tone is too sweet, the look on her face too guileless.

She's being used to find out information on me.

In a panic, I grab at her shoulders. "Ames, listen to me–"

Her laugh is hollow. "Months. I've been trying to get you to open up for months, and *now* you want *me* to listen?" She shrugs out of my grip and stands. "Too little, too late, Eevee."

She taps at her phone, barely glancing up to add, "It could've been me and you."

I hug my knees to my chest and frown at her. "What do you mean?"

She sighs, slipping her phone into the front pocket of her hoodie. "All these months. All your trips to the fae realm. I could've been coming with you, helping you. But instead, you iced me out."

I pinch the bridge of my nose. This is not happening right now.

"At least Ilinor trusts me."

No, no, no. My head snaps up. "Ames, don't tell me this Ilinor's taken you–"

"To Elfaeme? And why shouldn't I? Amelia is smart and helpful. I value her insight," says a bright voice near my window.

I twist on my bed, sheets and blankets knotting beneath me.

"Let me guess. Ilinor," I say flatly.

The fae girl in front of my window bows tauntingly, her silvery hair sliding forward in two waterfalls.

She straightens, her back as straight as a steel

rod. With a fluid motion, she tucks her hair behind her ears, revealing green eyes devoid of any warmth.

"Ilinor!" Amelia squeals in a whisper. "You got here so quick! I just texted you!"

She runs over and gives Ilinor a hug, which Ilinor reciprocates, her eyes never leaving my face.

"Step away from her!" I scramble off the bed, my voice high-pitched and panicky.

"Why?" Amelia breaks her hug with Ilinor to give me an incredulous look.

"Yes, Eevee, why?" Ilinor asks mockingly. The self-satisfied look on her face, like she's beaten me at my own game, is infuriating.

"Trust me," I say to Amelia through gritted teeth, ignoring Ilinor. "It's safer for you not to touch her."

Amelia laughs. "Trust you?" she whispers, hands flying to her hips, her chin sticking out. "Like you've trusted me, you mean?"

I rub at my temples, weary beyond belief. Is this how dad feels when I see him rubbing his temples during one of Greg and Charlie's frequent fights? Utterly bone-tired? Because that's how I feel right now.

All my months of subterfuge, thinking I was being sneaky and secretive, that I was successful at keeping my fae life and human life separate, appear to have caught up to me.

I'm starting to wonder if the promise I made to Sean, Shannon, and Quince was made for the right reasons. At the time, I'd told myself it was to protect my family and friends. Are good reasons and good motives enough to offset the consequences? Or, on some deep level, did I believe Quince and his Unseelie cousins when they said it would be better if no one else outside us four knew of our plans for the Winter Solstice Festival? If I think back to that night, the first Sunday after Homecoming, wasn't I secretly, selfishly relieved to make that promise? Didn't part of me think that Cam and Maggie, who had been so terrified the one time I'd brought them to Elfaeme, wouldn't be able to handle any more fae-related problems? Guilt sloshes in my stomach. I had completely dismissed any of my family as being able to help. Maybe Amelia, Cam, and Maggie aren't the ones with the trust issues.

I take a breath, loosening my jaw. "You're right," I say to Amelia, disregarding Ilinor, who has wandered in front of the vanity and is applying lip gloss.

Amelia blinks. "I am?"

"I should've told you what I told mom and dad," I explain. "Maybe not Jess or the dweebs yet—" our current term of endearment for Greg and Charlie "—but I should've told you."

"But you didn't." Ilinor smacks her glossy lips together and pockets the tube of lip gloss. "You kept your own sister in the dark." She tsks, then shoots me a contemptuous grin. "I guess the phrase, 'We're the Ackers, we stick together through it all,' doesn't apply to Evelyn Acker."

The way Amelia's face crumples in disappointment at Ilinor's words is an arrow strike to my lungs, taking all my breath away. Can this night get any worse?

"Eevee?"

The color drains from my face. Apparently it can.

I whirl around to face the figure sitting on my bed.

Quince "I've-got-the-*best*-timing" Florentz is all sharp angles and dark edges, his almost black hair rumpled, yet still somehow cute. But his eyes, usually twinkling with mischief, are dim with worry.

"You're late," he says. "Se–"

I leap forward, tackling him into the pillows in a full-body hug.

"We've got company," I whisper to him, quiet as a butterfly. He frowns at the tension in my voice.

"Hello, Quince," Ilinor says, her voice dry, detached. "I didn't expect to see you here."

I don't think Quince has ever broken an embrace so fast. He stands. "Ilinor." His voice is as stiff as his body.

As I stand next to him, taking his hand, a rage flares in Ilinor's eyes, so quick I almost wonder if I imagined it.

Her lip curls in a feral snarl. "Did the court not think I could handle this assignment?" I see red momentarily when it dawns on me that by "this assignment" she means tricking my sister into befriending her. "I'm surprised they sent you, of all fae, to check on me."

"And why's that?" Quince asks woodenly.

"Oh, don't act dumb. It doesn't suit you," she says, waving a hand dismissively at him. "The assignment is going exactly how I hoped, by the way," she concludes, examining the nonexistent dirt under her fingernails.

I gape at her, then turn to Quince, whose hand in mine is limp and sweaty.

"Oh. Em. Gee. I just realized I'm the only human in this room!" Amelia covers her mouth and giggles.

And you have no idea how much danger you're in because of it, I think.

Ilinor lifts her focus from her nails to Quince, who's still standing uselessly beside me, like a lump on a log. "So? Are you going to leave me to do my job now, or…"

The grin on her face is like the look a lioness has before ripping into the flesh of an antelope.

I feel Quince shudder, then shake himself. He gives my hand a squeeze and drops it.

The hand squeeze eases some of the tension in my back. It'll be okay. He'll stand up to Ilinor with me to help him, then we'll figure out what to say to Amelia.

"Absolutely," I hear him saying. "You look like you have it covered. So. Yeah. Uh…bye, Ilinor."

Quince "what-the-hell,-did-he-just-abandon-me-to-deal-with-a-random-fae?" Florentz doesn't even look at me before he takes a step and disappears.

My brain can't equate the stiff-necked, formal

attitude with Quince's usual energetic, passionate demeanor.

Who is Ilinor, and why did her presence make my kind-of-sort-of boyfriend act like a completely different person?

I'm not sure if I'm so terrified I'm numb, or if I'm just numb. But I can't let this feeling overwhelm me. Not now, not when Amelia is here and needs me to help her, even if she doesn't know the danger she's in. Fear is truly, of all base passions, the most accursed (thanks to *Henry VI, Part I* for that insight).

I feel about as prepared for this encounter as Cinderella was prepared for her ball. At least Cinderella had a fairy godmother to help her attend the ball in style. Something tells me I won't be quite as lucky.

As soon as Quince disappeared, the toothy grin dropped off Ilinor's face. She turns and studies me with her inexpressive green eyes.

"That never gets old, seeing someone–poof!–disappear, just like that!" Amelia gushes, snapping her fingers. She wrinkles her nose and adds, "You never told me Quince was fae, too."

"There's a lot Evelyn hasn't told you," Ilinor drawls, emphasizing each syllable of my name with a curled lip, like it left a bad taste in her mouth. Her eyes haven't left my face. She steps toward me until we're almost nose-to-nose. Or, we would be, if I wasn't so short. "You're the one trying to steal the Unseelie throne from King Nightglade." There's something in her eyes I can't understand–animosity? Jealousy?

Deep breath, Eevee, I remind myself.

Amelia's eyes go saucer-wide.

This is all part of the plan.

I straighten my shoulders and force my face into what I hope looks like a regal expression. "I am."

Who is Ilinor?

Ilinor's face breaks into a grim smile. "So you admit it. I have to say, that takes some courage." She eyes me thoughtfully. "You'll never overthrow him, though. Nightglade's power and connections are more far-reaching than you think."

"I'll take my chances," I reply, keeping my voice cool.

"Eevee, why did Ilinor say you're plotting to take over someone's throne?" Amelia asks, her whole face scrunched in confusion. "You don't actually have any claim to the throne, do you?" She looks at Ilinor. "Does she?"

"She does," Ilinor answers, again shooting me

that look of angry envy. "But that won't save her."
Ilinor moves to touch me, but I back away from her
spidery fingers, my whole body on alert.

"Stay away from me," I spit.

"I wish I could," she shoots back. "But I have
an assignment to finish."

Quick as a panther, she lunges at me. All I can
think is that I need to avoid any skin-on-skin contact
with her. I don't want to be dragged to Elfaeme against
my will, not now.

"Ilinor, what are you doing?" Amelia asks,
rushing forward, then coming to a stop.

Ilinor and I circle each other in the middle of
my bedroom. My hands, I realize, are crackling with
flame, but they're shaking.

"Stop this, both of you!" Amelia steps between
us, just as Ilinor lunges again.

I watch, like it's happening in slow-motion,
Ilinor's outstretched hands collide with Amelia's neck.
Amelia lets out a small, croaking gasp, and Ilinor's
fingers dig into her skin. A momentary look of surprise
crosses Ilinor's face, then sly satisfaction.

I reach forward, not caring that my hands are
still aflame, but my arms move slowly, like they're the
arms of a sloth.

Amelia's sweatshirt is almost at my fingertips.
Her head turns, her doe eyes wide, terrified.

And then they're both gone.

Time resumes its normal pace. I stumble, off-
balance.

"No!" I shout, aware I might wake up my family, but unable to stop. "Bring her back! Ilinor!"

It's useless, shouting at someone in a totally different realm, but I don't give a damn. She stole my sister.

My door swings open. I whirl toward it to see Jess, rubbing her eyes and blinking at me. Sweet Jess, who may be in 8th grade but still loves princesses and fairies and rainbows and any kind of animal, no matter how ugly.

"Wh-what's going on?" she asks in between a jaw-cracking yawn.

With everything that life's thrown at her, like having birth parents who cared more about their next hit than if their kid was fed, it always amazes me how she remains a glass half full kind of person. But here she is, thirteen years old, proudly wearing princess pajamas, and staring at my hands, mouth open in amazement.

"Your hands–they're–"

"On fire, yeah," I say, too tired and stressed to come up with an excuse. Not that I could lie anyway. I shove past her into the hall.

She follows after me as I head toward mom and dad's room. "I knew I wasn't imagining it," I hear her mutter behind me. "Mom and dad just acted like it was no big deal, but I knew…"

I barge into mom and dad's room and flip the light switch, bathing the room in a harsh, white light from above.

"Eevee? Jess? What?" Mom pushes herself up onto her elbow and pokes at dad's side. "Todd? Todd! The girls want something."

Dad jerks awake with a start, sitting bolt upright and looking around wildly. "What? What? What?"

When mom finally gets dad to calm down and wake up a bit more, they both blink sleepily at me and Jess.

"Well?" mom asks. "What is it that couldn't wait until morning?"

Jess raises her eyebrows expectantly at me.

"Can—can we have some privacy?" I ask, nodding at my little sister, who scowls.

Someday, Jess, I promise her silently. *Someday I'll tell you all about my wings and why I have fiery fists. But not today.*

"Fine. Jess, honey, why don't you lay back down?" dad asks thickly, still half-asleep. When she doesn't move, he adds, "Now," in his no-nonsense voice he only uses when absolutely necessary.

Jess stomps out of the room, shooting me an angry look I probably deserve.

As soon as her elephantine footsteps fade, I race to mom and dad's bed. Part of me wants nothing more than to crawl under the covers and snuggle between them, like I used to do when I was little and the shadows in the dark scared me.

Now I'm older and the shadows in the dark still scare me, especially now I know fae monsters are real, but I don't climb into bed. I haven't for years. Instead, I stop next to mom's side and try not to burst into tears.

"They've taken Amelia," I say, my voice cracking.

"What do you mean? Who's taken Amelia?" asks dad. He grabs at his glasses on the nightstand and fumbles in his haste, jamming them onto his face so they sit crookedly across his nose.

"Ilinor, she's this Unseelie fae, and…"

I stop, my heart dropping.

I can already see the fae magic at work. Both of their eyes go blank.

"Ilinor?" mom asks, her voice all vague and floaty. "Amelia's new friend?"

"That's nice," dad adds, his voice fuzzy.

"She didn't take her for a sleepover!" I say, fighting an urge to shake their shoulders. "She's taken Amelia to Elfaeme!"

Their expressions remain blank.

I sink to the bed, sitting by mom's side. "I don't–I don't know if you'll remember this." The tears I'd been fighting leak down my face. "Or even if you'll realize how bad it is that Amelia's been kidnapped by the same fae who are holding my birth parents hostage, but…" I take a shaky breath. "But you deserve to know that one of your daughters has been kidnapped."

"Thanks, dear." Mom pats my cheek.

I lean into her hand, wishing I could stay here forever with the two people who have always made me feel safe and loved.

But Amelia's been kidnapped, and the winter

solstice is less than a week away. I stand and step back from the bed.

"I'm going to save her," I tell them. "I promise."

They turn empty, confused faces toward me as I exit.

I close my door behind me after checking and double-checking the hall to make sure Jess isn't lurking nearby. The last thing I need is for Jess to get caught up in my fae life, too.

One sibling crisis at a time.

I sit on my bed, then immediately stand and begin pacing instead, anxiety driving me to keep moving.

As I pace, I weigh my options, trying to think logically while 90% of my brain shouts, "Your sister's been kidnapped by fae!" on repeat. Okay, probably more like 99%.

I can't follow after Ilinor and Amelia, as much as I want to. I can guess where Ilinor's taken her. If I'm right, I'd be captured as soon as I materialized. If I'm wrong and she hasn't taken Amelia to the Unseelie Court, then it would be impossible to pinpoint exactly where they've gone and I'd end up blindly stumbling around Elfaeme, which is less than efficient as far as rescue operations go.

Remembering Quince's tense behavior around Ilinor, I pace even faster, chewing on my bottom lip. Why was he acting so awkward around her? I check the clock on my nightstand. Almost midnight. Usually we'd be leaving Sean and Shannon's by now, after exchanging notes on the upcoming Winter Solstice Festival and going through some martial arts training exercises with Sean. It's a little terrifying knowing how many ways he knows how to kill someone with just his hands. But maybe Quince is still there–if he went back there after leaving my room.

Thinking of Quince doesn't fill me with fluttery happiness like usual. His response when she asked if he would leave her to do her job was, "Absolutely." Why? What's been going on at the Unseelie Court these last few months that he hasn't been telling me?

Decided, I ready myself to take the dizzying, disorienting step from human to fae realm, when I pause.

The strange, keening cries I'd heard last night coming from the second story room, Shannon's shifty behavior in the sitting room…there's something going on that they aren't sharing with me. Maybe what they're hiding will give me a clue as to what's going on in the Unseelie Court that Quince isn't telling me. Sean and Shannon still have their connections to the court, even if they don't attend it much anymore.

What if I materialize inside their house first, check out what Sean and Shannon are hiding, then fly out the window and knock on their door? They don't need to know I broke the fae code of honor by entering another fae's house without permission. They're not the only ones who can keep secrets.

Each minute I waste is another minute Amelia is in the hands of Ilinor and, most likely, Nightglade. I picture Sean and Shannon's second story room and gather my energy, then step forward.

My stomach jumps into my mouth then plummets to my feet. Am I upright? Upside down? I shake my head, which only makes the spinning sensation worse. The smell of something rancid, like lemons rotting on a pile of weeks-old meat, fills my nose when I take a breath.

I lean over and vomit.

Icy cold stings the palms of my hands as I push myself up and wipe my mouth.

Muffled voices reach my ears, and I slowly register where I am: on Sean and Shannon's doorstep.

"See? I told you it'd be a good idea to pay that little bit extra for the anti-theft charm." I clutch my stomach and swallow, fighting another urge to vomit. The voice is so amused and delighted, it can only be Shannon talking.

"A little extra?" I hear Sean splutter. "It cost us an arm and a leg!"

I try to stand, but my stomach protests and I lean over, retching, so I'm not sure, but it sounds like Shannon says, "Yes, but not ours," in response.

Their door opens and I'm illuminated by a

beam of warm candlelight in all my pukey glory.

"Oh, it's you." Sean blinks once, then steps back and opens the door.

"Eevee?" Shannon peers around the door, then raises an eyebrow. "What were you doing, setting off our anti-theft charm? We thought you knew better than to appear inside a fae's house."

If I speak, I'll throw up again. I shrug. Sean's gaze doesn't leave my face, and I get the uncomfortable feeling he knows I was trying to see what they're hiding upstairs.

"Well, come in," Shannon says with a flourishing gesture. I wobble to my feet, then sway as a wave of nausea hits me. He pats my back as I step inside. "The effects of the charm should wear off in an hour or so. At least, that's what the fae we bought it from told us."

I want to retort that he's way too cheerful about this, but my stomach heaves and I groan as I follow them down the hall.

We walk past the sitting room into their spacious kitchen, where Quince sits at the large mahogany table, cracking peanut shells and popping the peanuts into his mouth.

Peanuts!

I forget my nausea for the moment. "What the hell, Quince?"

Instantly, I pay for my outburst. The smell of rotting lemons and meat intensifies and I rush to the sink.

When there's absolutely nothing left in my stomach, I turn around and glare at Quince, who swallows a peanut and looks with interest at the bowl of empty shells.

"We hear you met Ilinor tonight," Shannon says in the silence, with a tone no different than if he were discussing the weather.

I laugh hysterically, covering my mouth just in case. Tears stream down my face, either at Shannon's underwhelming tone or at the situation I'm in, or both. I can't tell. My emotions are all over the place.

Quince stares at me, alarmed by my reaction. I don't blame him.

"Met her?" I finally say, lowering my hands. "She kidnapped my sister."

The color drains from Quince's face and he drops the peanut he'd been holding. Sean's eyes widen slightly, a large display of emotion for him.

Shannon gasps. "Why would she do that?"

"Ask him," I say, pointing to Quince.

Quince's face, which had gone from pale to a kind of ashen gray at the news of Amelia's kidnapping, flushes. He stands, pushing the chair back so hard it squeals against the stone floor.

"What is that supposed to mean?"

His dark eyes glitter with tears, not anger, but I think of the look of terror in Amelia's wide eyes when Ilinor kidnapped her. Ilinor had been reaching for me. It should've been me.

I glare at him. When I don't answer, his

shoulders stiffen. "I think I should go." His voice is as wooden as it was in Ilinor's presence.

"What's been going on at the Unseelie Court these last few months?" I ask, following after him. "What aren't you telling me?"

He turns, and his face sags wearily. "I know you're angry and scared for Amelia's safety. I am, too. I need you to trust me, Eevee. Stay away from Ilinor. We'll get Amelia back."

I study his face, the way there's a worry line between his eyebrows almost permanently these days, the way his eyes don't quite meet mine. I knew a relationship with him would be tough. How could it not be, when I live in the human realm and he stays at the Unseelie Court? When my very existence is a danger to those around me because of who my birth mother is? But I never thought he'd keep anything from me. Not until tonight.

"Who is Ilinor?" I ask, reaching for his hand. "Why do I need to avoid her?" He draws back, fumbling for the door, and exits without answering. "Coward!" I shout after him.

I turn to see Sean and Shannon both staring at me, nonplussed.

"That was unnecessary, "Sean says.

"He deserves it," I reply, but the words fall flat. I don't even know why I shouted at Quince.

Yes, I do. I'm angry at myself for not being able to protect my sister, and I took it out on someone who is clearly suffering, too.

I don't like what stress does to me, I decide.

"No he doesn't, and you know it." Shannon smooths his hair back. "You don't know what he's had to put up with at court."

"Because he hasn't trusted me enough to tell me!" As soon as the words leave my lips, I am wracked with guilt. Hadn't Cam, Maggie, and Amelia accused me of the same thing?

"You can't control what others choose to reveal about themselves or their lives," Sean says, examining the knife in his hand and polishing it. He pockets it. "No matter how much you may want to."

"You can challenge them if you think they're doing something stupid, though," Shannon adds.

"Which was not the case for our dear cousin," Sean says before I can say that I think Quince had been pretty stupid not telling me about Ilinor.

"Who is Ilinor?" I ask them when we're all lounging in the sitting room, since Quince wouldn't answer me. I can't sleep, knowing Amelia's in danger, and I don't feel like returning to my house just yet. The fire crackles and spits in the silence. Sean and Shannon exchange a look, the one that I've learned means they're having one of their telepathic conversations.

It's hard, making myself wait as they hold their voiceless discussion. I run through the weekend's events in my head as I wait, trying to pick apart all the things that have transpired. There must be some clue I missed, something which explains why all this is happening now, with the winter solstice so near at hand. Scamp's vision. The weird sounds coming from upstairs during my last visit, which are still unexplained. Dancing with the wild fae. Olearia's plea. Ilinor's visit. Amelia's kidnapping.

A couple thoughts that come to mind are: I've been naive, thinking Nightglade didn't have some plan to go after me and my family, and the Seelie King and Queen might be the answer to save not only Aspen, but Amelia, too.

"She deserves to know," Sean says aloud, his tone severe, inviting no arguments. "Protecting her from the knowledge will only do more harm than good in the long run."

Shannon shakes his head and exits the sitting room. I focus on Sean, who is rubbing his hands together and staring into the fire.

Have I ever seen Shannon disagree with Sean? "What do I deserve to know? Who is Ilinor?"

Sean is silent for so long, I think maybe he's changed his mind about telling me. His hands grip his knees and he takes a deep breath. When his eyes meet mine, they are kind, and sad. A pit of unease drops into my already unsettled stomach.

"She's Nightglade's daughter from one of his mistresses. So, for lack of a better term, kind of like a stepsister to you. You're both children of Unseelie royalty." He looks down at his clenched hands and speaks to them, his words coming out so fast I almost miss them. "And, as of a month ago, she was promised in marriage to Quince."

I take a breath to answer, then lean over and empty my stomach on the rug.

Night Time Chats With Centuries-Old Fae

Shannon returns with a pillow and some blankets. I cocoon myself beneath them and stare at the twins. I can't imagine what I look like. Probably like a zombie, between the late night, near-constant throwing up, and emotional trauma of losing my sister.

"So, how long have you guys known about Ilinor?" I ask once I'm comfortably situated beneath layers of blankets.

"About her existence, her parentage, or her betrothal to Quince?" asks Shannon. "Those all have different answers, you see."

"Any, all. I…" I bury my face in my hands. If Nightglade's goal is to tear my world out from under me and crush it to dust, he's succeeding. Whatever he's doing to Maeve with the curse of the revoked crown is going to end up killing my birth parents. He had Ilinor befriend my sister months ago, and she kidnapped her when she couldn't get at me. And *now* I find out my boyfriend has a secret fiancée—also Ilinor.

I can't think of her as my "stepsister for lack of a better term." What kind of person steals who, she thinks, is her half sister's boyfriend, then tries to kidnap that same half sister, only to kidnap her half sister's sister instead? It hurts my head to think about it.

I must have asked this out loud because Shannon clears his throat uncomfortably and Sean sighs.

"I'm going to get tea," Shannon says, standing. "Want some?"

Without waiting for an answer, he leaves, his batlike wings rising and falling with his steps.

"Like the rest of the Unseelie Court, Ilinor believes you are the true heir of Nightglade and Maeve," Sean explains. "It's a lie we've used to our advantage, of course. We don't correct anyone who claims you are their daughter, even if we know otherwise. You can imagine how jealous she would be, to find out about this true heir, when for years she thought *she* was the closest heir to the throne."

"She's no closer to the throne than I am."

"But she thinks you are. She believes you to be

her half sister," Sean says, taking out a knife from one of his pockets and shining it on the bottom of his shirt like normal people would do with glasses. "She thinks you both share a father. Nightglade."

"There have to be some in the Unseelie Court who saw Aspen imprisoned at the same time as Maeve," I argue. "Wouldn't they have put two and two together?"

"Nightglade has made it clear…" Sean stops, looks closely at me. "Aspen, did you say?"

Hot tea spills from the cup Shannon had been handing to me, dropping to the plush rug. I hand him a smaller blanket I don't really need for my blanket cocoon. As he dabs at the rug, I notice the scratches criss-crossing the back of his hands, which tremble like he's overtired. Whatever they're hiding upstairs, it's taking a lot out of Shannon. For the first time, I worry for his health.

He gives me a small, reassuring smile. "Drink up," he says. "It's best while it's hot."

While Shannon mops up the spill, I take a quick sip of the chamomile tea, wondering if it'll really help to calm my nerves like the tea boxes always promise.

"Aspen, of the wild fae?" Sean presses after a few sips. He hasn't taken his eyes off me.

I nod.

"You followed the cat," he guesses, his face thoughtful. The hand holding the knife starts fidgeting with it, rolling it between the fingers without once cutting any of them off (a feat I doubt I'd be able to accomplish without bloodshed).

"Yes." Was it only earlier today that I followed Scamp? I check the time on my phone. Technically, since it's well past midnight, it was yesterday when I followed Scamp to Elfaeme and danced in the meadow with the wild fae. And talked with Olearia. Her warning about the curse of the revoked crown, and her plea to me to go seek the help of the Seelie King and Queen, echo in my head.

"So many fae, wild fae like Aspen, Unseelie, Seelie, have petitioned the Seelie King and Queen to help release Maeve and Aspen from Nightglade's secret prison. But to each, they say, 'We will wait for the daughter of Maeve herself to come forth and ask. No other requests will be considered'...If you don't, Maeve's power will continue to wane, and there's no guarantee Aspen will be alive for you to save on the winter solstice."

"Now we know who Maeve has been with all these years," Shannon says, rolling up the blanket and tossing it to the side carelessly. I wonder briefly what they do to maintain such a clean household if that's typical behavior, but then I look at Sean, who has not a single wrinkle in his outfit or a hair out of place, and I don't have to ask.

Then I see Shannon glance at Sean.

"Uh-uh. No!" I scowl fiercely at the both of them. "You've kept secrets from me ever since I've known you. Like that thing you're hiding upstairs."

Sean grips the hilt of his knife and Shannon adopts an overly innocent look on his face. But neither of them deny it or offer any clue as to what it is. Fine.

At least it's out in the open that I'm onto them.

"No more," I say, staring hard at Sean, then Shannon. "Whatever you were about to say to each other, you can say it out loud." I set down the teacup without taking another sip and cross my arms. Neither of them, it seems, want to be the first to break the silence. "Well? You obviously have heard of Aspen. What do you know about my birth father?"

"You should say it," Shannon tells Sean. "You were the one who lived in Sweetbriar Wood with the wild fae there."

I lean forward, intrigued. I know Sean and Shannon have had long lives. They're over two centuries old, though they've never told me their exact age. But I never imagined them spending any of that time apart.

And then, in a voice as even as a calm lake at sunrise, Sean tells me what he knows about Aspen.

It isn't much, and he's done speaking after a couple minutes, to my disappointment.

Sean only spent a few years living in Sweetbriar Wood, which is almost no time at all for a fae who can live for many ages of men. During that time, his interactions with Aspen were fleeting.

"He was always coming and going, and very secretive about what his business was outside Sweetbriar." Sean pauses, and Shannon chuckles.

"I guess now we know where he was going," Shannon says, winking at me. A blush creeps over my face. Even though I haven't met them yet, it's still awkward to think about the romantic life of my birth parents.

A wrinkle forms between Sean's eyes. "I remember something. But," he hesitates. "I think, Eevee, you shouldn't put too much stock in what I'm about to say. Because Aspen was willing to have you raised by humans, which shows he's probably changed his thinking since I saw him."

"Or Maeve changed his thinking," Shannon says, sitting on the arm of the couch next to me and elbowing me with another wink.

I try and ignore Shannon. "Changed his thinking about what?"

"There's a theory," Sean says.

"A story, really," Shannon adds, "with absolutely no basis in fact whatsoever."

Sean nods at him.

"A theory about what?"

"About separating Elfaeme from the human realm permanently," Sean answers.

"Can it be done?" I ask, my tea now cold.

"It's a story only," Shannon scoffs. "No. Elfaeme has always been a step away from the human realm. Do you know why?" I shake my head. "Because fae *need* humans and the human realm. Elfaeme was born as a reflection of the human world. What would happen if we severed ourselves from the very image we were reflecting? What is in a mirror when the person or image in front of it disappears?"

"Nothing," I whisper.

"Nothing." He nods. "Even damaging part of the Earth in the human realm can affect the landscape of Elfaeme. You change the image, the reflection changes, too."

"And that image includes humans, whether we like it or not." There's a bitter edge to Sean's voice. I look at him, curious as to why. Did he also change his thinking about this story? Had he once hoped to be free of the human world?

Something tugs at my memory. The smell of grease and sweat, and the snout-nosed face of a goblin handing out pamphlets for the underground group of fae determined to reclaim (as they put it) Earth for the fae. They go by the acronym FREEDOM, I remember, conjuring up the image of the pamphlet in my head as best I can. What did it stand for again? I press my temples and focus. Fae Reclaiming the Earth…that was the first part. What was the second? FREEDOM. Oh, yes. My blood runs cold. Fae Reclaiming the Earth, End Dominion of Men.

"So if FREEDOM gets their wish and ends the dominion of men…" I say slowly, thinking of the leaflet shoved into my hands at the fall equinox. Quince had torn it into tiny pieces as soon as he saw what it was.

"It will have consequences here in Elfaeme that none could predict," Shannon says, finishing my thought. "You'll note, though, they also do not give any weight to the theory of separating the worlds."

"No," I say, my mouth twisting in disgust.

"They just want to possess both."

I understand now why some fae spend their lives on Earth helping in nonprofit organizations. They want to preserve the Earth and its inhabitants, humans and animals, as much as possible, to preserve Elfaeme. I understand the ones who are infuriated with humans, too. It has to be incredibly frustrating to know the fate of your world is in the hands of those who seem intent on destroying theirs.

I count to ten in my head and refocus. Whatever FREEDOM is up to, it has to wait until after the winter solstice, after Amelia and my birth parents are safe.

"Okay," I say slowly, trying to process what they've shared, which is difficult considering it's the early hours of the morning and everything that's happened today would be overwhelming on its own, let alone all within twenty-four hours. "So Aspen used to believe in the theory of separating the fae and human realms. But you don't think he still does?" I'm trying not to judge, but Aspen sounds like he used to be naive.

"No," Sean answers swiftly. "Not anymore. No matter what he used to believe."

I wonder at the swiftness of his response. Is he trying to reassure me that my birth father isn't a human-hater, when my adoptive family, who I love, is human? Or is there more to the story he isn't telling?

"I hope not," I conclude. A ridiculous thought crosses my mind. What would family get-togethers look like in the future if my birth father hates humans and my human parents immediately forget or downplay any mention of the fae?

"You know, Eevee," Sean says after contemplating the flickering fire, "Most fae are aware of the limitations of our shadow world." He smiles at me, but it's a sad smile. "The theory of the worlds separating, it's a thought experiment only. And most know that."

We settle into a pensive silence, with the only sound in the room the crackling of the flames.

"Would you like to hear about my years at the Unseelie Court without Sean?" Shannon asks. "It was around the time Maeve and Aspen would've been meeting in secret."

"You were not at the court entirely without me," Sean says, with a sharp glance at his brother.

Shannon flaps a hand at Sean. "You were barely there."

"I attended twice a week." Sean scowls.

Shannon, dismissing Sean's protests, launches into a tale of his exploits at the Unseelie Court right before Maeve disappeared. He's a master storyteller, animated at all the right parts and hushed when something important is about to happen. He might have been successful at distracting me from my sister's kidnapping, Quince's betrothal, Olearia's plea, and my birth father's possible hatred of humans, if it weren't for Sean.

Every so often, Sean interrupts Shannon to correct him on one detail or another, or protest vehemently, "I was there, I know that for a fact!", which always ends with them arguing about some minute detail or another.

"And thus," Shannon concludes, "though I pride myself–" At a look from Sean, he clears his throat and says, "I mean, WE pride ourselves on knowing everything that happens in the Unseelie Court, nearly twenty years ago we were bested by the Queen herself, who kept her intentions and her affair with Aspen hidden from everyone, including Nightglade. Until the day she left, no one would have suspected her of wanting to renounce the crown, knowing the curse–"

"And Nightglade least of all," Sean interrupts, shooting a warning look at Shannon with his piercing blue eyes.

"I know about the curse of the revoked crown," I say before Sean can berate Shannon for revealing too much.

I think how heartbreaking it would be, to wake up and find your partner gone with no explanation. To go from being confident of your life and choices, to having nothing but an empty throne next to yours and a collection of unanswered questions. I almost feel bad for Nightglade. I almost get why he wants Maeve to suffer.

And I don't enjoy feeling like I understand Nightglade. It feels wrong, like my insides are slowly turning rotten.

"What now?" I ask them. I have nowhere else to turn, not really. And no matter what they're hiding,

Sean and Shannon know Elfaeme better than anyone else I know.

Their identical sets of ice blue eyes both lock with mine and I'm struck by their chilling intensity. The moment is broken when I can't hold back a yawn.

"You're tired," Shannon says. He stands and stretches. "Frankly, so am I. Sleep, then attend school in the morning. That's what we do now."

He picks up my teacup with the grace of a gazelle and heads toward the kitchen.

"School?" I ask Sean incredulously. "With everything that's happened this weekend, I'm supposed to go to school?"

"*We're* going to school," Sean clarifies.

I know it's late, or early (depending on if you're a night owl or a morning person), so I figure I don't hear him right. My face cracks into the first real smile I've had for hours, and I laugh and laugh.

"Right," I say between snorts. "You and Shannon are coming to school with me. Okay."

"It's been ages since I've gone to an institute of learning," Shannon declares from the doorway. With all the snorting I'd been doing I hadn't heard him return.

"Calling Duluth High an 'institute of learning' is a bit of a stretch," I joke. They blink at me, totally unappreciative of my humorous comment on the modern day public education system in America. Don't get me wrong, most of my teachers do the best with what they've got, but the system itself could do with an overhaul.

"You can sleep in here," Sean says, gesturing to the room and to me, where I'm still cocooned beneath multiple blankets. "We'll wake you in a few hours, then travel to your house to get what you need for school."

I feel my eyes widen. "You're serious. You guys are really going to make me go to school tomorrow, after everything that's happened? And…" My nose wrinkles. "And you're coming with me?"

"Now she's catching on!" Shannon says cheerfully. "Yes, dear, that's the plan. But first–"

The keening cry of the mystery thing neither of them will tell me about interrupts him.

"Ex–excuse me," he says, sidling away. "See you in a few hours, Eevee. Try and get some sleep." He eyes me critically. "You look like you need it."

I lob a pillow at his retreating back.

"Why are you coming to school with me?" I ask Sean quickly before he can leave. The only reason I can think of is that they want to protect me. I'm kind of annoyed at the thought of Sean and Shannon acting as my personal bodyguards all day.

"Ilinor got to your sister by pretending to be a fellow student," Sean explains. His expression is so murderous, I hunker down in my blanket cocoon. "We want to see what other fae may be lurking at Duluth High under Nightglade's orders."

His lips press together, and I notice for the first time how the streak of black hair framing the right side of his face has a few gray strands in it. Have those always been there? Or have the last few months of planning and training aged him?

"So you're coming to school, then," I say, checking the time on my phone with a grimace. "In six hours."

"Yes, but we'll wake you up in three," Sean says, examining a silver pocket watch he's pulled out of nowhere.

I groan. "Why?"

He looks like he wants to chuckle at my response but doesn't. "To get ready, of course."

With that, Sean leaves me to get what little sleep I can.

"More of a nap than anything," I grumble to myself. My head no more than touches the pillow and darkness takes me.

Sean and Shannon Get Schooled

4 Days Until the Winter Solstice

Nightmares keep me tossing and turning all night. Or rather, the rest of the night. In one of them, I'm at my birth parents' cottage in the Seelie woods, and Nightglade opens the door before I can knock.

"I've been waiting for you," he says. His gray eyes gleam as he reaches for me. I'm not quick enough, and he grabs my arm, which turns into a bouquet of flowers. With a tug, he rips it from my body. Blood splatters everywhere, covering the flowers and his face. Unperturbed, he raises the bouquet to his nose and sniffs.

The one that wakes me up involves Quince. I'm

running after him, but he's always at the edge of my sight. Finally, I stop running because even in my dream my lungs scream for air and stars dance before my eyes. Then I feel his hand on my shoulder, but when I turn to face him, I'm eye-to-eye with Ilinor. She grins to reveal pointed teeth like a wolf before she transforms into a full wolf and lunges.

I scream, my heart pounding. Sleep is impossible, so I lie awake, staring into the dull red embers of the fire until Shannon comes to get me.

He's got a cut on his forearm I know for a fact wasn't there a few hours ago, but I'm more distracted by his clothes.

"What are you wearing?" I ask, sitting upright and accepting the steaming mug of coffee he offers me. It looks like he's put the coffee in a beer stein, but I'm not complaining. It's filled to the brim and is made just how I like it—strong and black—which means more coffee for me. At this point I'd take an IV of coffee if that's what's needed to get me through the day so I can save Amelia.

"This?" Shannon asks, looking down at his outfit in confusion, then back up at me. "I don't understand. From the little I've seen of American movies, I thought football players were popular?"

I pinch the bridge of my nose and sigh. This is going to be harder than I thought. After a sip of the coffee, which revives me, I say as patiently as I'm able, "Yes, but they don't usually wear their uniforms to school, especially in the middle of winter after football season's done."

He slaps his helmet. "Of course! It's winter in Minnesota. So…hockey then? I think I have a hockey jersey somewhere…"

"Let's stay away from sports," I suggest, extricating myself from the blanket nest. "Is your dressing room still in the same place?"

I crane my neck as we walk up the stairs, hoping for a glimpse of the creature Shannon's caring for, but with no luck. The house around us is sleepy and quiet, which makes sense since it's four in the morning. When we get to the room in their house dedicated solely to clothes of all kinds and spanning centuries of fashion, Sean is there already. I choke on my coffee.

"You–what–" Words fail me, and I gape open-mouthed at Sean.

Let's just say I have chills and they're multiplying. But not in a good way.

"Like it?" Sean asks, pleased. His long hair is tied back in a ponytail at the nape of his neck. He's swooped and greased his bangs with so much gel his hair shines. Sean pops the collar of his leather jacket and smiles at himself in the mirror.

"I love it! Shannon exclaims, removing his football helmet. "You've captured the modern cool kid look perfectly."

I focus on sipping my coffee and choke again. When I've swallowed, I say, "He's mastered it perfectly if this were the fifties. Nineteen fifties," I clarify.

Sean's leathery wings droop. Crud, I've hurt his

feelings. "You look great," I say with as much enthusiasm as I can. "It's just…when have you ever seen me or Quince wearing an outfit like that?"

Shannon eyes my clothes. "So…we should wear pajama pants and wrinkled t-shirts?"

"Do you even own pajama pants and t-shirts?" I counter, walking between two racks of clothes and running my hands along the smooth silks. I miss Quince. He'd be laughing with me right now at Sean and Shannon's costumes, his dark eyes crinkling like they do when he smiles.

"Why would we?" Sean asks, following behind me. "We sleep na–"

I whirl around, holding my hand up. My face reddens up to the pointed tips of my ears. "Don't finish that sentence," I say. "I don't want that visual in my head."

Shannon guffaws and even Sean cracks a grin.

By the time I coerce the two of them into wearing somewhat normal outfits–jeans and button-up collared shirts–it leaves me with only half an hour to get ready for the day myself. Shannon pushes Sean to the side so he is centered in the mirror and adjusts the sky blue bow tie he's insisted on wearing no matter how much I tell him most high school kids wouldn't be caught dead wearing one.

They each take one of my hands and I guide them from their house in the fae realm, which has become my safe haven in Elfaeme, to my room in Duluth. The Acker house is showing some signs of life even though it's still dark out. The shower down the hall is running, and downstairs the microwave hums and beeps. I check my phone. Dad must already be driving Greg and Charlie to the morning care program at their elementary school. He usually takes them since his schedule is less crazy than mom's.

Just mom and Jess are here, then. Amelia's absence weighs on me. I know it's not my fault, but I can't help feeling guilty for what she's going through. The sooner I can save her, the better.

Sean and Shannon are wandering aimlessly in my room and I panic for a second, looking around. I didn't leave out anything embarrassing, did I? I scan the room and breathe a sigh of relief. It's messy, with clothes covering the floor and my backpack's contents spread out in no order whatsoever on my desk, but there's no bras or underwear on display.

I kick them out to the hall so I can change. "If you see my mom or Jess, don't tell them you're fae," I hiss. "Just—stay there."

They amble down the hall and stop in front of my mom's wall of art at the top of the stairs. The wall is covered from ceiling to floor with six foot wide cork board, though you wouldn't know it because every single inch of that is covered with overlapping layers of paper. She agonizes over what to keep up and what to save. Before any of the pieces of art are put into a box in the basement (she has four, each labeled with our names), she snaps a picture of it with her phone. "So I don't forget," she always says. She even has a few pieces of Cam's hung up, since Cam has been like an honorary sibling for years now. Luckily, I don't have anything humiliating on the art wall, just a still life of a fruit bowl I did in art class last year.

I leave Sean and Shannon to examine the artwork and rush to my closet, throwing on some leggings, a sweatshirt, and, after a sniff, a bit of deodorant. I pull the sweatshirt back down over my stomach. Amelia calls this my tourist shirt because across the front are the words "North Shore" in big block print. I don't care that it makes me look like a tourist rather than a local. I got it cheap at a thrift store and it's so warm and comfortable, like being surrounded by a hug. I could use a little comfort today.

Catching a glimpse of myself in the vanity mirror, I run my fingers through my hair, fluffing it up on top and trying in vain to flatten the back. I shove my school books into my backpack and my math homework on top, then join Sean and Shannon in the hall.

They're still examining the artwork with interest. Shannon is squatting, his face inches from a picture of a pink and blue dinosaur Greg had painted.

"Remarkable use of color," I hear him murmur.

Watching them from behind, I'm struck suddenly by how empty their backs look without their wings. Their ears, though. I bite my lip. Those could be a problem.

I almost have them convinced to wear hats until they see the options available: a pink hat, a unicorn hat

with sparkles, and a couple of dinosaur hats Greg and
Charlie aren't wearing today. Mom's earmuffs do
nothing to cover the pointed tips of their ears, and dad
must be wearing his this morning (he's a one hat kind
of guy). I grab my hat before Sean can. It's a mottled
green with a little golden pom pom on top.

It takes some convincing to get them to put on
any of the other winter hats available, but eventually
Shannon settles on the unicorn hat and Sean takes
Greg's blue dinosaur hat.

I check the time on my phone. Cam will be here
any minute.

Eyeing Sean and Shannon in their unicorn and
dinosaur hats, I place my hands on my hips, looking
like a puffed up bird with my winter jacket.

"Now, listen, you two," I say. "I've kept Cam
and Maggie in the dark these last few months like you
asked, and it hasn't been easy. But Amelia's been
kidnapped, and you both are coming to school with me.
I think the time for keeping them out of the loop has
ended, don't you?"

They look at one another. I can't actually hear
what they're saying, but I know they're having a
telepathic debate.

"Stop talking to each other so I can't hear you,"
I say irritably. "I mean it. Release me from my promise
not to tell them anything. They need to know what's
going on."

After what seems like eons, they break eye
contact with each other and Sean gives me a curt nod.

I send out a silent thank you to the universe that luck seems to be with me so far today. Cam's old family van, which is more rust than van but still manages to drive on the icy roads in a Minnesota winter, pulls into the driveway as soon as I get Sean and Shannon out the door.

The two of them stop dead in their tracks and stare at Cam's van, their eyebrows raised so high they're hidden by their hats.

"We could just realm-hop," Shannon offers. "Meet you there."

"That takes a lot of energy," Sean says automatically, though he frowns as if calculating just how much energy and if it would be worth the risk.

Cam, who's heard plenty about Sean and Shannon from me but has never met them before now, holds back a laugh.

"Suit yourselves," I say, buckling myself in the passenger seat, "but I'm kinda surprised you two are scared of riding in a car."

They both stride down the driveway and climb in without a word. Cam backs out into the road, but stops when Shannon clutches at the door handle and shrieks. I show them how to buckle themselves in and by the time we pick up Maggie, whose car is in the shop, they seem to be enjoying themselves.

"It's like flying, but takes no effort," Sean observes, leaning forward and looking at what Cam is doing. "You just need to turn the wheel!"

"There's a little more to it than that," Cam says,

barely able to keep a straight face.

Neither of them are willing to give up their window seats, so Maggie squishes herself between them and grins at me.

"You didn't tell me it was bring your friend to school day!"

I shrug, and Maggie zones in on my mood right away.

"What's going on, E?"

I update her and Cam on what was, without a doubt, my worst Sunday to date on the way to school.

"You've GOT to be kidding me," Maggie fumes in a barely controlled voice. Cam pulls the van into a parking space. Sean and Shannon are already fumbling at their seatbelts, their eyes on the school, but Maggie stays motionless between them. Her dark brown eyes flash angrily. "Nightglade sent his bastard child to kidnap you, but when she couldn't, she took Amelia instead?" She unbuckles forcefully, the metal buckle whipping Shannon in the arm, right where the newest cut from the mystery creature is located. He flinches and a hiss escapes his lips, but Maggie pays no attention to him as she storms past him out of the car.

In the driver's seat, Cam says nothing, but there's a pulsing tic in their jaw and their knuckles stand out white against the steering wheel. I can only imagine what they're thinking. That my fae life is spilling over into my human life as much as I tried to prevent it.

How long until Cam decides we've had a good run? Over a decade of friendship and tears and laughter and inside jokes are piled between us, like a mountain of memories. But when we became friends in invisibility back in elementary school, I doubt Cam realized I had a magical ability to remain hidden from the human eye when I want to. And on top that mountain of memories is one I doubt I'll forget. Cam's words from this last weekend. *She's not a person. She's a fae.*

I try to catch Cam's eyes, but they are reaching for their backpack and don't notice me. Would I have said something like that, if our positions were reversed? If my best friend one day told me they weren't human, would I still be driving them to school like Cam does for me?

I don't know.

Outside the van, Maggie is chatting with Sean and Shannon. Shannon, I notice, is keeping his distance from her as she gestures wildly.

"Crazy! So you guys don't really get cold then? What about if it's like negative fifty?" They open their mouths to answer, but she cocks her head and jabs a finger at their hats. "If you don't get cold, what's with the headwear?"

"They're older than me, Mags," I say, closing the van door behind me. "Their ears are harder to hide than mine."

"So?" She raises an eyebrow at me. "It'd be easier to tell people they're wearing elf ears than try to fight Ms. Lowell on her no-hats policy."

I frown. Maggie's found the flaw in my plan. I

kind of figured as long as we avoided Principal Lowell we'd be fine. Plus I wasn't sure if the hat policy applied to guests. But maybe Maggie is right.

"We can't lie about it," I point out. "If someone asks about the ears."

Sean and Shannon have already stripped their hats off and toss them into the van with relish.

"Cam and I got you," Maggie assures me. "Come on, we gotta get them visitor badges. Let me do the talking."

Silently I bless all things wonderful for whatever brought Maggie Roberts into my life. She doesn't have Quince's fae ability to charm the people she talks to, but she's got the human equivalent. Once she's done talking with old Mr. Jives in the office, Sean and Shannon have matching pink visitor badges stuck to their chests and are shaking hands with him.

"It's so rare to have visitors scouting for acting talent," he says, shaking Sean's hand vigorously. "We have a great program here. Ms. Wilson, the high school director, she does it all. She's really built the drama department from the ground up."

"Don't tell Ms. Wilson they're here," warns Maggie. "It'll ruin the point of scouting for raw talent."

Sean and Shannon grin widely as Sean withdraws his hand from Mr. Jives' grip.

"I gotta ask, though." Mr. Jives lowers his voice to a whisper. "What's with the ears?"

"They work for a Renaissance festival acting troupe," Cam answers promptly.

Maggie rubs her hands together and shoots Cam a smile. "Sure do!" She turns a stern look to Mr. Jives. "But you didn't hear that from us."

"Of course, of course," Mr. Jives says, tapping at his nose and lowering himself into his chair. "You can count on me."

"Thanks, Mr. J!" Maggie says, her voice bright and cheery.

He salutes her before returning to his crossword puzzle.

"Okay," she grabs my elbow and pulls me toward her, keeping her words to a whisper. "You should be good now. If anyone asks why they're here, you can tell them truthfully you heard someone in the office say they're scouting for acting talent for a Renaissance festival troupe, which explains the ears. But the rest is confidential."

"What would I do without you?" I ask.

"The world may never know," Maggie replies, pulling me even closer until she envelops me in a hug. Ever since she started her job at the Java Jive, she smells faintly of coffee and vanilla. I love that smell. "You get those bastard fae who kidnapped Ames and your birth parents," she whispers. "They're making this personal and they deserve everything they've got coming for them." She pulls away and winks at Sean and Shannon, who are staring at the mass of students passing by in the hall. To be fair, an ample number of students are staring back at them.

"Come on," I say, dragging Sean and Shannon

down the hall.

Cam trails behind us. "What can I do to help?" they ask, moving between me and Shannon.

I slow to a stop in front of my small animal care classroom. "I'm not sure."

"Keep an eye out for anything suspicious," Sean tells them. "If anything feels off or not quite right, let us know right away."

"We're dealing with fae who are trained in staying hidden," Shannon adds. "So you might not see anything. Think back to the last couple months. If anything comes to mind—"

"Let you know right away," Cam interrupts. "Got it." They sling their backpack over their shoulder and adjust their faded blue hair, which had flopped in front of their right eye, then slouch away.

I turn to Sean and Shannon, who both look so out of place in the sea of students around us. "Ready to go to class?"

The uncertainty in their eyes echoes how I feel about having them here at school with me.

"Come on," I say, trying to sound cheerful as I lock arms with each of them and lead them to my first class. "It's time for the two of you to get some learnin', as my grandma Alice says."

Finding Fae in Strange Places

"You know that shimmer you can see when another fae does magic in the human realm?" Sean asks me in a whisper so quiet I know no human ear could pick up on it. My small animal care class is well underway, now that Mr. Kinsley has finished explaining the day's assignment and set us to work. He had briefly acknowledged Sean and Shannon's presence in the beginning of class, but not even a fire could derail Mr. Kinsley from his lessons.

"Of course I know about that," I say confidently, as if I hadn't just learned of my fae heritage months ago. "Why?" I lower my voice to be as quiet as he was. "Did you see something?"

"No," he says. "But you were staring off into space with such concentration, I thought you might've."

I roll my eyes at him. "I was thinking."

Shannon looks over my shoulder at my worksheet. "Proper veterinary practices for fish?"

"People bring their fish to the vet, too!" I hunch over my paper so he can't read it. "Aren't you guys supposed to be looking for, you know…?" They blink at me. "Fae?" I mouth.

"We've already checked the room," Shannon says while Sean uses the reflection in the window to fix his hair. "We're relatively certain no one in here is fae. And you told us we can't search through the school without you."

"You can't," I reiterate, my heart skipping a beat just thinking what kind of trouble they would get in. And me, for bringing them here.

"It would help us track down the fae more quickly," Sean says as I scribble at my assignment.

"We don't even know for sure there are any other fae here," I point out. I scratch my chin and look down at the question on the second page. What is the procedure for treating fin rot again?

"There are," Shannon replies, crossing his hands serenely in front of him on the desk. "We just have to keep an eye out."

I hope they're right. I would love for Ilinor to be the one on the receiving end of my fiery fists, but I'll settle for any other fae who may be lurking around

Duluth High. No one messes with my sister. She's an Acker, like me. Even if the four of us are from different parents originally, we're all Ackers now, and we'll stick together through it all. Now that I think about that phrase, though, I don't think dad had fae abductions on his mind when he said it.

According to Sean and Shannon, no fae spies were in attendance in my world religions class, so when I settle into my desk for biology class with Mrs. Field, I resign myself to another forty-five minutes of attempting to make myself work while worrying about my kidnapped sister and entertaining Sean and Shannon who, I've found out, have even less of an attention span than I do when it comes to school.

Not when it comes to frogs, however. I look up to see Shannon staring intently at the terrarium where Mrs. Field's pet frog, Sparky, lives.

"Stare at him long enough and you're going to make him blush," I joke.

Shannon jumps and his expression darkens. "Oh really?"

He stands and stretches, casually making his way to the terrarium, while Sean continues to pepper Mrs. Field with questions on the energy flow of the food web.

Mystified, I watch Shannon as he closely observes Sparky the frog, then Quince's words from the fall equinox come back to me.

"Of course, none of the fae folk appear as their true selves in the human realm. Some fae, fairy folk like you and me,

look like humans. But others like that goblin? They appear as animals."

Now I'm eyeing Sparky the frog with suspicion, too. What if all this time Sparky has really been an undercover fae spy?

Like Folsom.

Ugh, what if Sparky the frog IS Folsom? I've picked him up and fed him dead flies.

He's peed on my hand!

I glare at Sparky, my science worksheet forgotten. If Sparky's actually Folsom, he has a lot of explaining to do.

Tense seconds turn into minutes, and the bell rings. Sparky spent the class period doing nothing more suspicious than croaking.

"Maybe Ilinor was the only fae he sent here on reconnaissance," Sean muses. "But it doesn't seem like Nightglade. He likes to have backup plans for his backup plans."

"We could go back to square one," Shannon suggests. "Focus on our Winter Solstice Festival plans. It's a guarantee Nightglade will have everyone out on display that night so he can gloat–Maeve, Aspen, and now Amelia."

Beneath the lunch table my foot taps incessantly. I don't like that plan. I mean, I do like our winter solstice plan, as much as I'm able to like a plan which leads me into a certain trap where I might not make it out alive. But I don't like the idea of waiting until the winter solstice to do anything.

Olearia's plea has been on my mind a lot today. If I can go to the Seelie Court and beg for their help, maybe this can all be resolved before Nightglade gets his chance to trap us.

"At least you're still keeping up with your routine, Eevee," Cam says. "Penny would freak out if you skipped."

"If she wasn't affected by the fae magic," I reply glumly.

We're all quiet, because that's what happened with Amelia. This morning, mom called to tell the office Amelia was at a friend's and she wasn't sure when she'd be back. Maggie somehow tracked down this information, which she shared with me to be helpful, but it only depressed me.

"You'll find her," Maggie says, squeezing my hand. "I know it."

I wish I had her confidence. She sees my fae powers and thinks only of the adventures. I have a hard time getting her to realize how serious it is that my birth parents and sister are in the hands of someone who not only has a twisted mind but magical powers at his disposal.

I smile at her but it feels forced. I focus instead on my lunch, even though I don't have much of an appetite. Sean and Shannon are both picking at theirs.

"Come on," I say, nudging Shannon. "Eat up. We gotta keep up our strength." To demonstrate, I spork a bite of limp, steamed vegetables into my mouth.

He picks up the cheese-covered, brick-shaped bread and eyes it. "This is nutritious?"

"It's the best you're going to get right now."

He nibbles at a corner of it and I make a silly face at Cam, who smiles and opens up their home lunch–salad with hardboiled eggs.

"Why can't we have that?" Sean asks, pointing to Cam's salad. Cam hunkers down, placing their arms as shields between their food and Sean.

I'm almost done with my lunch when someone taps me on the shoulder. Between my frayed nerves, lack of sleep, and excess amounts of coffee, I'm surprised that all that happens is I jump a foot out of my seat and bang my left knee on the lunch table.

"Ow!" I rub at my throbbing knee and turn to give the shoulder tapper a piece of my mind, but the words die on my lips.

"Shoulders guy!" I blurt out. He blinks, confused, and Maggie snickers. "I mean, Trent. What's up?"

He looks like someone has sucked all the life out of him and left behind a pale shell. His face is chalky and he has purple bags under his eyes, which are red-rimmed. Has he been crying?

"Do you–" He swallows, his Adam's apple bobbing. His voice is gravelly, like he's worn it out by talking too much. Or sobbing. "Do you know why Amelia's ghosted me? I figured I'd ask her today at school, but I can't find her anywhere. It's like, I dunno, like she's avoiding me?" He scratches the back of his head, then shrugs his immense shoulders. "Figured you might know since you're her sister."

Oh god. How do I explain Amelia's absence to shoulders guy without telling him the truth and really freaking him out?

Quince must be on my mind today because I remember how adamantly he talked about learning to tell the truth to hide the truth. Something I'm finding many fae excel at. I don't usually fault Todd and Penny Acker for how they've raised me–how were they to know I wasn't human and might someday need unique skill sets?–but sometimes I think their "honesty is the best policy" rule has really set me up to struggle with this basic fae talent.

"She's somewhere without cell service," I hear Cam explain in their quiet, calm voice. I share a quick look of surprise with Maggie, who, between the three of us, I would've expected to say something first. Truthfully, I'm just grateful Sean and Shannon haven't said anything. They're still attracting more attention to us than I'd like, even with all my efforts to get them to blend in.

As Cam concocts a believable story to explain Amelia's absence from both school and social media, I lean over to Maggie. "But where there is true friendship, there needs none," I quote.

"Shakespeare?" she asks with a small grin.

"*Timon of Athens*, if I'm not mistaken," Shannon says, swallowing his last bite of cheesy bread.

"Mom got me a book of Shakespeare quotes for

all occasions," I explain to Maggie. "She seemed to think I knew the Bard's insults too well and should branch out."

Maggie throws her head back and laughs. "Oh Penny! I love your mom."

Trent plods away and Cam turns back to us.

"Thanks Cam. I owe you one."

"You're welcome," they reply, frowning down at their salad, which has noticeably less lettuce in it than it did before. I fix Sean with a death stare, but since he's busy looking anywhere except at me or Cam, I doubt he sees it.

"Hey," I say quietly, placing my hand on Cam's arm. "I know all the changes in my life are affecting you, too. I really do appreciate the support."

Is it my imagination, or do they stiffen when I touch them? I take my hand away and they look at me out of the corner of their eyes. "I know," they say. "I wouldn't do it if I didn't know how much it meant to you."

I want to ask, "Even though I'm fae, not human?" but I don't.

In the hall outside the library, I slow to a stop. The library doors are covered with signs demanding silence and cooperation.

A SILENT

STUDY HALL

IS A

PRODUCTIVE

STUDY HALL

QUIET
STUDENTS

=

HAPPY
TEACHER

Somehow the class period I thought would be the easiest part of my day has become the most torturous, especially now I don't even have Quince to share it with.

Taking a breath, I push the door open and do a quick scan of the room. Jim is over at the computers already, and the other study hall students are scattered throughout the library at tables, computers, or wandering among the shelves and chatting quietly. No sign of Mr. Abscons, the notoriously foul-tempered librarian, yet.

"This way." I gesture at Sean and Shannon to follow me. They stare down some sophomore kid as he passes by us, and he giggles nervously, shuffling away to a table with his friends.

I watch them scan the room. "Any of them fae?" I ask quietly.

"Not that I can tell," Shannon says as he locks eyes with a freshman girl who blushes and drops the book she was holding. "Too high strung. Definitely teenagers."

"Amelia thought Ilinor was definitely a teenager, too," I remind him.

The bell to start study hall will ring shortly. I herd Sean and Shannon past the checkout desk, heading toward my usual spot at the computers next to Jim, but slow down in front of the checkout desk. Abscons is running late today. This could be a chance to mess with him.

Ever since Mr. Abscons took over for Ms. Burns earlier this year, the student body as a whole has come to a consensus about our substitute librarian. He sucks. I haven't taken part in any of the pranks against him yet, but I can't pass up this opportunity.

"Hold on," I whisper to Sean and Shannon, who are having way too much fun intimidating my peers with their unnerving stares. I sneak around the desk and start rifling through the stacks of books and papers. Some teachers have sticky notes attached to worksheets that need copying. I consider switching the sticky notes, but decide against it. Yes, it would make Abscons look incompetent, which he hates, but it would also mess up the teachers' plans for their classes.

Some of the papers in a large pile to my left shift, unbalanced from my rummaging, and a sliver of yellow appears. I frown, removing the papers, to reveal a notebook with badly drawn fairies on the cover.

Not just any notebook.

MY notebook, the one I thought I'd lost months ago.

The one with all my notes about Maeve and her clues to help me find her in the fae realm.

I snatch it up, relief and horror and realization swirling in me until I'm dizzy. If Abscons has had my notebook this whole time, then…

"Evelyn!"

I whirl around at the sound of Abscons' shrill voice. His ratlike face is contorted with anger.

"What are you doing behind my desk? Go to your seat now, or it's deten–tion…"

His voice quavers to a stop and I swear his whole body turns as white and see-through as a moonbeam.

"No," he whispers. "Not you two. Not again. Gods, no! No!"

He turns, takes a couple of weaving steps, and

then bolts for the door.

Sean and Shannon dash after him into the hall. Still clutching my notebook, I run to them.

"He's gone," Sean informs me as he walks back into the library, his face unnervingly calm. "I don't think he'll be back."

Stick to the Plan, Don't Do Anything Stupid

Study hall erupts into chaos until Principal Lowell herself strides in to hear excitable students talking over each other in their eagerness to share the gossip: Mr. Abscons has fled.

Unfortunately, Principal Lowell is fluent in excited student and all accounts end with mentioning Abscons' reason for fleeing. My two guests.

"Evelyn?" Principal Lowell asks, marching over to me. Her hair is held back in a bun so tight it pulls at the skin of her face. She's wearing her usual pantsuit, her whole outfit harsh lines and no-nonsense. "I'd like to hear your side of the story." She crosses her arms and her face settles into an expression I know well because I usually see it on my dad's face. The "I'm-not-going-anywhere-until-you-talk" expression. Her gray eyes are cold and offer no mercy. "Let's start with these two guests of yours. Where are they?"

Her question takes some time to sink in. I spin around.

"Son of a biscuit! Those toad-spotted traitors!" Harsh, I know. But if Edgar can call Edmund a toad-spotted traitor in *King Lear* for his villainy, I can certainly use the same insult for Sean and Shannon for abandoning me at school.

"I don't know," I answer truthfully when I turn to face Principal Lowell.

C: *u left school?*

M: *E*

M: *E, where r u?*

M: *???*

M: *did u guys FIND SUM1*

M: *was it Abscons?*

M: *cuz that dude was sketch and no1 liked him*

C: *yeah i heard he ran out of study hall, was it cuz of u?*

M: *EEVEE WE NEED ANSWERS*

I'll answer them soon. Probably. If I remember. Cam and Maggie deserve an update. Right now I'm too upset by the letter I'm holding.

I tried Sean and Shannon's house first, as soon as Principal Lowell was convinced I had no knowledge of where they were. Just excused myself to go to the bathroom and ended up in Elfaeme instead. You know, like you do when you're a teenage fae whose fae friends just abandoned her at school with no explanation whatsoever. I figured, if I were them, I'd go back to somewhere I knew was fortified and safe.

But when I got there, the house and grounds were empty and quiet, the ice on the walls and windows sparkling in the cold, early afternoon sunlight.

I had spent a good five minutes banging on their front door and flying around their property. I was not going to make the same mistake I had last night when I tried to appear directly in their house. It makes me queasy just thinking of the smell of rotting lemons and meat.

In an infuriating turn of events, I found a letter in their second story window where I had spied on them (okay, tried unsuccessfully to spy on them) on Saturday night. It wasn't marked, and I missed it on my first couple fly-arounds. But the third time I stopped and hovered in front of that damn second story window, wondering where they could be and if they left the mystery creature at their house or took it with them, when I saw it, a small sliver of white poking out from beneath one of the frost-covered panes of glass.

I broke three icicles while retrieving it. Hovering in the air while prying a small envelope out from beneath a window is not as easy as one would think.

And now, here I sit, on my bed, staring at a letter and ignoring my phone.

"Dearest friend," the letter begins, in big letters with extra flourishes. I grind my teeth as I read through the letter for the thousandth time. There's no doubt in my mind I'm the "Dearest friend," even if they carefully kept my name from appearing anywhere in the letter, out of caution.

Dearest friend,

The presence of that fae—Abscons, did you call him?—changes our situation, I'm afraid. In the Unseelie Court he goes by the name Banethistle. He is known by all and trusted by none, except Nightglade, to whom he owes his life. Anything Nightglade needs, Banethistle will do. Even if it means his own hands are stained red with blood.

Banethistle saw us with you, though. We're not safe. Not that we were before, but now our association with you has been discovered. You are not safe, either.

We've gone into hiding for the time being, and it is pointless to try to find us. No one has ever found us when we choose to be hidden. You will see us again in a few days.

Stick to the plan. Do not stray from the plan, and don't do anything to attract attention to yourself.

Your friend,
Shannon

P.S. Sean says don't do anything stupid.

I crumple up the letter and toss it across my room, where it bounces harmlessly against my wall and settles on a pile of clothes. Don't do anything stupid. Right.

So I'm just supposed to sit here, go to school, follow through the motions of my human life until Friday night, when the Winter Solstice Festival begins and our plan will officially be set in motion?

No. I send a quick text to Cam and Maggie and pace my room. I'm glad no one is home yet. I'll probably be punished for leaving school early, but then again, maybe not. The fae magic affecting my parents has made them worrisomely forgetful this week.

If this were a year ago, I'd probably tell mom I had a bad headache or something.

But now that I'm a full-grown fae, I can't even try to get away with that excuse. Don't get me wrong, being a full-grown fae comes with excellent advantages, like my flaming fists and being able to pick up on animals' emotions. I've found cats are the easiest for me to sense, but when I visited the aquarium in Duluth with my family last month, I ended up with a headache from sensing all the fish emotions. They were so hungry, and so territorial. Especially the little ones. Honestly, even with the confusion that comes from

158

sensing emotions that aren't mine, I'm kind of excited about what that second ability might mean for my future career as a vet tech.

But these powers, cool as they are, have their limits and come with a price. Like the number one rule all fae are bound to: *fae can't lie.*

I remember Quince telling me other rules, but it was on Homecoming and we haven't talked about that night, preferring to focus on the hope of the future than on the pain of the past. There are many rules fae are bound to, but he said there were three major ones. I frown, forcing myself to think back to that night, before the cottage, when we had just left the Reflecting Pool and had no idea what we were getting into. Obviously, the first is the one that affects me the most on a daily basis. But the second has something to do with one's true name, given at birth. That one worries me, because the two people who know my true name are in Nightglade's clutches. I don't even know what Maeve and Aspen had named me, before giving me into the care of Todd and Penny Acker. The third eludes me, though.

Thinking about what my true name might be and how, unlike other teens, I can't lie to my parents even if I want to, sends me down one of my "what-if" thought spirals. What if Maeve and Aspen had raised me, rather than Todd and Penny? Would they have done something similar to Jerry and Myska, Quince's parents, and encouraged me to practice the art of telling a truth to conceal the truth? Quince isn't bound by the rules of the fae, yet. Not for another twelve days. At least he'll be ready when the time comes.

These "what-if" spirals always leave me feeling unsettled, like a piece of dandelion fluff blown away, never finding a place to land, always drifting.

My room is suddenly too small. I leave and pace through the house, eventually making my way to the kitchen. I brew some coffee and stalk the kitchen until the pot is full, which seems to take forever.

The rich, bitter smell of coffee fills the kitchen as it brews. When the hum of the machine comes to a stop I pour myself a mug and sip, my brain working furiously.

Sean and Shannon are in hiding.

Abscons is a fae named Banethistle, who works for Nightglade, *and* he's a notebook thief.

Nightglade has ramped up his efforts in the last few days to…what? Remove me from the equation before I can get to the winter solstice? Slowly eliminate all the good things in my life so the next best option would be to go to him? I don't understand the purpose behind everything that's happened. Is he growing impatient? How can he do all of this to me if he thinks I'm his daughter?

I pour myself more coffee, and though it's hot, my blood turns to ice. What if he knows I'm not his daughter by now, and this is his twisted way to get back at Maeve, by torturing me and playing head games? Sending Ilinor to befriend Amelia and sow distrust between us, then having her kidnap Amelia when she couldn't get to me. Instructing Abscons to spy on me and steal from me. Kidnapping and, most likely, torturing my birth parents, Maeve and Aspen, before I could meet them. Arranging a betrothal between Ilinor—who he may or may not think is my half sister, either way, it's sadistic of him—and Quince.

Sitting down, I drain my second mug of coffee. I'm repeatedly hitting my forehead on the kitchen table when I hear the chair across from me scrape on the linoleum floor.

"Eevee?" Cam asks. I sit up. Maggie stands behind them on her phone.

"Why?" I wail.

Cam's face wrinkles in confusion. "Why what?"

"Why is he doing all of this?" My voice is hoarse, and I feel pathetic and weak, but Cam looks at me with concern, not pity.

"Nightglade?" they ask tentatively.

"Yeah, him." I tick off all the ways Nightglade has worked his warped plans from afar.

"Classic case of power-hungry narcissism," Maggie explains, still looking down at her phone. "He's separating you from the people you care for, keeping tabs on you so he knows your movements, and trying to make it so you'll come to him defeated and he can mold you how he wants."

"That will never happen," I snarl.

"'Course it won't," Cam assures me. "Because he can't separate us."

Can't he? I stare at Cam, and maybe they see

the question in my eyes because they break eye contact and clear their throat.

"He doesn't need to separate us," I say, misery expanding painfully in my chest. "I was doing that well enough on my own with all my secret keeping."

Cam takes a breath, then pauses, their head tilting forward so their hair flops in front of their eyes.

Maggie helps herself to the pot of coffee I brewed, which is somehow half gone already, and pours an unnecessary amount of creamer into her mug. "E, we might be a little offended you didn't talk to us about this winter solstice stuff from the beginning, but we'll get over it. You need to get over it, too. Besides," she sits down and plunks her phone onto the table in front of me, "we need to get better at protecting ourselves so no one else gets kidnapped like Amelia."

I study the pictures on her phone, then scroll through the articles while she cups her hands around the mug to warm them. "You really think this will work?" I ask.

She shrugs and takes her phone back. "Worth trying, anyway. Cam says they can get their hands on some of the supplies we need from the set build at school."

"I just heard from Jim, he says he'll set it aside for us," Cam confirms. Maggie tenses, the skin around her eyes and mouth going tight, but the pain must be fading for her because she smiles and the tense moment is gone. I'm glad. I've brought enough troubles to our friend group. We don't need Jim Mortensen, Quince's best human friend, coming between us.

"What about the–"

"We're going to drive around to a few places and see if we can track it down after we pick up the stuff from Jim," Maggie explains.

"We'll make sure we make enough for your whole family to wear, plus us," Cam assures me.

"And then some," adds Maggie, her face determined. "We're not going to let some fae folk capture us, E."

Her voice is steely, her dark brown eyes glinting. She's going to make such a great journalist someday, with her combination of making everyone feel trusting and her steel backbone.

"Sounds like you've got your mission."

But what's mine?

What can I do?

"I'm not waiting for the winter solstice," I declare aloud. I see Cam give Maggie one of their "I-told-you-so" looks. "I'm not," I say again, my resolve hardening. "No matter what Sean and Shannon say. They're not the ones whose immediate family members are being held captive. I can't afford to be as cautious as them, not when my birth parents' lives are on the line. And Amelia's."

"I get it." Maggie's face softens. "But what can you do?"

"I'm going to ask King Oakspirit and Queen Hibiscus for help. But," I fiddle with my now-empty coffee mug, wondering if I should refill it, or rethink my idea, or both, "I don't know where the Seelie Court is."

"Not trying to poke a hole in your plan, Eevee, but–"

"It's not so much a plan as an inkling of an idea," I tell Cam. "Poke away."

Their smile is small, faded, and their right hand fiddles with their hair as they speak. "If you don't know where the Seelie Court is, how do you plan to get there and back in time for the winter solstice?"

"I'll tell you what I can't do," I say as I stand and refill my coffee. "I can't just wander around Elfaeme, hoping I find someone who can help me get to the Seelie Court." You'd think, with all the planning I'd been doing with Sean, Shannon, and Quince, one of them would've brought out a map. No such luck. I'm starting to wonder if a map of Elfaeme even exists. But without Sean and Shannon's help, and in the absence of a map…

I pause, my hand holding the coffee pot trembling. There is a certain fae who might help me, for the right price. One whose motives I've never quite been able to figure out, but who knows a lot more about the fae realm than he lets on.

No, I can't ask Folsom for help. Who am I kidding?

He would offer it, though, I bet. For a price.

"What about…what's-her-name? That old fae with the rams horns you met yesterday?" Cam asks.

"Olearia." She'd help me, but… I shake my

head as I sit down at the table. "I don't know how to find her. I traveled to the meadow with Scamp's help. I don't think I'd be able to travel there again on my own. I don't know it well enough."

"So find Scamp." Maggie shrugs as if this were the most obvious answer.

I set down my coffee cup a little harder than I intend, and Cam winces at the sound.

"*You* try and find a stray cat who travels between both realms," I snap. "When you do, let me know."

Maggie looks about ready to shout back at me, but she huffs and storms away instead. "I'll be back in a minute," she calls over her shoulder, her voice shrill with anger.

Cam and I lock eyes. They stare at me, shock and concern written all over their face.

"What?" I grumble. "Scamp IS hard to track down."

Okay, that's not the point. They know it, and I know it.

Maggie comes back to the kitchen after a minute and points at my coffee. "Alright. Usually you know I love the stuff as much as you, E, but I don't think any amount of coffee is going to help much right now. All it's doing is making you more jittery and on edge."

There's an unspoken "and shitty to your best friends" message in there, too, and I hear it even if she doesn't say it.

At a nod from Maggie, Cam delicately removes the coffee mug from my grasp while Maggie pours out the rest of the coffee from the pot.

A flash of irritation burns through me, but I grit my teeth into a smile. "You're probably right." To her credit, Maggie doesn't respond with an "I told you so." She just places the empty pot back on its burner and turns off the coffee maker. "But Mags, Scamp can be gone for weeks or months at a time. He's a stray cat with two worlds at his disposal. Not exactly reliable. That's all I was trying to say."

"Okay, fair." She frowns and turns to me. "Wait, hold up. Why don't you just ask Quince?"

Cam's eyes light up. "Yeah, doesn't he have friends in the fae realm that you met at the fall equinox celebration? You'd think he'd know–"

"He's engaged."

Maggie eyeballs me, one eyebrow raised. "Like...busy?"

"Like to be married."

Her jaw drops.

"To Ilinor."

Cam's mouth hangs open to match Maggie's.

Ilinor again. I've known about her for less than a day, but she's been a pawn in Nightglade's endgame for months. The thought of the two of them scheming together to threaten me and my family makes my blood boil.

"How...? Why...? What?"

"Nightglade arranged it," I answer Maggie,

whose journalist brain at least is kicking in and getting her to ask the right questions, even if not in the most coherent fashion.

Anger and sadness scramble together in my heart and I stop talking.

"That's next level messed up," Maggie finally says. Cam's face is pale as they stare at me. "But I don't get why you can't ask Quince, even if he is engaged to your evil stepsister."

A ghost of a smile appears on Cam's lips at the evil stepsister comment. "Yeah, he can't exactly be happy about his engagement."

"He's not."

"So?" Maggie starts typing furiously on her phone. "No reason you can't ask him for help."

"He didn't tell me!" I burst out. Maggie stops typing and looks at me, cocking her head like a dog who hears something he doesn't quite understand. "He's been engaged to Ilinor for about a month now, and he didn't tell me. Sean and Shannon were the ones who broke the news, after Ilinor kidnapped Amelia, probably because they felt I deserved to know something about the person who literally stole my sister. And my kind of boyfriend." My knuckles crackle with flames and I stand and pace the kitchen, flapping my hands angrily to put out the fire before it gets even more out of control.

"Here," Cam says quietly. They lead me to the kitchen sink and guide my hands below the faucet, careful to avoid touching the flames, which have only gotten larger with all the frantic swinging. They turn on the faucet and douse my hands with a spray of cold water. Steam rises and stings my eyes as my knuckles sizzle. Beneath an onslaught of water, the flames fizzle out quickly. Cam turns the faucet off.

"Thanks," I say when they pat my shoulder.

Maggie hands me a kitchen towel, her eyes sparkling as they always do when she sees the fae side of me come out.

I take the towel from her and absentmindedly pat at my hands.

"Earth to Eevee." She snaps in front of my eyes and I blink, then focus on her. The towel is still in my hands, which are dry. How long have I been zoned out?

"Sorry, what?"

"Not sure where you went there," she jokes, "but I was just saying it's no wonder Quince didn't tell you about Ilinor." She holds up her fists. "He was afraid you'd react like that."

Part of me squirms in disgust at myself, at my inability to control my feelings or my flaming fists. If I can't control one, I can't control the other. And does it say more about Quince or me, that he was so hesitant to tell me about his betrothal?

I know Maggie meant it in a joking way. It's Maggie, she deals out her advice with a smile, which is partly what makes her so easy to talk to. It doesn't make her comment any less true, though.

"Even if I do message him, he may not want to help me," I say, thinking of how I shouted "Coward!"

at him last night when he was leaving Sean and Shannon's. "And he doesn't always respond right away. He can only make short trips to the human realm, and he's probably being watched even more now that Abscons has seen Sean and Shannon with me."

Suddenly I'm frozen in fear for Quince and his family. What will Nightglade do to them when he learns who was with me at school today?

"Hey," Cam says, tentatively nudging my shoulder. "You can't control that. But you can reach out to him and hope for the best."

"She already did," Maggie says. It's then I notice she has my phone. She hands it to me. "As did I. E, will you be okay here while you wait for Quince to get back to you, or do you want to come with us?"

Staying on the move, doing something productive like track down items around town to make fae protection charms sounds so much better than sitting idle at home with anxiety as my only company, waiting for a text that might not come.

"I can't," I say with regret. "I should stay here, in case…"

I don't finish the thought, but Maggie and Cam both nod. "We'll try to be quick." Maggie's already slinging on her jacket. "If you hear from Quince and you have to leave suddenly, just know we'll be back soon with some protection for your family."

"You don't know for sure that it'll work," I warn.

"You don't know it won't," she retorts.

And with that reassurance, they leave me to my anxious, exhausted thoughts.

Burnt Out

There's not much time until Jess gets home from school, so I refill the coffee pot because I'm feeling contrarian, and busy myself with stalking a path from the kitchen to the living room and back as I think. My brain's a jumbled mess. I know I should use this time productively somehow, but I can't think of what else to do, save travel to the fae realm and wander around, hoping whatever fae I come across would be willing to help me.

Like Folsom, my brain whispers. *I know where he lives, he was there the first time I traveled to Elfaeme, he was there Homecoming night, too, and he doesn't strike me as the kind of fae who would wander far from his home.* Unless he were reinstated to his position in the Unseelie Court, of course.

A sense of peaceful calm tugs at the edge of my mind and I freeze, the hairs on my arms standing on end. I'm anything but peaceful right now.

So where is that feeling coming from? More specifically, from whom?

Has Nightglade sent an animal to finish what Ilinor started yesterday? It isn't too much of a stretch of the imagination to picture the stern-faced Nightglade instructing a wolf or some other animal to come to my house and kill me, his gray eyes glinting like steel as he sends the animal to take care of me once and for all.

But then I hear a low, buzzing sound and I breathe a sigh of relief. "Hey Slink," I say, opening the door to mom and dad's room.

The sense of peacefulness is more powerful the closer I get to him. Setting my coffee cup down, I climb onto the bed carefully, so as not to disturb him, and curl myself around the dark ball of fluff. He's warm against me, his fur sleek, and as I bury my face in the fur on his side, I breathe in the smell of the outdoors. His buzzsaw purring stops and annoyance emanates from him, but when he realizes I'm not moving anymore, he settles back into a watchful sleep. I want to stay here forever, snuggling next to Slinky's warm, comforting body, but my anxiety won't let me. Not right now.

I kiss Slinky on his silky head and continue obsessively pacing through the house, checking my phone about fifty times a minute, and practicing some of the self-defense moves Sean had been teaching me.

None of it helps, and I feel so ineffectual, so useless, I want to scream.

Careful planning hasn't helped. Aspen is in danger of dying before the winter solstice, and who knows what torture Nightglade is forcing Maeve to endure. Secrecy hasn't helped. It kept me from being open with my friends and Amelia, and even led Amelia to trust Ilinor instead of me. Look where that got her.

I grind my teeth. What is it Grandpa Jon used to tell me? I picture his wooden rocking chair on his front porch, where he liked to sit and watch the sunset, rocking back and forth and drinking a beer. As a kid, I told my grandpa Jon everything, including my most secret wishes. "Evelyn," he'd say, tipping the beer back, "If wishes were horses, beggars would ride."

I can't change what I've done or not done since Homecoming night. But I can take action now, before the winter solstice.

Deadlines help. I chew my lip as I think. Quince usually takes at least a couple hours to a day or more to respond. I don't have that many days left until the winter solstice, so if I don't hear from him before tomorrow morning, I'm going to the fae realm without him and looking for Folsom.

I send a quick text to Maggie and Cam.

E: *i might not b at school tmrw or the rest of the week if i have 2 leave suddenly*

As usual, Maggie's response is rapidfire.

M: don't worry about that E
M: we got u

She sends me a selfie of her and Cam at some greenhouse.

Having a plan with a timeline calms me, like adding aloe to a sunburn. I check the clock in the living room. Jess should be home by 4:00 at the latest, depending on how quick the bus driver is, which gives me about another hour at home by myself.

Sean and Shannon's warnings play on repeat in my head as I think of traveling with Quince or Folsom to the Seelie Court. Stick to the plan. Don't do anything stupid.

I'm definitely not sticking to the plan. And I might just be doing something incredibly stupid, whether Quince replies to me or not.

In a weird way, I think they'd approve.

The clock ticks by. Less than an hour until Jess gets home. I walk up the stairs, thinking if I had a fitness tracker I'd be way over ten thousand steps by now with all this pacing, when I pass my room.

I back up, and rush to my bed, panic gripping me. What if Nightglade sends more fae here? Ilinor was within feet of my adoption box with its medical records, card, photo, and note from Maeve. If she had found it, how could they have used that against me?

Maybe they can't. Maybe they know all they need to know already, but I can't shake the thought that I should get rid of any evidence I can. I kneel down next to my bed and pull out the cardboard box. I haven't opened it in a few weeks, not since the Sunday after Thanksgiving when our Sunday meeting at Sean and Shannon's involved more jokes and fun than actual planning. I had come home that night filled with longing to have a night like that with my birth parents, had wondered if they'd be as quirky as Shannon or as tempestuously calm as Sean. Or maybe even as cheerful and radiant as Quince.

On top of the papers is the music box with its glittering, blood-red jewel adorning it. There's no inscription identifying me anywhere on its surface, but I don't think I could bring myself to destroy it even if there were. Inside, tucked away safely, is the baby doll seen in the only picture of me taken by one of my birth parents. She had carried a note to me across time, a clue to finding Maeve someday.

But I was too late.

I lift the music box out and grab at the adoption packet beneath, where all the papers and notes are stored. I've studied them so much I have their contents memorized.

The papers removed, I place the beautiful music box back in the plain cardboard one and slide it in its place under my bed. I would hate to lose the music box and doll, if a fae does come to the house and find them, but they're too bulky to bring with me to Elfaeme.

Backpacks don't work well with wings, so I need to pack light.

The papers in the large manila envelope feel heavy, like I'm carrying bricks, and my steps are slow as I carry them to the bathroom. A thought occurs to me as I set them in the tub, and I go collect the yellow notebook Abscons stole from me. At this point there's no question he's passed on all its contents to Nightglade, but at least I can prevent anyone else from reading it. In the hall, I glance up at the smoke alarm. Can't have that going off and disturbing the neighbors. Old Mrs. Grimsbee next door already complains enough about the racket Greg and Charlie make between the two of them.

I turn off the smoke alarm and return to the bathroom, the tile floor cold against my feet.

Once everything is assembled in the bathtub, I pause. It looks insignificant in the bottom of the tub, this small pile of papers topped with a yellow notebook. Insignificant, and yet, in the wrong hands...

I shake my own hands and crack my knuckles. "Okay, Eevee, you can do this," I whisper to myself. "Just like Shannon taught you. Find the fire within."

A few minutes later, I'm holding my hands up to my face and shouting at them and seriously considering getting the lighter from the junk drawer, which I probably should have done in the first place. Not even thinking of Amelia being kidnapped or Quince's betrothal to Ilinor is enough to set my knuckles aflame. Probably because my anger about both of those situations is all tangled up in guilt.

When was the last time I was truly angry–just purely angry?

The night Jess first saw my flaming fists springs to mind.

"Stupid Damian," I growl. Even thinking of him now, thinking of all the months we were together and how it ended with him first breaking up with me, then wanting me as his booty call when he was home from college, makes my ears spout steam. I really hope he grows out of being a self-involved tool, for his own sake.

Orange and yellow flames crackle then burst to life over both my hands. Huh. I guess Damian's good for something after all.

Quickly, I touch my hands to the papers in the tub. As they catch fire, I blow on my knuckles and shake them. "Cool the fire," I mutter, the phrase Shannon taught me to say when my fists no longer needed to be wreathed in flames.

On impulse, I reach into the tub and grab the photograph of me as a baby, rescuing it from its fiery fate. The edges are charred, but otherwise it's unharmed. I fold it into my phone case, hidden away.

I don't know how long I sit on the toilet seat, watching almost every bit of physical evidence that ties me to my birth parents go up in flames. Long enough to see the papers smolder into embers and, finally, crumble to ash.

It feels final, this act. I don't know why, really.

I've gone to the fae realm dozens of times since finding out I was fae. But I can't shake this feeling of foreboding, like my next trip might be my last.

Of course, I don't have the gift of foresight as far as I'm aware, so I really hope I'm wrong.

I turn on the shower and lift the nozzle, aiming it at the gray ashes until they're all washed down the drain and the tub is white and clean, no sign of any charred papers to be seen.

All my wired, anxious energy seems to have followed the ashes down the drain because I sag to the floor, dropping the nozzle and letting my arms hang limply over the edge of the tub.

I'd stay here all afternoon, my arms dangling, forehead pressed to cool porcelain, if it weren't for my phone buzzing. I pull it out of my sweatshirt pocket and fight down disappointment. It's not Quince.

It's Maggie, though. They've found everything they need and are heading to Cam's house to put it all together.

Good. I hope it works and they'll be protected from any fae who may try to kidnap them. After Ilinor took Amelia last night I've developed a new phobia: having my friends and family abducted by the fae.

I sense Slinky waking up, so I drag myself to my feet and go to him, scooping him up in my arms. He's gained weight as he's aged. We have diet food for him, but it doesn't work because he gobbles it all up and then goes and steals food from the trash or begs Greg and Charlie for treats, the little glutton.

Shutting myself and Slinky inside my room, I collapse on the bed and hug him to my chest. He squirms free and curls up at the end of my bed, so I burrow under my covers and, for the first time in all the craziness of the last few days, I let myself cry.

Big, wracking sobs hurt my chest and my pillow becomes wet with tears, but still I cry. I can't stop. I'm crying for everything. For my kidnapped sister, with her poor boyfriend, shoulders guy, who thinks she ghosted him, and her quick smile, and her love of cheese. For the birth parents I haven't met, and may not ever, if any part of our winter solstice plans (my current plan, and Sean and Shannon's plan) fall through. For this divide I feel between me and Quince that's caused by more than living in different realms. And for the opportunity that Nightglade stole from me. When I knocked on my birth parents' cottage door on Homecoming night, I was ready to meet them. But Nightglade had gotten there first and stole our reunion from me before it could even happen. I will never forgive him for that.

At some point my sobs die down, and I open my eyes, which feel puffy and raw, to see Slinky has scooched closer to me and is eyeing me, concern dimming his big, yellow eyes.

He doesn't protest when I bring him under the covers with me, and it's with his fluffy body snuggled up next to my stomach that I finally give in to the exhaustion and fall into a deep sleep.

Ready, Set

3 Days Until the Winter Solstice

When I wake up my room is dark and Slinky is meowing at the door. I rub the sand out of my eyes and stretch. All my limbs are heavy and slow, reluctant to move. I must've slept in the same position the whole time, because my joints creak like I'm eighty, not eighteen, and I feel stiff and sore all over.

Slinky meows again, so I force myself to stand and hobble over to the door. He streaks into the hall like a shadow escaping the light and is quickly gone from sight.

How long did I sleep? I yawn and check my phone. Just after midnight. No one woke me up for dinner or anything. Or, if they tried, I didn't realize it and fell right back asleep.

My gut clenches. What if no one woke me up because no one's here? I was sleeping so deeply, I could've slept through a tornado, let alone a fae invasion.

As quietly as I can, I step into the hall, my heart thudding in my ears. *Please don't be gone*, I silently pray. I can't lose anyone else, I haven't even recovered the others who were taken from me. I tiptoe toward Jess's room first, since hers is closest. Loud, snuffling snores reach my ears and I breathe a sigh of relief. Jess is notorious for her loud snoring, it's why sleeping in a camper with her results in a lot of sleep-deprived Ackers by the end of our camping trips.

Greg and Charlie's room is next. I stand outside their door, which is cracked open. The light from their dinosaur night-light spills into the hall, and my ears pick up the quiet sounds of their breathing. I listen to it a moment longer, my heart rate slowing. They're okay. Jess is okay, too.

I think they sense someone's in the hall, because I can hear their beds creak as they both shift in their sleep. I press a kiss to my hand and place it on their doorway, then sneak over to my parents' room.

Their door is closed, so I press my ear to the cool wood, then slump against it in relief. Everyone's safe. For now.

Everyone except Amelia. I straighten and, for the first time since I woke up, take out my phone. Still nothing from Quince, but I have a bunch of missed messages from Cam and Maggie.

C: *we got it all done!*
M: *i am NOT crafty*
M: *ugh*
C: *we'll drop off the ones we made with ur fam tmrw. it took a little longer than expected to make them*
M: *just say it, Cam*
M: *say it*
C: *…*
M: *SAY IT*
C: *Maggie kept breaking the stems*
M: *yep. sure did.*
M: *but we got it done!*
M: *cu tmrw, E*

Mission accomplished. Now we'll find out if their efforts were worth it or if they spent their Monday night tracking down items and crafting for nothing.

No texts from Quince, though. I wonder if he's awake. He's a night owl, and a lot of the texts I get from him come from this time of night. I head to my room and softly close the door, reminding myself that I have until the morning. If I don't hear from him before I have to go to school, I'm going to Elfaeme instead.

I realize I never read the text Maggie sent Quince from my phone.

E (but really M): *RED ALERT NEED HELP ASAP*

It's quick and to the point, no information leaked that shouldn't be, and the caps certainly convey a sense of urgency. Not exactly written in my style, but I guess that isn't the point.

I plug in my phone and set it on my nightstand. After sleeping all afternoon and evening, I'm wide awake while the rest of the world sleeps. I gaze out my window at the winter wonderland in my backyard. I love how the snow glows in the moonlight, giving the land a ghostly appearance. The snow monster (not a snow man or woman, but a snow monster) that Greg and Charlie built stands next to our porch, all eight stick arms proudly at attention. They spent an entire afternoon building it last week. I wonder how long it'll last before they decide to demolish it. Or if I'll be around to see the next snow monster they build.

Stop thinking like that, Eevee! I admonish myself, turning from the window. I can't think past the winter solstice, and what might or might not happen. But I also can't say there's no doubt I'll see another Greg and Charlie snow monster this winter. There's definitely doubt. A fair helping of it.

My phone lights up and I'm not rushing to check it, which is why I don't end up banging my toe on the corner of my nightstand.

Okay, I do. And why does it hurt so much when it's such a little toe?

False alarm. It's an email, and a spam email at that. I swear I'm not usually this obsessive about texts from Quince, but I can't shake the thought I had earlier: that something might have happened to him and his parents. How swiftly will Nightglade act once he hears of Sean and Shannon's association with me? And what will he do to Quince, Myska, and Jerry for the simple crime of being related to Sean and Shannon?

I sit on my bed and rub my shoulders. It's infinitely less satisfying than Cam's shoulder rubs, but it'll have to do, because my shoulders are as tight as if I'd spent all afternoon lifting weights with shoulders guy, not sleeping.

I know what I want to do. The only thing stopping me is my self-imposed deadline giving Quince a chance to get back to me.

Only a few more hours remain. Then, with or without Quince "might-have-been-arrested-by-a-narcissistic-fairy-king" Florentz, I'm going to Elfaeme. Maybe it means I'm doing something stupid, but I can't sit here and wait for Friday night to arrive for Quince to text me.

So I text him instead.

E: *im going 2 where we met F that night. leaving b4 school Dec 20*

Someone in Elfaeme needs to know of my (most likely) stupid plan. Might as well be my sort of boyfriend.

The last few days have made one thing abundantly clear to me: my fae connections are limited at best, especially with two of them in hiding, one possibly being detained by Nightglade, and the others in a part of Elfaeme I've only visited once with the help of an unreliable stray cat.

But Folsom, he's even more desperate than I am. And I bet he'd do anything to recover his position at the Unseelie Court. Including, I hope, delivering me willingly to Nightglade after I convince him to escort me on a detour to the Seelie Court.

Crazy? Maybe. Stupid? Probably. But the best chance I have to help everyone I care about (or am related to—the jury's out on if I'll actually like Maeve and Aspen, though I hope I do) lies in the Seelie Court.

The hours pass so slowly I am convinced the clock is tricking me and adding extra seconds to each minute, extra minutes to each hour. At one point my stomach grumbles like a drunken pirate so I risk a trip down to the kitchen to make a peanut butter and jelly sandwich. The whole thrilling experience takes only ten minutes, and then I'm on my bed again, my eyes glued to the clock on my phone.

I must doze off, because when I open my eyes again, mom is knocking on the door.

"I'm heading to the office. Make sure you get up and are ready to go before Cam gets here, Eevee."

I'm immobilized by conflicting desires. I want to rush to the door and wrap mom up in a hug and never let go. And I also want to avoid touching her or seeing her because it'll hurt too much, knowing what I know about Amelia, knowing I'm leaving for Elfaeme soon and, if Folsom turns out to be stronger than he looks, probably not coming back.

I gurgle out a reply that kind of sounds like I tried to say "good bye" and "I love you" at the same time: "Goove bou!"

She's used to my incoherent pre-coffee mumblings, though, so she takes it in stride. "Goove bou to you too, honey. See you tonight!"

No, you probably won't, I think. My brain, after so many hours of staring at my phone and willing time to move faster, is slow-moving, but I get up and slip my phone in the front pocket of my hoodie, then pull on a pair of shoes.

I don't know how long I stand in the middle of my room, listening to the sounds of my dad and brothers and Jess getting ready for their day. Jess is worried about some homework assignment for science and crashes down the hall, wailing that she'll never be able to study chimpanzees like Jane Goodall if she fails 8th grade science. Greg and Charlie are like mini hurricanes, shouting at each other and wrestling their way into their clothes and out the door. Dad calls up the stairs to say goodbye to me.

And then there's silence.

Is this my last morning at home? Will I never hear the chaotic sounds of my family getting ready in the morning ever again?

It's not too late, Eevee, I remind myself. *You're the one who gave yourself a deadline. You're the one who's determined to go to Elfaeme to find the Seelie Court, even though Sean and*

But the plan was made before Amelia was kidnapped and before I knew about Maeve's power waning and the danger Aspen was in.

I ready myself to travel to the glade in the In Between where I last saw Folsom, the glade where one stone, with a little of my blood, could take me to my birth parents' now abandoned cottage.

And I can't do it. My whole body is as rigid as a stone statue. Images from Homecoming night rise fresh in my mind as if I saw them yesterday, not back in October.

The first impression I had that night after opening the door to their cottage: furniture ripped apart, books everywhere, apples strewn on the floor.

A tang of blood in the air.

Slick streaks of blood on the floor and the windows, like there had been a struggle.

A tuft of brown hair, curled on the floor.

And, resting on the splintered table, a folded note.

It was difficult to get to the table without stepping on blood. Most of the blood looked normal, like human blood. But in the moonlight, some of the streaks and drops of blood glittered black.

My hands shook like leaves in the wind as I reached for the note.

Behind me, I could hear Quince's gasp of surprise and horror as he entered the cottage.

I forced my eyes away from the carnage and

looked down at the note.

The only words on it were "*I look forward to the flowers.*"

My parting words to Nightglade burned in my ears. When he insisted I thank him for saving me and Quince from the fae who attacked us, I'd said, "I'll send you flowers."

Nightglade's message was clear. Come see me, I have your birth mother and her lover.

Bring flowers.

My phone buzzes, breaking me from the hold of the memories. I reel and sit on the floor, my legs too weak to move to my bed. Anytime I think of the blood and wreckage of that night, my heart starts racing like I've run a marathon.

I've tried so hard since that night to downplay the effect it had on me, seeing all that blood and destruction. After all, I'm going to be a vet tech someday. Or at least, that's the plan, as long as I don't die in the fae realm first. As a vet tech, I'll be dealing with blood on a regular basis.

But the way that black blood glittered in the moonlight…

No. I swallow, mentally pushing the images away. Because it's not just the blood. It's the sickly sweet tang of it in my nose, and the shuddering knowledge that blazed through my body when I touched a finger to the wet drop of blood on the back of a wooden chair.

Somehow, I knew, when I touched that drop,

that I was touching Maeve's blood. Maybe I inherited some of her blood magic, because there was no doubt in my mind whose blood was on my fingertip. I spent a lot of time washing my hands when I got home that night.

Anger at Nightglade simmers and bubbles like acid in my stomach. My phone buzzes again.

Oh yes. I'm in my room, in Duluth. In the human realm, where I can get texts on my phone. And it's only three days until the winter solstice.

Sometimes when I feel too many emotions all at once, I end up feeling numb instead. Like when I had to ride back to Duluth from Winona with Damian's parents. That was an awkward car ride, to say the least.

Right, my phone. Still numb, I unlock the screen and look down at the messages, blinking a couple times until the words come into focus.

Q: *are you okay?*
Q: *I'll meet you there, but we can't stay long. F might be watching.*

I almost laugh. That was my hope, that Folsom was spying on the circle of moonstones. He can't stop himself, he's always looking for another opportunity to claw his way back to the Unseelie Court with his sticky-padded fingers. But Quince has come through, he can help me.

Not only that, but he's able to text, which means he came to the human realm, which means

Nightglade hasn't done anything to him or his family yet!

It's like a weight has lifted off my shoulders. I don't have my wings, but I feel like I could float right now.

This time I don't think of anything but that circle of moonstones. I stand, close my eyes, and step forward.

After facing Sean and Shannon's magical security system head-on, the slight queasiness and disorientation I feel when traveling from one realm to the other is nothing. It's like a single bug bite compared to a full-body poison ivy rash. And, growing up in Minnesota, I'm unfortunately all too familiar with both of those unpleasant sensations.

A cool breeze tickles the small hairs on the back of my neck and I open my eyes. My bedroom has disappeared, replaced by a quiet grove. The clearing I'm in is surrounded by skeletal trees dotted with green buds, all of the land shadowed in the fog of an early spring morning. I've appeared in the center of a circle of stones, each of which glow with an undulating light. Any one of these can, with the touch of a finger, take me almost anywhere in Elfaeme…so long as there's a moonstone at the other end. It's admittedly not my favorite way to travel through the fae realm. Though the fae realm is smaller than Earth, it's not small by any means. I have no idea how long it'd take me to walk or fly from the remote, snow-capped mountains of the Unseelie lands to the rolling, grassy knolls of the Seelie territory. I've never tried, but I imagine it would take longer than the three days I have until the winter solstice.

Once again, I make a mental note to ask Quince about acquiring a map of Elfaeme. I've never been the greatest at reading maps, but I'd make an effort with that one.

Someone taps me on the shoulder and I jump, my wings fluttering madly, and bob up and down in no orderly fashion whatsoever before I collect myself and turn mid-air, lowering to the ground so I'm facing Quince "scared-the-crap-out-of-me" Florentz. He's wearing his usual Unseelie courtier outfit, with a dark, form-fitting waistcoat and forest green pants. His waistcoat is unbuttoned, as if he were in the process of getting dressed and decided that buttoning wasn't worth his time. Beneath it is a wrinkled white satin shirt.

The joking comment I was going to make dies on my lips as I take in his face, which is the color of egg whites. His dark eyes are wide and terrified.

All the anger I'd been holding against him for hiding his betrothal from me dissipates at that scared puppy look.

"What's going on?"

He holds a finger to my lips, then crushes me in a hug.

"Not here," he whispers in my hair. His voice is hoarse, like he'd been shouting or crying. "You-know-who might be nearby."

We're in Folsom's neck of the woods. He's called this part of the In Between his home for decades at least. But the woods are large. He probably isn't nearby. Certainly not near enough to hear a whisper.

Part of me is a little disappointed I don't see Folsom anywhere. Don't get me wrong, I'm glad Quince is here, even if he's squeezing me so hard I think my ribs are cracking. And I didn't really want to have to strike a deal with the frog-faced Folsom. But I have the insatiable curiosity of a toddler. He and I have unfinished business. What was his plan for me on that first trip I took to Elfaeme? What had he meant the last time I saw him, when he turned his bulging eyes to me and said, "I never told him. Remember that"?

I open my eyes a crack and peer into the murky shadows beneath the trees, on the alert for any sign of movement. My ears perk up when I hear a distant rustle, followed by a splash.

Quince hears it, too. His whole body stiffens against mine.

"We need to go," he says. "Now."

"But—"

"I'll explain when we're somewhere safer."

He pulls me to one of the moonstones. Not THE moonstone, the one which, with a drop of my blood, would take us to the secluded cottage in the humid forest.

"Wait, Quince—" I cry out. "You're hurting me. I haven't had a chance to tell you my plan or—"

He loosens his grip on my hand, but doesn't

release it. We're standing in front of one of the
moonstones, its surface a kaleidoscope of shifting white
light.

"We need to go to the…" He leans in quickly,
and in a whisper that tickles like a fuzzy caterpillar, says,
"the Seelie Court."

I step back, our hands still linked, and I'm not
sure if it's his hand or mine that's sweating, but our
palms are slick against each other.

"Are you a mind reader?" I ask, staring at him
hard like if I try, I might be able to bore through his
skull to discover the thoughts he's hidden beneath.

He scratches at one of his small, black horns, a
line appearing between his eyes. "What?"

"You can't be, right? You haven't turned
eighteen yet, you haven't come into your full powers
or–"

"Eevee," he stops my confused rambling and,
with a sob, pulls me into another hug.

This erratic behavior scares me. The paranoia
about Folsom, the terrified eyes, the crushing hugs and
the apparent mind-reading. Quince, *my* Quince, is
impulsive and energetic, and more prone to laughter
than tears. I want to ask him what happened at the
Unseelie Court, but his paranoia is contagious and now
I'm starting to think he's right and we shouldn't catch
up with each other where Folsom might hear us. I send
out a silent promise to Folsom that I'll see him again,
and when I do, we'll have a little chat.

"Okay," I say to Quince, my voice muffled

from my face squashed against his chest.

He releases me, looking down at me with haunted eyes. "Okay?"

"Let's take a moonstone. You can explain to me on the way how you knew that's where I needed to go."

Now he's gazing at me like I'm the mind reader.

"I'll tell you later," I say.

He nods, silent sobs making his shoulders shake, but takes our intertwined hands and touches the moonstone in front of us.

The last thing I see as the grove of trees fades is bulbous, shockingly yellow eyes staring at us from the gloomy underbrush.

Quince Has a Map

We emerge next to a moonstone in a forest clearing much like the one we left behind, and I gasp, clutching at my chest. Moonstone travel for me is like falling off a swing and landing on my back. Both experiences are sudden, startling, and leave me gasping for breath. Ignoring the uncomfortable feeling, I focus on our surroundings. Above us, through spindly branches, a pale morning sky peeps through, bespeckled with the last remaining stars of the night. The balmy breeze winding its way through our hair and wings is the first hint I have that we're no longer in the In Between, where each day shifts from spring to autumn. The warmth of the wind on my skin can mean only one thing in the fae realm: we're in Seelie territory now. But the question I had before remains. Where, within the Seelie lands, is the court of King Oakspirit and Queen Hibiscus?

"I'm going to need my fingers eventually," I joke with Quince, trying to keep my voice light.

When he doesn't answer, I look up into his face. Tracks of liquid silver run from his eyes to his chin. With my free hand I reach up and trace one of the tracks. He doesn't look at me, doesn't release his grip on my fingers. We stand as if frozen in time, our hands clasped, my finger grazing his cheek. Then, like my mom used to do with me when I was little, I wipe the tear away and cup his cheek in my hand, tenderness for this person who's come to mean so much to me stabbing at my heart.

"What happened?" I ask quietly.

He drops my hand and turns away from me, stepping angrily across the clearing, crushing wildflowers and sweet grasses beneath his stamping feet. "What else?" he asks, his voice bone-deep weary.

"Nightglade," I whisper.

His whole body tenses at the name. He's silhouetted against the sky, but I can see his shoulders hunch and his black, feathered wings quiver.

I step over to him as cautiously as if approaching a wild animal. "Did he hurt you?"

Quince scrubs at his face and looks at me. His eyes are fathomless, two empty black holes. "Hurt me? Nightglade? He'd never get his own hands dirty to hurt a bastard of both courts like me."

The bitterness in Quince's voice knocks me backward. I take a step away from him. "Don't call yourself that."

"Why shouldn't I? It's what everyone else calls me."

"Quince, you're not…" I pause, wondering why I never thought to ask before now. "You're not the only child of both courts at the Unseelie Court, are you?"

"I'm the only one he's parading around. Nightglade likes to make sure I'm visible. I'm his token child of both courts, his way of showing the Unseelie fae he's not as bigoted as everyone claims him to be."

"That's awful."

"The worst part, aside from being an object of intense interest from a bunch of fae I don't know, is knowing if I step one toe out of line, do anything Nightglade doesn't like, he'll use me as an example of how unruly and willful children of both courts are."

He takes to the air, flying like his life depends on it.

Maybe it does.

I launch into the air after him, my gossamer-thin butterfly wings working hard to catch up to him so we're level.

"What we're doing now… Nightglade isn't going to like this."

He doesn't answer. Why should he? We both know what we're doing is directly against the wishes of the Unseelie King. *On some level, Nightglade must be scared, I muse.* Otherwise why would he expend so much effort to stop me from coming to the Winter Solstice Festival and claiming my right to the throne? I'm young, I've only recently come into my powers, and I'm new to the fae world. If he wanted, he could crush me easily.

I'm pulled from my thoughts when I realize Quince is talking. All I catch is the last part of what he's saying. "...which is why we have to get to the Seelie Court."

"How did you know that's where I needed to go?" I ask him, trying not to sound out of breath. It's a lot of work, making these wings fly. I love flying, but I don't get to do it often.

He slows his pace. His large, black feathered wings beat steadily, and he isn't even breaking a sweat.

"I wondered when you said that earlier. What do you mean, you were already planning to go to the Seelie Court?"

As we fly, I tell him everything I told Sean and Shannon about Scamp, the meadow, dancing with the wild fae, and Olearia's desperate request.

"I wasn't seriously considering going," I conclude. "And then…"

"Amelia was kidnapped," he finishes. He doesn't meet my eyes. "Eevee, I'm so sorry I froze like that in front of Ilinor and left you in the lurch, it's just–"

"You're seventeen and weren't prepared for a

standoff between your kind-of-sort-of girlfriend and your betrothed?"

His face crumples, and he turns it away from me. "Kind of sort of?" he mutters to himself.

We've never officially established our relationship more than "I like you, you like me, let's steal some kisses between preparing to overthrow the Unseelie King's rule and simultaneously rescue my birth parents." Not that he hasn't asked. Every week.

Actually, thinking back, he stopped asking around when he and Ilinor would've been announced as betrothed.

"Does your fiancée know you're flying to the Seelie Court with me?"

"No," he answers shortly. He descends toward a small clearing in the teeming, tropical forest below us.

The forest we land in is most likely the same one where my birth parents hid for years from Nightglade. I have no idea how large it is, though, or where we are in comparison to where their now abandoned cottage is, but breathing in the air that always smells like rain and fresh earth reminds me of that night. Unlike the eerie quiet surrounding Maeve and Aspen's cottage, this part of the forest is overflowing with life. Birdcalls, welcoming the morning, come from the treetops around us, interspersed with melodies of frogs croaking and insects humming. I focus on the sounds, which are so different from the silence of that night as I land beside him.

"We need to find a moonstone," he explains.

"There's only certain ones that lead to the Seelie Court, just like the Unseelie Court. It's a way to protect the courts from attacking each other. You can leave the courts without a moonstone, but moonstones are the only way in."

"Oh," I say, considering this. I suppose it's harder to send an army a few at a time through a moonstone than all at once through the land or air. "Makes sense."

"Right," he nods. "So not all moonstones work to take us to the Seelie Court. My mom–" His face crumples again.

"Quince?"

He turns to me and takes a breath. "Mom and dad are on house arrest."

My heart tightens. It's like I feared.

"Nightglade can't risk appearing too capricious in front of his court. He has a lot of power, but there are many in the court who watch him eagerly for any sign of weakness or waning mental faculties. Making a case for either of those could lead, at the very least, to a long legal battle for Nightglade to keep his place as Unseelie King."

"What's keeping everyone from doing that?" I ask bitterly, thinking how we wouldn't have had to make such risky plans if the Unseelie courtiers had decided to petition for Nightglade's removal.

"Nightglade knows how to stay in power," Quince answers simply, his expression stormy. "He's been doing it for centuries."

"But if he were to revoke your dad's place in court…" I muse. "He'd be going back on the promise he made only months ago, when he restored Jerry to his old position."

"Right," Quince says. "And that's exactly what Nightglade is trying to avoid. He doesn't want to give the court any reason to petition for his removal. Folk at the court are already talking about some of his questionable decisions of late. In whispers, of course. He hears the rumors, though. He has spies for his spies."

"So he can't just throw your parents into prison."

"No." He shudders. "Not without a good reason. The Iron Prison is probably where he wanted to send them, but instead he sent his guards to bind me and my parents and move us to a new house which he fortified with iron to prevent us from escaping." His face whitens with rage. "The guards told us we would be expected to make appearances at court as if nothing were wrong. If we didn't do this, we would be punished."

"I'm so sorry," I say, wrapping my arm around his waist. He leans his head on mine.

"Dad's lost so much weight these last few months," he says into my hair, and I can hear the fear in his voice. "And mom is a ball of anxiety. Now…" He pauses, his jaw tightening. "I don't know how much longer they can hold up."

"What'll happen to them, since you escaped?"

"I don't know." He wraps his arms around me, holding me tight. "I don't know. Mom forced me to go, though. She told me as much as she could, and she and dad distracted the guards so I could escape. I couldn't realm-hop inside the house, but," he grins, but it looks forced, "I guess my dad really is related to Sean and Shannon. He had the guards so confused they didn't know their lefts from their rights, and mom snuck me out the door behind them. She can be sneaky if she wants to be. I think it's her mousiness."

I remember the first time I met Myska, at the fall equinox celebration. Mousy is a good way to describe her. She had been nibbling on cheese, and the fact she has a mouse-like tail really enhances the image.

"I was supposed to go straight to the Seelie lands as quickly as I could, but I couldn't leave without checking on you, so I traveled to Duluth first, and that's when I got your texts."

"And now here we are."

"Here we are." He hugs me, then lets me go. "I'm glad I risked going to Duluth first. Now I don't have to go to the Seelie Court alone."

He looks at me with so much warmth, I can't quite meet his eyes. What use will I be? If anything, it'll be even more dangerous for him to travel with me than on his own.

"It almost would've been better if your parents hadn't gone back to the Unseelie Court at all," I say, still not meeting his gaze.

"Nightglade left them no real choice," he

reminds me, his voice brittle. "We were to join his court and prove ourselves to be good Unseelie courtiers, or go into hiding and never have a place to call home, never have any friends for longer than a few days or weeks, living in isolation until Nightglade…" He stops himself, unwilling to tempt fate and say what he and his parents really want to have happen to Nightglade.

We may be alone in this clearing in the Seelie forest, but in Elfaeme, even the trees have ears.

The morning here is warm already, the sunlight hazy through a light fog swirling around our feet. Quince has moved out of the clearing and is on a footpath beneath the trees, examining a piece of paper. I peer over his shoulders and almost knock him over in my excitement and relief.

"Is that a map?!"

It looks nothing like the hastily sketched map of the In Between Maeve had made, one of the clues she left for me to find her. The map in Quince's hands is intricate, the words written in a spidery script, the images of the woods and surrounding areas drawn with such detail, I half expect the trees to sway. If I touch the snow-capped mountains of the Unseelie lands, I wonder if they'd be cold to the touch.

It's a map of Elfaeme, all of it, completed with loving labor.

For the first time, I'm seeing the world of my birth parents, my world, laid out before me in its entirety on a single piece of paper.

And I could almost cry from the beauty.

The fae have preserved the natural wonders of their world with as much vigor as it seems some humans give to destroying Earth's resources.

Down the center of the map is the In Between. Not all of the In Between is deciduous forest, like where I first appeared. Some of it has plains and pine forest, even a large lake. I see the river where Quince and I had once collected water to reveal a hidden message on the Mage Stone, the large, now-dormant, moonstone. The Mage Stone is also labeled, as is the nearby market where fae congregate to trade their wares. I wonder if this market is where Sean and Shannon bought their home security charm, or if they attend more nefarious markets.

To the east and north of the In Between are the Unseelie lands. Crystal Lake, where the wyverns are, is located just south of the mountain range, which extends from north of the In Between all the way to the furthest eastern edge of the map.

But not all Unseelie territory is frozen in perpetual winter. In fact, much of the southern Unseelie land is covered in swamps and bogs, and even a desert.

To the west and south of the In Between are the Seelie lands. Most of the lands west of the In Between are filled with hills, rivers, and lakes, some large enough to be small seas.

But in the southwest, where we are now, is a lush forest, similar to the rainforests on earth. I can see why my birth parents chose to hide here. The forest is large, and the furthest possible place away from the Unseelie Court while still being in Elfaeme.

Pressing against the Seelie forest and the woods of the In Between in the south is another mountain range, smaller than the one in the north, but with several lakes and active volcanoes listed.

I squint, leaning even further over Quince's shoulder. This fog is making it hard to see. Where is the Seelie Court? I don't see it anywhere in the forest we're in currently. Then, in small letters, right at the edge of the Seelie forest and at the base of an active volcano, are the words "Land of the Seelie Court."

I'm fascinated. I want to spend all day studying this map until I have every marking memorized, but Quince rolls it up and places it in an inside pocket of his waistcoat.

"Where'd you find that map?" I ask.

He smiles. It's a faded smile compared to his usual joyful grin, but it's a smile nonetheless. "You like it?"

I nod. "It's beautiful."

"My dad made it," he admits, the pride in his voice unmistakable. "With my mom's help. They used their combined knowledge of the different realms. I guess it was kind of their pet project they worked on together all those years living in Duluth."

"Well, he did a wonderful job," I say. "Truly, Quince. I love it. I've been wishing for a map."

"Mom thought I'd need it." His face, which had brightened with momentary joy and pride, darkened again. "She didn't have much time, though, so all she said to me was to be careful of the creatures as I traveled, and then pointed out where some of the moonstones are that would take me to the Seelie Court."

We walk down the path together, my steps not quite as light as his but still quiet. "Most of your time in the fae realm has been in safe places, Eevee," he says, and I feel his eyes on me. "The fall equinox celebration. Sean and Shannon's house. The Mage Stone. But–"

I hold up my hand. "But it isn't all safe. I know." I remember how Cam and Maggie and I had barely escaped from the vengeful tree spirit, how the wyverns had swarmed us as soon as they were aware of our presence, how Quince and I had been attacked and nearly killed before Nightglade, for some reason, chose to save us.

"No, it isn't. Some fae are just as willing to attack or trick other fae as they would attack or trick humans. Even more, now."

"Why more now?" I ask, alarmed.

The path snakes away in front of us as we walk. In the distance I can hear the soft sounds of waves lapping against a shore.

"Keep an eye out for a moonstone near the water's edge," he says.

"Okay, but–"

"Your question." His lips quirk in a half grin and he bumps my shoulder with his. "I was getting there. Earth has become less appealing to many fae.

The pollution stinking up the air and reducing the overall air quality, the trash, it can make it unbearable for some of the more feral fae."

My face wrinkles in confusion. "Feral fae? Don't you mean the wild fae?"

"No." Quince is usually amused or surprised by my ignorance of Elfaeme, but right now he just looks grim. "I mean feral. The wild fae are fae who don't align with either court, Seelie or Unseelie, but they still have their own moral codes which govern them, and they tolerate humans as much as the next fae."

"So…not a lot," I comment.

He nods his agreement. "But feral fae have no moral code and no love of humans. Yes, they'll make short trips to Earth. And like most fae, feral fae love making mischief or causing harm. But they don't go to Earth as often or stay as long as they used to."

We slow. With the fog getting thicker around us, it's becoming hard to make out anything. The path could've disappeared and we wouldn't have known. And where did the sun go? Wasn't the sun coming out when we arrived not that long ago?

"Many of the more feral fae," Quince continues, "stay in Elfaeme and attack or play pranks on each other instead of wasting their energy by realm-hopping to Earth."

I shiver. Why is it so cold? My hand finds Quince's. The murky fog is as thick and cold as whipped cream, but nowhere near as delicious. I lick my lips, which are beaded with cold drops of condensation.

"I didn't see fog listed on the map," I joke. It's hard to breathe, let alone speak, in this oppressive fog.

I can see Quince's head move, but even though he's right next to me, all I can make out is a vague shape turning this way and that. I lace my fingers with his, goosebumps erupting down my arms.

"This fog isn't natural," Quince says, his voice muffled like he's speaking through a pillow.

"No shit, Sherlock," I say weakly.

Neither of us laughs. We've stopped moving, and stand as if waiting for something.

"Do you know what it is?"

Quince's hand in mine is clammy. I feel him lean in next to me. I can't even see the hand I hold up in front of my face. Everything is a white fog. If there's anyone else out there, we wouldn't know until it was too late.

"Mom's told me about the creatures in the Seelie lands," he whispers, his breathing labored. "I grew up listening to her stories. There was one she told about a type of fae creature who comes with the fog." He has to pause to catch his breath, then, in a low, whispery voice that tickles my ear, he sings.

"Beware, beware
when fog is in the air
and mists cover all the land.
It's at times like this the gwyllyon walks
silently through shrouded paths

calling always for her lost betrothed.
Should you hear her mournful cries
your fate is in her hands.
Beware your presence does not anger her
or on foggy paths you'll ever walk
searching for all you've lost
never to be found again."

His whispered song comes to an end, and, as if waiting for its cue, we hear a long, low, mournful wail coming from the mist all around us.

Fog and Furry Friends

The gwyllyon's wail fills the air all around us, echoing and reverberating, infused with anguish.

All I hear, all I feel as the sound penetrates my ears, is pure despair. Is my face wet from the fog or the tears? I no longer know.

"Quince." His name comes out of my mouth as a sob more than a word. It's hard to say anything through this lump in my throat. "How do we keep from angering her?"

We can't anger her. If we do, we'll end up lost, like in the song Myska used to sing. And if we're lost, how are we going to find the Seelie Court?

His forehead presses against mine and I breathe

in his fresh smell, which reminds me of the creek running through my cousin's yard. It's a sweet smell, like wildflowers and spring grasses and pine trees, with a touch of earthiness.

"I don't know," he admits, his voice trembling. "There's nothing in the song about how not to anger her. It just says not to."

I close my eyes. With how thick the fog is, I can't see anything anyway. This way, with my eyes closed, I can focus on the pressure of his forehead on mine, on our shuddering, shaky breaths mingling together, on our fingers interlaced.

"I could try charming her," he says in a whisper. I clutch his hands at the sound of another mournful wail. Is it my imagination, or does the gwyllyon sound closer? Her cries are louder, anyway.

"No," I whisper fiercely, my eyes flying open and my heart hammering so hard I can feel it in my stomach. "You haven't fully come into your powers yet, you're not eighteen!"

I know he has some power to charm those he talks to. I saw him use it on Ms. Burns, the school librarian who Mr. Abscons was subbing for. But I've also seen his charm do absolutely nothing at all to the rogue ice troll we encountered lumbering around outside Sean and Shannon's.

"You have to trust me," he whispers back, just as fiercely. "I can do this, Eevee."

"What if you can't?" I say, unable to keep the fear from my voice. He regards me with his glittering black eyes, an air of seriousness about him I'm not used to. A small whimper escapes my lips, immediately overshadowed by another low groan from the gwyllyon.

"There's only one way to know."

His forehead leaves mine, but the smell of him stays with me in the fog.

Then he's pulling his hands from mine as well, his fingers slipping from my grasp, and I lose all sight of him as he stands and steps away from me.

"No!" I whisper-yell, angry and terrified. For the first time since the fog appeared I'm totally alone in it, separated from Quince, from everyone, lost in a mist so thick I don't dare move for fear of running into something or falling into a pit.

My whole body is heavy as stone. Maybe I'm turning into a statue, I think wildly. Maybe when the gwyllyon leaves and the mist dissipates, it'll reveal the crouched form of a young fae with butterfly wings, terror etched on her face.

Then I hear Quince speaking from somewhere in front of me. His voice is quiet, calm, not a hint of a tremble in it, and his words are warm and rich, even with the damp cold of the fog.

"Love can be so full of pain, can't it?" he says. His tone speaks of honey and the sweet understanding that passes between people under the cover of the stars. The gwyllyon wails again, even louder.

"I know," Quince says, as if he understands what she's saying with her wordless cry. "It can be awful to love someone with your whole being and not be able to be with them."

Her cry turns to a whimpering moan. I'm breathless as I listen, caught between terror that it won't work and small bubble of painful joy. Can he mean me? Or is he just saying whatever comes to mind to soothe the gwyllyon so she goes away?

"It's the worst kind of pain," he continues, "because it's all tied up with memories and good feelings, too, and you can't separate it, you don't want to. It's bittersweet."

His voice lowers, and I strain to hear what he'll say next. The gwyllyon is now letting out small, hiccuping sobs. He's doing it. He's calming the gwyllyon. We're going to get out of this.

Even the fog is fading. I can see! Not far, but enough to see the form of Quince a little to the left, about ten feet in front of me. Before him is a thin woman with black, matted hair which reaches down to her feet. I creep nearer, staying low to the ground, then freeze in place when her features come into view.

Her skin, what's left of it, sags from her skeletal body. If her hair is black now, it's from the mold that covers it from her scalp down to the raggedy edges by her feet. Where her eyes should be are empty sockets, and her frame is wrapped in a garment as gauzy as the fog that surrounds her.

I try to keep myself from gagging at the sight of her. How does Quince stay so calm as the mists fade and the gwyllyon's form is revealed right before where he stands?

"Sometimes you wonder," he's saying to her as she watches him with her empty eye sockets, "if they're also suffering when they can't touch your skin or hear your voice."

The gwyllyon nods her head, her rotting, moldy hair falling forward, obscuring her unnerving lack of eyes. A soft moan escapes her desiccated lips.

"It hurts," he whispers. The fog is almost gone now, and above, I can see the sun trying to pierce the clouds. Quince glances around, sees me, and steps to his right so he's between me and the gwyllyon, who is now sobbing silently into her hands. "I get it. I'm not free to be with who I love, either."

I catch my breath. He does mean me. But he's never mentioned that he loves me! We've kept our relationship undefined these last few months. And, sure, I've felt my feelings for him growing even more than I'd expected they would, enough where it's terrified me sometimes how strongly I feel. But with everything else going on, and him living in Elfaeme while I was still in Duluth, it didn't ever feel right to bring it up. Plus, I don't want to come on too strong and scare him away. It was easier to focus on the Winter Solstice Festival and our plans to save Maeve and Aspen rather than on how my chest gets all gooey and warm inside whenever his hand brushes my skin.

The gwyllyon's sobs bring me back to the present. If it weren't for the gwyllyon, would Quince have said that he loved me at all? He has to know I've heard him, that I've guessed he's talking about us. His back is to me, so I can't see his face to try and discern any meaning from it.

Does it matter, Eevee? I chide myself. We're young, and he is betrothed to Ilinor because of–

"...because of Nightglade," I hear him say out loud, finishing my thought by coincidence.

Immediately I know Quince has made a mistake. The gwyllyon, who had almost faded away like the fog she came in on, returns in her full, rotten glory, her face transfigured into an expression of pure rage.

The sky above us darkens and fog swirls around our feet. I scramble up and, without thinking, run forward and grab Quince's arm.

"We have to get out of here!" I shout as the gwyllyon's mouth opens, revealing mossy teeth and a mottled black tongue. A cloud of noxious, yellow gas pours forth out of her mouth, along with an unending howl of anger.

With our free hands we cover our mouths and noses with our shirts. Quince looks upward, then back to me, and I nod. My hand still clutching his arm, we launch ourselves into the air. Every movement of my wings takes effort, the fog growing heavier each second, as if it's trying to drag us down, but I force myself to follow Quince, to stick with him. Why are we flying so slowly? Does this fog never end?

We make it no more than twenty feet in the air when my wings give out.

We drop instantly, my weight dragging Quince down with me.

I don't want to let go. I need to let go. At least one of us can get out of here.

I loosen my hold on Quince's arm, but it's too late. The heavy, wet fog drags us both downward until we crash to the ground and fall with a thump on the moss-covered earth.

Quince rolls over with a groan. I land feet first before falling forward onto my left hand, my right still holding my sweatshirt over my mouth and nose. My feet and my wrist sting, but I don't think I broke anything. Quince, though, landed on his back.

"My wing," he says, wincing. The fog is back, almost as thick as before, this time with swirls of the noxious yellow gas floating in it. I can barely make out his form next to me. He sits up and sucks in a hissing breath as he shifts his weight and flexes his wings. The left one is bent at an unnatural angle that twists my stomach when I look at it.

His breathing…is it more labored than it was before? I tear my gaze from his broken wing and look, with horror, at his face.

His uncovered face. He's been breathing in the yellow gas.

Whatever the gas is, its effect is nearly immediate. He gags and splutters as I watch helplessly, then his whole body convulses, his eyes rolling back into his head, before he collapses forward onto the ground.

"No!" I yell into my "North Shore" sweatshirt, my words drowned out by the gwyllyon's wordless roar.

My head swims. How long can I last before my sweatshirt is no longer enough to keep out the poisonous yellow gas?

I drag Quince's twitching, unconscious body about twenty feet away from the gwyllyon when I have my answer.

Oh.

Pain sears down my throat and in my nostrils. My insides are on fire. That's the only explanation for this feeling. I fall next to Quince, desperately holding onto consciousness, but it's slippery and keeps trying to evade my grasp.

With my last ounce of strength, my vision spotty and my limbs twitching like Quince's, I lay my body over him. At least I can protect him from harm a little longer.

The last clear thought I have before everything goes black is that I've failed. I won't save my birth parents or Amelia, and I won't get to tell Quince I love him.

Then the pain takes over and I think and move no more.

Everything hurts, and my mattress is lumpy. Why is it moving? My brain feels like cotton as I try to work out this puzzle. Beneath me, my mattress continues to rise and fall. I can think of no reason for this.

And what is that licking my face?

"Slink, stop." My voice is thick, like my mouth is filled with the same cotton which has taken over my brain.

With monumental effort, I crack open one of my eyes, then close it.

No, that doesn't make sense.

I open it again, staring into the green-eyed gaze of Scamp, whose head is tilted questioningly. When he sees my eyes open, he sits back on his haunches and meows.

Beneath me, my mattress shifts at the sound.

Mattresses don't do that, my brain informs me.

"Is this a dream?"

It has the feeling of a dream. Everything around me is vague shapes in a misty fog, except for Scamp, who is so close I could reach out and touch him.

Fog.

Something sparks in my mind and the encounter with the gwyllyon comes rushing back.

As quickly as I'm able, I roll off Quince, who is stirring and muttering but still unconscious. I listen intently, but can hear no unearthly cries. The gwyllyon has gone, but the mist remains.

Scamp steps up to me and, to his displeasure, I scoop him up and squeeze him to my chest.

"How did you find us?" I ask, my voice still thick and raspy. According to the song Quince sang about the gwyllyon, if we angered her, we'd be lost on foggy paths. Well, we definitely angered her, between Quince mentioning Nightglade and us trying to fly away. What did Nightglade do to anger this particular gwyllyon so much?

Scamp squirms in my arms and I look down at him. Is that a collar around his neck? That's strange. Until I learned he was more than the typical cat, I'd always assumed he was a stray because he never had a collar.

On the collar is a small pouch. It reminds me of a miniature fanny pack. Both the collar and pouch are made out of the same warm, brown leather.

My fingers don't want to work. They fumble with the strings on the pouch for a frustrating minute (frustrating for both me and Scamp) until it finally opens. I pull out a small slip of paper, the pouch's only contents, and release Scamp so I can read the message.

All it says is:

Glad you decided to help. ~Olearia

A Broken Wing Isn't Our Only Problem

Scamp stalks restlessly back and forth as I shake Quince's shoulder, trying not to jostle him too much. The way his left wing bends outward, compared to his right wing, which is at rest and tucked against his back, is unsettling. Every time I glance at it, I have to look away again at something else. Right now I'm staring at the ground by his head. Some of his wing feathers are strewn around him on the ground, glossy black against the mossy forest floor.

"Quince," I whisper, too afraid to shout in case the gwyllyon is nearby somewhere. I shake his shoulder again, then sit back when he groans.

"Eevee?" His voice comes out in a croak, and he swallows, wincing, his eyes closed. "Are we safe?"

I glance at Scamp, whose skinny, dusty-colored body is barely visible through the fog. "I'm not sure," I admit.

He opens his eyes and struggles into an upright position. "The gwyllyon?" he asks, panic on his face.

"Gone, I think."

He relaxes, then his eyes take in the fog and widen. "Lost in the fog," he whispers in his croaky voice. "I couldn't calm her, then."

"You *were* calming her, though," I say, trying to reassure him.

"You heard what I was saying to her?" he asks. "Of course she heard," he mutters to himself before I can answer, "it's not like you were whispering to the gwyllyon."

I blush and look down at my hands in my lap. "S-so about what you said–"

"I'm glad you heard, actually–"

We both stop talking. I force myself to look up at him. When my eyes meet his, there's something there, behind his gaze, a desperation and longing that makes my heart skip a beat. I look away and clear my throat.

"Anyway, she was almost gone after…after what you said. You would've done it, I think, but…"

The fog swirls around us with a chill wind, reminding me that it's the gwyllyon's fog we're stuck in, and she might be able to hear us still.

Scamp meows impatiently and Quince's head snaps around to stare at him, having noticed the cat for the first time.

"That's Scamp," I explain to Quince.

"The cat from the diner?" he asks in a daze, still staring at Scamp. "The one who gave you the vision and brought you to the wild fae?"

"Yeah. He's here to help us." I show him the note from Olearia.

"He can lead us out of the fog?" Quince asks, scanning the note quickly and handing it back to me.

I glance at the scrappy, one-eared cat. "He certainly seems to think so," I say. "I can sense him in my mind. He's not feeling unsure at all, not even a bit. In fact, he's mostly…" I frown. "Annoyed and grumpy."

"So, a typical cat," Quince mutters, standing slowly.

"Yes, but…" I bite my lip and eye Scamp, who blinks up at me, then continues to pace back and forth. "But he found us in the fog, didn't he? So it stands to reason he'd be able to lead us out the way he came."

"Maybe." Quince looks unconvinced.

"Do you have any better ideas?"

He shakes his head, then sways dangerously on the spot. His face turns five shades paler than usual, almost the color of the fog surrounding us, and he slumps to the ground.

"I just…need a minute," he says through gritted

teeth.

I sit down next to him, ignoring the peevish feelings from Scamp. "Take all the time you need," I say, shooting a stern look at the cat, who looks about ready to pounce on the next mouse he sees.

To distract Quince from the pain of his broken wing, I recount Sean and Shannon's reconnaissance mission to Duluth High with me. A little color comes back into his cheeks as I talk, and a small smile tugs at the corners of his lips when I describe how intently we all observed Sparky the frog. But as soon as I reveal Mr. Abscons' true identity, Quince's eyes narrow with anger and Scamp growls.

"You've heard of him?" I ask. "He seemed to know of Sean and Shannon, anyway. He turned and fled at the sight of them!" I chuckle again, recalling Abscons' terrified face when he saw who was in his study hall with me.

Quince's laugh is low and grim. "Oh, I've heard of Banethistle. If I had known who he was, he wouldn't have lasted long as our substitute librarian."

My brow furrows. This intense hatred, this isn't like Quince. "Why?"

But Quince doesn't answer. He stands and tries moving his wings, but his left wing won't move. It reminds me of a robin I nursed back to health the summer after 6th grade. It had crashed into one of our windows and I rushed outside to find it laying on our porch, dazed, one of its wings broken from the fall. Even then I had a desire to help animals. The easiest way to set a wing is to take bandage tape and, putting the wing in its natural resting position, wrap it around the whole body to make sure the wing stays in place. The robin's wing hadn't been bent like Quince's though. I gnaw at the inside of my bottom lip as I think.

"What?" Quince asks when he sees my look of concentration.

"Your wing," I say. "No chance you have any of Sean and Shannon's healing salve on you, do you?"

He shakes his head. "It doesn't heal broken bones, anyway. Only minor injuries. Why?"

"It should really be realigned and splinted before we go anywhere, then. So it has a chance to heal properly." I frown, trying to peer through the fog. We're in a forest, or at least we were. If I can just find one with the right sized branches…

"You're right. Let's just stop at the doctor first, and then we'll be on our way," Quince says sarcastically.

I know his wing hurts and something about Abscons has upset him, but I bristle at his tone. "Neither of us can leave this fog to go to the human realm, or I might suggest we do just that!" I snap back. My nose wrinkles as I realize that, in the human realm, his wings wouldn't be there at all. "Wait…"

"I'd still feel the pain," he says with a ghost of a smile on his face. "But no human doctor would be able to see or feel my wing in order to do anything about it." He rubs wearily at his eyes. "Sorry for the snark. It's just, my wing really hurts, and I'm mad at myself for failing to get rid of the gwyllyon and landing us both here. And I still can't believe Banethistle's been our substitute librarian this whole time."

I want to ask why Banethistle incites such murderous thoughts in him, but at the pain causing his face to look drawn and exhausted, I hold my tongue and force myself to smile. "We're going to get out of this," I tell him with more confidence than I feel. "We've got Scamp, and..." I pause, looking around.

"Cat got your tongue?"

"Seriously?" I raise an eyebrow. "You think *now* is a good time to joke?" I smile, this time for real. "Also, that joke was awful."

"Best I can do at the moment."

I turn in a slow circle, my smile fading. No sign of the cat, but I can't see far in the fog. What's even more worrisome is I can't sense him in my mind anymore, either. His grumpy presence is gone.

Swearing loudly, I stomp over to Quince. "I don't believe it." I fume. "He's gone! I thought he was here to help us."

"Maybe he went to scout a path," Quince suggests, but his voice is wooden.

"Yeah. Maybe." I glance at Quince out of the corner of my eyes. His normally sharp-jawed face is now slack with pain. "Right," I say crisply. "We shouldn't stray too far in case Scamp comes back for us, but we can at least take care of that wing."

He stares at me, startled, eyes wide in alarm.

"I helped a robin with a broken wing once," I

say before Quince can protest. "And I've learned a little about emergency first aid in class."

If possible, his eyes get wider. "But you've never actually done emergency first aid, you've only learned about it, what if—"

"It's called emergency first aid for a reason," I cut in smoothly. "Nobody really expects to use it, but it's helpful to know in case. And if we don't take care of that wing, I don't know how well you'll be flying once it heals."

Eventually Quince helps me look for a couple of strong, straight sticks. I take off my North Shore sweatshirt, removing my phone from the front pocket and placing it in the phone pocket on my leggings instead. The screen won't turn on, so I can't check the time. It's probably due to the enchanted fog, which is chilly against my skin. I shiver as I lean over to place my sweatshirt on the ground next to the sticks.

"Hey," Quince says, stepping over to me and running his hands up my arms, my skin immediately heating wherever he touches. He raises his fingers and traces the orange flower markings on my temples, then looks me in the eye. "Thank you for doing this," he says quietly.

I blush. "Don't thank me yet. I haven't realigned your wing or splinted it."

"I mean, thank you for caring about me," he says, his face open and vulnerable and tense with pain.

"Of course." I swallow. Electricity crackles at my temples where his fingers continue to trace the flower patterns. "You'd do the same for me."

He's so close to me, I realize. If I lean forward an inch, our lips would touch. I can feel his breath on my face–

And then something in his eyes shutters closed, and he drops his hands from my temples like my skin burns to touch.

What just happened? I bite the inside of my cheeks and look down at the ground, my chest feeling like a balloon that is suddenly deflating. Looking at the sticks and sweatshirt on the ground, I'm reminded of my task.

"We should take care of that wing now," I say, bending down and picking up the sticks.

We keep the conversation on the wing, carefully avoiding any mention of our almost kiss, what he said to the gwyllyon, or his betrothal status. I attempt the splint on his unbroken wing first, which is good, because the sticks keep slipping on his glossy feathers. No matter what I do, every time I try to wrap the sweatshirt around the wing and body, looping it around one of his shoulders, over the wing, and beneath the other wing and armpit, and go to tie it in front, the sticks slip from their position.

"I saw some vines earlier," Quince says after I growl in frustration when the sticks slide out of place for the third time.

We move slowly through the fog, staying close enough where we can see each other, to where Quince had seen the vines.

They make all the difference. With the vines we break off, each about ten feet in length, it's easier to hold the splint in place until the sweatshirt can be wrapped around to keep the wing close to his body. Once I'm satisfied with how the splint looks on his good wing, I remove it and turn my attention to his broken one.

"This is going to hurt," I warn him, the first words either of us has said in a while.

His face is covered in a sheen of sweat. "Just do it," he says.

I take a breath. I've only seen videos on realigning broken bones, I've never actually done it myself.

I focus on the broken wing, pretending I'm a vet tech already and I'm tending to a humongous bird. Like an ostrich. *It's just like the robin*, I tell myself. *But bigger.* My hands shake, but I reach out my right hand and grip the wing above the break.

"Okay, I'm going to align your bone now."

Quince's head moves imperceptibly in a nod, so I gently place my other hand on the wing beneath the break.

"Ready? One, two—" Like in the videos I've seen, I pull and push with firm movements until the wing looks like its unbroken counterpart. As fast as I can, I take the sticks and place them on the front and back of the wing, tie it closely, but not too tightly, to his body, then wrap it all in my blue North Shore sweatshirt.

"There," I say, standing back and examining the splint. I avoid looking at Quince's face. "That's the best I can do. You still need medical attention, but that should hold for now."

"Thank you," Quince says, holding out a hand and stopping me as I circle around him to inspect it from all angles. "I don't know what I'd do without you, Eevee."

I remove my arm from his grasp and turn away. "You'll figure it out."

He's quiet for a minute, and I take the opportunity to scrub at my face and run a hand through my hair. *Don't cry now. Neither of us can do anything about his betrothal to Ilinor.* "Alrighty then," I say brightly as I face him. "We've given Scamp enough time to come back. With or without the cat, we need to get out of this fog. What do you think? This way?"

And without waiting for him to answer, I march off into the fog.

This is the Fog that Never Ends

"If you sing that song one more time, I make no promises you won't end up with another broken bone," I warn Quince before he bursts into yet another verse of "This is the fog that never ends."

His dark eyes twinkle merrily at me. "What? It's true. The fog is never-ending. Can't I have some fun? Or do we have to spend every moment contemplating our doomed fate to wander the misty paths forever?"

It's been what feels like hours now, and no matter which way we decide to walk, the fog follows us. No forest sounds penetrate the fog, either, but we walk by trees and underbrush. I wonder if this is what it feels like to be a ghost, wandering aimlessly in a murky fog for eternity.

"Not every moment," I concede. "I don't think I can take any more of that song, though," I add hastily when he inhales and opens his mouth to sing again.

"What should we talk about then?" Quince asks, slowing down and looking at me curiously.

I draw a blank.

In the silence, Quince cocks an eyebrow. "We could finally discuss how we handle this 'kind of sort of' boyfriend/girlfriend thing now that I'm engaged to marry your birthmom's husband's daughter."

"How's that wing doing?" I ask, flustered.

With all the walking we've done, I'm worried it'll have jostled the splint, but I fall back to check it and it seems to be holding. As I touch the broken wing, I purse my lips. The part nearest the break is hot to the touch, even through the feathers and sweatshirt.

"You can't just bring up my broken wing every time you want to change the subject, you know," Quince comments teasingly.

I hate how my cheeks flush red anytime I'm flustered, and definitely not because I'm embarrassed. Because I'm not.

Now that I think about it, are his eyes glittering unnaturally bright? My brows furrow as I look up into his face, which has a waxy sheen to it. I place the inside of my wrist to his forehead, like my mom used to do whenever I'd wake up with a...

"Fever," I mutter.

"If I'm feverish, it's because you're so hot," he

says, winking at me.

"And delusional," I add, my cheeks probably the color of red wine at this point. My brain kicks into overdrive, my thoughts racing and tumbling over each other. This fever isn't good. He needs medical attention. We're stuck in the fog, with no way out.

No way out. Who knows how long we've been wandering? It only feels like it's been a few hours, but it's hard to measure the passage of time with all the endless fog and our phones not working.

"Some people started walking in it not knowing what it was, and they'll continue walking in it forever just because…" Quince sings softly to himself. I don't yell at him this time. What's the point? He's burning up with fever, he doesn't know what he's saying. Or singing. I wince as he starts the song over with extra gusto. Or how badly he sings when he has a fever.

His song stops abruptly, and I look up, suddenly worried he might've passed out or something, but he's standing, and awake, a cautiously excited look on his face.

"Isn't that the cat that was supposed to help us?" he asks me, tugging on my arm and pointing.

I squint at the shape he's pointing at. It does look kind of cat-shaped.

Quince is already walking over to it. "Here, kitty, kitty," he says in a high, sing-song voice that I'm sure Scamp would hate.

I step after Quince, then pause.

"Here, kitty, kitty," Quince says again, walking

closer to the cat. I don't know why, but my feet don't want to move. Something feels off, but I can't put my finger on what it is. Maybe it's the fog messing with me. I screw up my eyes to try and see Scamp better through the cloud-murk.

Quince's words, rather than encouraging Scamp to come closer, only make him scuttle away from Quince's clumsy approach.

He wheels to face me where I stand with my feet rooted to the forest floor. "Scamp's hurt!"

Fear constricts my chest. Had something gotten to Scamp after he left us? Is that why he hasn't returned until now? I rush forward to catch up with Quince, and slow down when I am about a foot behind him. Is the fog taking on new properties, trying to separate us? Why am I slowing down when I get closer to Quince? He crouches down and alternates between clicking his tongue and making hushing noises, which he most likely intends to be soothing, but Scamp's green eyes widen and he hobbles further away from us.

"It's okay, kitty," Quince says, inching toward the cowering cat. "We won't hurt you."

Why do my feet not want to obey my brain? I need to go check on Scamp's injuries. Instead, my feverish, wounded, kind-of-sort-of boyfriend is the one who is trying his best to soothe Scamp, who keeps scooting just outside Quince's outstretched hands.

Poor Scamp. I follow after Quince, willing my feet to take me closer. Who knows what's happened to the poor cat. He's probably in pain, and terrified, and—

I halt, my heart jumping to my throat.

I know what feels off.

My mouth moves to form Quince's name, but no sound comes out.

Given that danger seems to lurk almost everywhere we go in Elfaeme, I think it's too much to ask that the fae in front of Quince has good intentions.

That creature may look and sound like Scamp, but it's not the cat I know who loves sausage links and only consents to head scratches if you tempt him with food first.

I say "that creature" because the part of me that can sense animals is totally dormant, even though I'm well within range to sense it.

Which means the "kitty" Quince is reaching toward is definitely not Scamp, and, in all likelihood, not a cat at all.

I open my mouth again to warn Quince, and again, no words come out. Quince's form is becoming more and more blurry to look at as he follows the thing pretending to be Scamp. Alarm bells go off in my brain. Where is it leading him? I highly doubt to a hospital to treat his wing and fever.

If only Quince really were a mind reader! I've been screaming internally for the last thirty seconds. There's no way Quince wouldn't pick up on my wordless terror if he could read minds even a little.

He and Not-Scamp are so far from me now I can barely see them through the mist. Willing my legs to move, I march my way over rocks and around trees to keep Quince in my sight.

"Quince!" I manage to whisper when I am close enough to touch his wings.

"Come here, kitty," he says with exasperation. "Let me look at that leg, huh?"

Not-Scamp turns its green eyes plaintively up at Quince, then shoots a quick glance at me where I stand behind him. For a split second, the eyes transform, like the creature accidentally lets its fae glamour slip for a moment. In their place are two devilish black eyes, full of malicious loathing. Its glare roots me to the spot.

Then the illusion returns and it looks like Scamp again. It cowers away from Quince's reach and lets out a pathetic-sounding mew.

"Quince," I whisper. "That thing, it–"

Not-Scamp hisses and spits at me, a malevolent gleam in its eyes. Its lips are curled back in anger.

"It's hurt, I know," Quince says. "If I can just get it to stay still, maybe you can tend to its leg like you did my wing and then it can lead us out of this stupid fog." His face shines with fever sweat and delirious thoughts of escape.

"I want to get out of this fog, too, but–"

Not-Scamp renews its pitiful meowing and limps a few steps out of Quince's reach. He's about to step forward when a yowling, hissing ball of fur comes crashing into him, knocking him sideways.

My brain is flooded with anger and fear, but it's not mine.

Scamp!

The two Scamps are locked into a full-on cat fight. Miraculously, Not-Scamp's leg seems to have healed, because I can't tell them apart. Howls and hisses fill the air as they tumble and claw at each other.

"There's two of them," Quince says blankly. He looks up at me with glassy eyes from where Scamp, the real Scamp, knocked him to the ground. "Why are there two of them?"

"It's what I was trying to tell you." I help Quince to his feet. Scamp and Not-Scamp claw and bite at each other furiously. "The one you were following. It isn't Scamp, it just looks like him."

"How did you know?"

I tap my temple. "Couldn't sense him like I usually do. Didn't think of it at first, but I felt something was off. Then I realized what it was."

"You couldn't sense the fake Scamp at all."

Shaking my head, I say, "I tried to tell you, but..." I trail off.

"We should separate them, shouldn't we?" Quince asks, indicating the dusty-colored ball of claws and teeth.

"How?"

He shrugs. "I dunno. You grab one and I grab the other?"

The yowling intensifies.

"We should do it now, before they kill each other," I say. That's what Scamp wants to do—kill the creature that looks like him. It comes across as a sense of wordless rage in my mind, distracting me.

We circle around the cats, who pay no attention to us.

I nod to Quince, and we run in, lightning-fast, each grabbing the scruff of a hissing, spitting cat.

"Now what?" Quince asks, holding Scamp or Not-Scamp away from his body to avoid the claws.

"Stay there," I say, an idea dawning on me. Backing away from Quince and the cat he's holding, I survey the cat in my hands. *Are you Scamp, or are you something else?*

Fear and wordless rage still prickle at the back of my mind. *Maybe you are Scamp*, I think, looking down at the squirming cat. Quince and Scamp-or-not are only a dark, wriggling shape in the mist. A few more steps and I won't see them anymore.

The part of my mind that senses animal emotions goes silent and I freeze mid-step. I turn my gaze slowly down at Not-Scamp in my hands. The urge to throw it and run is so strong my arm holding the creature shakes.

"What are you?"

It twists in my grip and breaks free. As it tumbles to the ground, the dusty fur darkens and lengthens into quills that cover its entire back. It lands on two feet and turns its face up to me. I find myself gazing into the black, devilish eyes I had seen earlier. In its true form, the eyes are bulging and close set above a bulbous nose. It comes up no higher than my knee, and almost looks like a humanoid, evil hedgehog. It sneers at me, revealing pointed, gleaming teeth, then runs off into the mist, disappearing from view almost at once.

Eager to put distance between myself and the evil hedgehog creature, I step forward again until I can see Quince, who has a tight grip on Scamp, and sense Scamp's panicky emotions bubbling and bursting in my head.

"I'm okay," I call. "It's just me. The creature ran off."

I tell Quince what the creature looked like before it ran off, and he drops Scamp in surprise and horror, his arms hanging limply at his sides as he gapes at me.

Scamp growls at the insult of being dropped so unceremoniously and his irritation hits me like a heat wave. With hesitant steps, Quince walks over to where the creature had last been prior to Scamp's appearance. When he returns, he has a hand clapped over his mouth and a look of alarm on his face.

"Pukwudgy," he says, taking a shaky breath. "If Scamp hadn't shown up and knocked me over when he did, I would've tumbled over into a ravine. I don't know how deep the fall would've been, it's hard to tell with the fog, but…"

He shakes his head wordlessly, and I feel the blood drain from my face.

If he had fallen, he wouldn't have been able to catch himself with his broken wing. He would've plummeted the whole way down. Maybe to his death.

In the back of my head I feel Scamp's pride and satisfaction with himself and his daring rescue.

"Yes, you're very heroic," I say, kneeling next to him. "But the real question is, can you lead us out of this fog so we can get to the Seelie Court?"

He flicks his tail as if to say, "Of course," and trots off, stopping after a few steps to look back at us expectantly.

I take Quince's hand in mine and lace our fingers together. His hand is burning up. If we don't get help soon…I push the thought away and smile up at him.

"No chasing after wounded creatures anymore, okay?"

He nods and says, "I'll leave that to you from now on."

Scamp, his tail swishing, eagerly takes the lead.

I'm Allergic to Daisy Chains

2 Days Until the Winter Solstice

Scamp has to be lost. Why else would we spend ten minutes walking in one direction only to turn and head in the opposite direction? We've done this a few times now. And our pace, which had started out brisk, has slowed down to a snail's crawl as Scamp stops often to sniff the air and look around, though I'm not sure what he can see in all this damn fog. The slow pace is torturous for me. I would rush everywhere if I could. Quince is struggling with the pace, too, but for a different reason. I cock my head, listening to his labored breathing, and gnaw at my lip. His heartbeat thuds against my hand from his wrist. There's no romantic motivation for continuing to hold hands. Actually, if I didn't have to hold his hand right now, I wouldn't. Quince's hand is hot and slicked with sweat, like the rest of his body. The white undershirt he's wearing under his open waistcoat is stuck to his chest, and his hair is damp. He looks like he's just come in out of the rain.

In front of us, Scamp's tail goes rigid and he meows, nosing at a spot before his face.

"Did you find something, buddy?" I ask, stepping closer and pulling Quince with me. I glance at him out of the corner of my eye. He's been unusually quiet this whole time, but I imagine his wing is hurting more than he's letting on.

I reach through the fog to where Scamp's entire body is pointed, almost like a hunting dog that has found its quarry.

My hand touches warm, balmy air, and I pull it back in surprise. After who knows how long stuck in the damp cold of the fog, the summery air on my hand felt like I had taken it out from under a wet washcloth and dunked it in a bowl of sunshine.

At my side, Quince is humming. "...that never ends, it goes on and on, my friends..."

"I don't see anything, though," I say to Scamp, who is blinking up at me with those vivid green eyes, the triumph on his face so apparent I would've known how he felt even if I couldn't also sense it in my mind.

He holds a paw up to the spot I'd had my hand in a moment ago and meows, as if to say, "Come on, dummy, you can figure this out."

I put my hand on his paw and feel the warm, balmy air again. I stand and drag Quince with me as I walk around the spot in a wide circle. As far as I can see, the fog is never-ending, just like Quince is singing to himself right now.

I stand next to Scamp. "If we walk through this exact spot, we'll be out of the fog?"

As if satisfied I finally understand, he rushes toward the spot and disappears. The last we see of him is his flicking tail, and then that's gone, too.

Quince lets out a cry of surprise. "Eevee, he–"

I tug at him eagerly and step through the exact spot where Scamp vanished.

Like it had never been there to begin with, the fog fades away instantly. We're not where we had been before the gwyllyon had found us, but we're still in the Seelie woods somewhere. Crickets chirp and frogs sing to each other beneath a sky twinkling with stars. Ahead of us, a lake as smooth as glass reflects the stars above, but as I can't see any glowing moonstones around it, I don't think this is the lake we were looking for.

Pride fills my mind. In the dark it's almost as hard to see as it had been with the fog, but Scamp must be somewhere near us. I scan the ground until I find a lump that could either be Scamp or a cat-shaped rock and make for it. The lump turns glowing eyes up at me.

"Scamp," I breathe, letting go of Quince's hand to pick up the smug cat. "You did it! You got us out!" I twirl around in excitement, relief flooding me from my head to my toes. "We're free!"

At a warning growl from Scamp, I set him down and he takes a few unsteady steps away from me.

"We did it, Quince!" I cheer, turning to him.

He smiles weakly at me. "Yay." His voice is faraway and faint.

Right. Quince needs help. I turn to Scamp. "Any chance you know where we can take Quince to get medical attention in the middle of the woods?"

"What do you mean?" Quince asks, putting on what he must think is a brave face. In reality, he looks constipated, but I'm not going to tell him that. "I'm fine!" He throws his arms out wide, but winces from the pain and sways on his feet.

"You're right. You're a picture of health, Quince Florentz," I say drily.

He grins ruefully at me. "Okay, I'm not in the best shape right now, but I'm well enough to get to the Seelie Court and–"

"Not without getting some medicine for that fever," I cut in.

I look down at Scamp, who is circling us and meowing, all concern and confusion. He doesn't know how to help us with this. Scanning our surroundings, the glassy lake, the impenetrable trees of the vast forest, and the starry sky above, there's only a few places I can think of to take him, and none of them are in this realm.

We could risk going back to my house, but a part of me that's cowardly doesn't want to see my family. If I see them, I might not want to leave them, and then what? Amelia still needs saving.

Pulling out my phone, I check the time. Now we're not in the fog anymore, the phone is working fine, thankfully. It's after two in the morning. My stomach drops. That means it's Wednesday, barely. Two more days until the Winter Solstice Festival at the Unseelie Court. The run-ins with the gwyllyon and the pukwudgy have set us back about a day.

Hopefully the delay isn't fatal to Aspen, considering what Olearia told me. I wonder…is that why she sent Scamp?

Next to me, Quince hisses with pain as he shifts position. *Focus, Eevee*, I tell myself. First thing's first. I can't go to my house, so…Cam or Maggie's would be an option. Is this a week Maggie's dad is out driving his truck route or not? I can't remember. If it isn't, I wouldn't want to show up at her house and wake him. He's nice enough, but values his sleep.

"We're going to go to Cam's," I say, pocketing my phone and crossing my arms. "Just to get some medicine at least."

Quince is slow to answer. "I don't know," he finally says. "To go to Duluth then back here would take a lot of energy. We may get stuck in one realm or the other until we rest. At the very least, we'll be more vulnerable to attacks in Elfaeme with our energy depleted."

"Yes, or you may get so sick that we're stuck here and vulnerable to attack anyway," I point out stubbornly. "Besides, no one's going to attack us at Cam's."

Eventually, I convince Quince it's in our best interest to take a quick detour to Cam's before continuing our search for the Seelie Court.

I pick up Scamp, who squirms on principle in my arms but stills when I whisper to him that we need him with us because he's so very brave and knowledgeable, and when we return to Elfaeme he can protect us on our journey.

He purrs in my arms like a buzzsaw and I feel his pride swell.

"Ready?" I ask Quince, shifting Scamp to one arm and holding out my hand. I'm reminded of our first trip to Elfaeme together, when we located the Mage Stone and deciphered the first of my birth mother's clues. He'd held out his hand to me in much the same way in the parking lot at Chummy's Bar and Grill.

Maybe he's remembering it, too, because something softens in his face as he takes my hand.

I close my eyes, not because I need to, but because it helps me concentrate, and think about Cam's room. How the walls are plastered with artwork by their favorite artists. Their bedspread, never made, features an assortment of Pokémon even though they're a senior in high school. (To be clear, I'm not knocking their Pokémon bedspread. I have brothers and sisters who have been forced to grow up before they were ready, and mom and dad try their best to get us all to be kids while we're kids. I think it's cool that Cam's parents also encourage Cam's creativity and inner child. Besides, Cam is one of the most responsible people I know. Enjoying and embracing "childlike" things does not necessarily make you childlike yourself.)

I open my eyes and we're in Cam's room. It's exactly like I pictured, but with more clothes and art supplies in haphazard piles on the ground than when I was last here. And in the bed is Cam, fast asleep.

"Huh," Quince whispers, looking down at his chest, nonplussed. "Odd. Eevee, what does my back look like?"

He turns so his back is to me. I love the slope of his shoulders. They're not overly muscled, but the waistcoat he's wearing emphasizes their shape. There's no denying it. Even feverish, he looks dashing.

Then my gaze travels to the splint I had made and my eyebrows raise. Anything that had been touching the wings is invisible. I run my hands through where his wings should be, but they pass through air without touching anything. My sweatshirt and the vines look like they just cut off at his shoulders, yet they remain in place, as secured as ever.

"Weird," I mutter. Quince turns around and I explain what I see.

He rubs his chin, looking thoughtful. "Not sure I've heard of many fae who stick around in the human realm when they're injured," he says quietly. "Maybe this is why. Kind of hard to treat anything when you can't touch it or see it. I wasn't sure what would happen with the splint and everything, though. Honestly, I kind of thought it'd just fall off me without the wings there anymore."

"Hopefully it'll be intact when we return," I say. "Or it's goodbye, comfy sweatshirt."

Quince pretends to be offended, clutching at his heart. "Not, oh no, Quince is hurt, hope he's okay. You're worried about your sweatshirt."

I shrug. "It's a good sweatshirt. Alright, I'm going to wake Cam. Hold on."

Holding my finger to my lips, I creep forward, Scamp as silent as a well-trained predator in the crook of my arm, and gently nudge Cam's shoulder.

At least, that was the plan. But somehow, though I intended to move forward toward the bed, with each step I find myself further from Cam until I'm as far from the bed as I can be in their room. I drop Scamp, who lands with a soft "fwump" and lets out a low growl. Cam shifts in their sleep but doesn't wake. I scratch urgently at my arms, my head, my neck, every inch of my body I can reach. It all itches so much my skin feels like it's on fire. Dimly I'm aware that Quince is furiously scratching at himself as well, and even Scamp, who has stayed at my feet at the far edge of Cam's room, is nibbling at his skin.

Was it something we touched in the forest that had some kind of slow-acting irritant on it? Maybe I'll ask Cam for some calamine lotion as well as pain medicine. Still scratching compulsively, I make for Cam's bed to wake them. Somehow I end up next to Scamp again. His tail is in his mouth and he's gnawing on it furiously.

I want to tear my skin off and run. Did some fae bug bite all of us? Is that a thing? I grunt in frustration and Cam stirs and sits up.

"Whoozere?" they ask, their blue eyes wide as they stare into the darkness. They fumble for their phone and raise it, turning on the flashlight. Quince and I are illuminated in the glow of the phone's flashlight, scratching like mad at our arms and torsos.

Cam leaps out of bed at once.

"Eevee! Quince! What are you doing here?" they ask in a hushed but forceful voice, stepping toward us.

I can't answer. I'm too preoccupied with scratching this infernal and all-consuming itch. I have to get away, get out of this skin. Quince is now next to me and Scamp. I'm both pressed up against the wall and using it to scratch my back.

Cam stops, a puzzled look on their face. Then their hand goes to their wrist and they grin.

"You tried to wake me up, didn't you?" they ask.

I nod, scratching behind my ear.

"It works," they whisper, their round face radiant in the light of the flashlight.

"What works?" I snap, rubbing behind my ear and on my stomach simultaneously.

"This!" They hold up their wrist. The green flannel pajama sleeve falls back to reveal a bracelet of daisies. Some of the petals float to the floor as they brandish it proudly.

Quince and I both press ourselves flatter against the wall, which I didn't think was possible, and pinpricks of pain cover my entire body, like being stabbed with a thousand sewing needles.

"Er, sorry," Cam says, lowering their wrist and twisting the bracelet off. They throw it on the bed behind them. As soon as it leaves their hands, the painful itching sensation subsides and I breathe a sigh of relief.

"Why do you have a daisy chain?" Quince asks. His skin looks blotchy and red where he scratched at it.

"It's not just a daisy chain," Cam says. "It's a daisy chain wrapped around an iron wire."

"Iron to repel, daisy chain to prevent abduction," Quince mutters.

"Why aren't we itching anymore though?" I ask.

Cam frowns. "When did you stop itching?"

"When you threw it behind you. And we were fine in your room until–"

"Until you tried to approach Cam," Quince says. "Then the charm activated."

Cam reaches to pick it up and slip it back on their wrist. "Try to walk toward me again," they say.

Quince and I both try, but are immediately overcome with the same burning, itching sensation as before. No matter how hard we try, we can't get close to Cam.

They remove it from their wrist and put it in the breast pocket on their pajamas. The symptoms ease, and we walk toward them again.

"It has to be touching human skin for it to work," Quince says. "I never knew that."

"You seem to know a lot about fairy protections, though," Cam says.

"Well, yeah," he says, a look of surprise on his face. "Why wouldn't I? My parents always made sure I knew what to avoid so I didn't end up acting too strangely around the human kids I went to school with. There was this one kid's birthday party I went to where his little brother, weird kid, loved wearing his clothes inside out. Any time he came near me I had to make some excuse for why I suddenly needed to go somewhere else. He ended up crying by the end of the party because he thought I didn't like him."

Daisy chains. Iron. Wearing clothes inside out. Okay, that last one finally makes sense to me though. Jess sometimes accidentally puts her shirts on inside out and doesn't notice. It always irritates me when she does and I avoid her until she switches her shirt around. Now I know why.

"I hadn't planned to test the daisy bracelets like this," Cam explains, their cheeks flushed with excitement. "But at least we know it works as protection, right? I'm actually drying out some daisy chains to encase them in resin for longer-lasting protection, but these'll have to do for now." They point to their front pocket on their pajamas where the daisy chain bracelet currently resides.

"Cool," I say feebly.

"Anyway, you never did answer, what are you doing here?" Cam asks, looking from me to Quince and down at the cat. "Maggie and I figured you'd be having some kind of feast or something with the King and Queen by now when you didn't show up at school today."

"That was the plan," I say. I exchange a look with Quince.

"We had a bit of a setback," he tells Cam.

"What kind of a setback?" Cam asks, looking alarmed. They brush their blue hair out of their eyes.

"Do you have any strong pain medicine and," I consider, looking at Quince, who may be wingless now but won't be when we return to Elfaeme, "as much bandage tape as you can spare?"

Fanny Packs and Froggy Fae

Cam loads up one of their mom's old fanny packs with pain meds, bandages, and any other medical supplies we can get our hands on, including a small instant ice pack that I can fold and shake to activate. Quince wanted to help, but we gave him some pain medicine and a large glass of water and told him he was in charge of Scamp. After we sent him from the room, I picked up Scamp and told him *he* was actually the one in charge of Quince. He turned his keen green eyes to me with a "no duh" expression, then slipped out of my arms to follow after Quince.

I check in on them, poking my head into the Bradleigh's entertainment room. Quince is asleep, laying on his side on the large, plush sectional, a fuzzy rainbow blanket draped over his body, with his feet sticking out the end. Scamp is curled up on Quince's legs, a tiny dustball. I smile. He's purring.

They both look so peaceful. I wish I didn't have to wake them soon, but every second counts.

"So what delayed you guys?" Cam asks quietly, handing me the fanny pack, which is stuffed so full it looks like the seams might burst. I doubt Cam's mom has used it in years, maybe not since the 90s. It's neon pink and green, like a wedge of fluorescent watermelon. I take it from them and clip it on my waist.

"It all started when we ran into this gwyllyon," I say with a shudder. I recount the whole, hellacious experience to them. By the time I get to the pukwudgy almost luring Quince into a ravine, they're staring at me in horror.

"You guys are lucky to be alive. And not wandering in magic fog for eternity, getting lured into traps by…what'd you call them? Puck wedgies?"

"Pukwudgies. I know."

A line appears between their eyes. "But you guys are fae. When you took me and Maggie with you to Elfaeme to prove to us you were a fairy, that tree spirit nearly killed us when she realized we were human. Why would fae attack other fae?"

"Keep in mind, that tree spirit was willing to let me die with you and Mags," I remind Cam. "But it's the way fae are, even to each other. They can't resist pulling pranks or—"

"You call what they did to you a prank?" Cam asks incredulously.

"Possibly a fatal prank, but yes."

"Oookaaayyy…"

We head to the kitchen and, after so many years of play dates and hang outs and sleepovers, I know exactly where Cam's mom stashes her candy. I make a beeline toward it. She thinks it's a secret, but Cam and I have been stealing from it for years.

I unwrap a piece of chocolate from its aluminum wrapper and pop it in my mouth. I always intend to let it melt on my tongue, but I never do. Too impatient, I guess. I chew the piece in my mouth and reach for another.

"You have to go soon, don't you?" Cam asks, taking a piece of chocolate as well. They don't crumple the aluminum into a ball like I do, though. They flatten it out against the cool concrete countertop of the kitchen island and fold it until it's a tiny square.

"We can't really afford to wait too long," I say through my third piece of chocolate. "Maeve's powers waning and all…"

Cam looks down at their hands and fiddles with the aluminum wrapper square.

"So you might run into more fae who want to…" They shoot a glance up at me. "Play pranks on you."

"Not if we can find one of the moonstones that'll take us to the Seelie Court sooner rather than later," Quince says from the doorway. He looks exhausted, but the fever gleam is gone from his eyes at least.

A smile slowly spreads across Cam's face. "I think I can help with that."

They hurry off, and Quince's gaze drops to the overstuffed fanny pack at my waist. He quirks an eyebrow. "Stylish," he says, sounding like he's holding back a laugh.

Pretending I don't know he's laughing at me, I add, very seriously, "And useful. I might invest in one of these myself at some point."

We dissolve into muted giggles, and warm relief spreads from my chest to my fingertips. He's going to be okay. And once we're at the Seelie Court, I'm sure King Oakspirit and Queen Hibiscus have a court physician or something who can tend to Quince's wing. We just need to get there first.

We're still shaking with silent laughter by the time Cam returns with one of those huge camping lanterns.

"I put new batteries in it," they say, handing it to Quince. "It should last up to a whole day on full power." Their eyes are misty, faraway with some memory, and a smile plays across their lips. "Dad got it when he was in his camping phase."

"I remember that!" I exclaim. "That was the summer you guys joined us at Lake Carlos State Park."

"Dad never did figure out how to set up the tent properly," they say with a groan.

"Yeah, bad luck you joined us on the rainiest

weekend of the summer."

Our eyes are suddenly blinded by the lantern. I fling my hands up to cover them.

"Dude, why?" Cam asks.

"Sorry," Quince says, fiddling with a few buttons and turning it off. "Experimenting."

"I told you it had fresh batteries."

"That's…bright," I comment, blinking away the spots.

"Should help us find that moonstone faster, though," Quince says, a satisfied look on his face.

"With any luck, we'll arrive at the Seelie Court in time for breakfast," I say. My stomach growls at the mention of food, and, thinking on how long we were in the fog, I realize the last time I had anything to eat, aside from Mrs. Bradleigh's candy, was more than a day ago.

"In case you don't…" Without finishing their thought, Cam rushes off again. I shrug at Quince.

They return shortly with another fanny pack, this one a blue almost as electric as their hair, and rummage through the cupboards for snacks. Peering over their shoulder, I see them stuff granola bars, fruit snacks, crackers, and protein bars, plus some of Mrs. Bradleigh's secret candy stash in the fanny pack. On top of it all, Cam jams two miniature water bottles. A cracker or two may have gotten smashed in the process. With determination on their face, they manage to zipper it shut, then hold out the overstuffed fanny pack to Quince.

"I've got the lantern, though," he says, stepping backward and wielding the lantern like a shield.

"I'm not wearing two fanny packs, and there's no way we're clipping it on Scamp's back, it looks like it weighs more than he does," I say.

"But–"

"Besides," I interrupt, my face breaking into what must look like a mischievous grin, "it's stylish. You said so yourself." I take it from Cam, wrap my arms around Quince's waist, and clip on the bright blue fanny pack.

Cam snickers. "You two look like a really dorky couple about to go hiking."

"Nah," I say. "We're a really dorky couple about to go hiking with our cat." I snatch at Scamp, who had slunk into the kitchen looking bleary-eyed, and hoist him into my arms.

"Wow," Cam says, surveying the three of us. "That's a whole 'nother level of dorky."

Quince is looking down at me with a goofy grin. "You said we were a couple," he comments when I raise my eyebrows at him questioningly.

I drop my gaze. "Yes, well, a couple of dorks is what I meant, obviously," I say, flustered. "I mean, with our fanny packs, and the cat, and–"

His lips press against mine, and whatever else I was going to say is lost. He tastes sweet, and I have a sneaking suspicion he snagged some of Mrs. Bradleigh's secret candy stash while it was out on the counter. My heart flutters in my chest as I kiss him back, and when we pull away, I'm light-headed.

"What do you say?" he whispers, while Cam busies themself with putting the kitchen back in order. "Will you be the better half of a dorky couple with me?"

Scamp struggles to break free but I tighten my hold on him, looking up into Quince's eyes. Hope makes his whole face light up. I can't think of any excuses to say no to him anymore, and to be perfectly frank, I don't want to. Except...

"Your fiancée wouldn't–"

"She's not my fiancée by choice."

"No, but–"

"We're trying to take the throne from Nightglade, right? That's part of the reason we made all those plans to save Maeve and Aspen at the Winter Solstice Festival, when we knew they'd be out on display. Nightglade is the one who ordered the betrothal. If he's removed from power–"

"Big if."

"If he's removed from power," Quince repeats, "and yo–"

"Cam?" A sleepy voice calls from down the hall. "Is that you? I didn't know you were going to help us at the brewery this morning."

With each word, the voice sounds louder, closer.

"You have to go!" Cam hisses at us, shoving us out of the kitchen and into the dark entertainment room. "Hey dad," they say in an overly casual voice.

Looking back, I can see Mr. Bradleigh's large form lumbering into the kitchen in jeans and a faded purple Vikings sweatshirt. Cam looks a lot like him, but where Mr. Bradleigh is comfortable with his bulk, Cam always tries to make themselves look smaller than they really are.

Quince reaches for my hand. Worried that he's going to be left behind, Scamp digs his claws into my arm.

"Ow! Scamp, quit it. Yeah, we should go." I spare one more glance towards the kitchen. Cam's dad is clapping them on the back, so they must've agreed to help at Beer on the Hill this morning.

I send a silent apology to Cam for wrecking their chance of getting any more sleep.

Quince's hand tightens on mine.

"Ready, dork?" I ask.

We reappear in the Seelie forest, out of breath and slightly disoriented from realm-hopping. This time, we're more prepared, with two fanny packs and a lantern (not to mention a fairly knowledgeable cat).

"Wondered when you'd come back."

I freeze. I know that voice.

We look down into the wide, froglike face of Folsom.

He stares up at us, his brown robe rippling in the warm night breeze, and I hate the crafty glee in his protuberant yellow eyes.

"Hello, princess," he says, sweeping into a bow, one webbed hand clutching his walking stick. He straightens, his froggy face hardening when he looks at Quince. "And her motley-blooded suitor." Quince's lip curls in a snarl. "I've been waiting for you to return."

The Moonstone by the Lake

"What do you mean, you've been waiting for us to return?" Quince demands. "How did you know where we were to begin with?"

But I recall the conversation Quince and I had in the In Between and the round, yellow eyes I had seen before we appeared in the Seelie forest, and I think I know how Folsom knew where we'd be.

"Filthy spy," I mutter so quietly even I can barely hear myself. But there's no mistaking it. Folsom's eyes flicker quickly to me, then back to Quince.

A frog with ears like a bat, I think grimly.

"No way," Quince says. "You're not coming with us." In my arms, Scamp growls softly in agreement. I feel his distrust of Folsom, which only solidifies my own misgivings.

Folsom looks to me, as if only my opinion matters. I shrug at him. "If Quince and Scamp don't want you to come with us, I'm not going to argue with them."

The look Folsom gives me is indecipherable. "I think you'll find," he says in his old, croaky voice, "that you'll want me with you in the end. I'm on your side, *E.*"

He says "E" with special emphasis. It was how I had introduced myself to him when I first met him. I had been fresh off of doing some obsessive research into the world of the fae after discovering my birth mother's note, and was wary of revealing too much about myself to the first fae I'd met. Which, if you ask me, was for the best, since I've never been able to figure out Folsom's motives.

So when he says he's on my side, I can't quite believe him. True, fae can't lie, but for all I know, he says he's on my side because he believes I should be brought to Nightglade to face my fate and that would, in fact, be somehow in my best interest. Some folks (fae and human alike) will do mental gymnastics to justify their actions.

"Will you take me with you?" Folsom asks, planting his staff on the ground and leaning on it.

Scamp launches himself out of my arms and lands on the ground in front of Folsom, hissing and spitting at him.

"I don't think Scamp wants you with us," I say calmly, my heart hammering against my ribs. Why is he being so insistent about joining us anyway?

Folsom regards Scamp warily, seeming to notice him for the first time. Scamp hisses and growls, his hair standing on end and his tail puffed out.

"What are you doing here?" Folsom asks Scamp with a look of recognition on his froggy face. He stumbles backward away from one of Scamp's swiping paws. "What do you want with her?"

Scamp springs at Folsom's face, claws extended, and Folsom dodges, retreating even further. He's spry, for an old frog who relies on his walking stick.

"I'm here to help, same as you!" he shouts at Scamp, who yowls and bats at the place where Folsom's left leg had been only a second earlier.

"They can understand each other?" I ask Quince, who shrugs one shoulder, his eyes on Folsom and Scamp.

"Apparently."

I look back at the two of them. They circle each other like boxers about to start a match, then Folsom catches my eye.

"Call him off. You'll want me with you in the end," he pleads. Scamp takes advantage of the distraction and jumps at Folsom, knocking him over.

As Folsom hits the ground he lets out a quiet "Oof."

Then ribbets of pain wrench through the air. Scamp's paws are blurred, he's slashing Folsom's chest and face and arms so fast.

I don't know why I do it, I don't care for Folsom at all, but I run forward and pull Scamp off of Folsom's trembling body.

Folsom curls into the fetal position on the ground, shaking violently from head to toe, his large eyes shut tight.

"You've made your point," I whisper into Scamp's only ear. He growls, staring at Folsom, but stops struggling in my arms.

"I think you should leave now," Quince says to Folsom, who is struggling to his feet.

His gnarled walking stick lies on the ground near my feet. I pick it up and hold it out to him. He snatches it from my hands without so much as a thank you.

"I could help," he grumbles, but at a warning growl from Scamp, he hastily backs away. As he disappears into the forest, I hear him muttering to himself, but the only words I can pick out clearly are, "...will be disappointed...no way I'll get back...I've failed..."

"He's probably upset he's losing out on another chance to earn his spot back at the Unseelie Court," I say scathingly to Quince after we've put a few minutes of walking between us and Folsom.

"Hmm?" he asks, not looking up from the map. He's holding it in one hand, the camping lantern in the other to illuminate it.

I marvel again at the amount of detail his

parents had put into the map. My finger traces along the Seelie Forest. "So where are we?"

He taps at a place near the southern edge of the map. "We're really close to one of the moonstones that'll take us to the Seelie Court is supposed to be. See here?" He indicates a small splash of blue. "There should be a lake somewhere around here." He folds up the map and puts it away in a pocket of his waistcoat, studies our surroundings, then heads off to the left.

I hear a *zzziiiip* and see Quince has stopped and unzipped his blue fanny pack. He pulls out some granola bars and water, turns to me, and, with a grin on his face, launches them in the air.

I'm not in sports for a reason. My hand-eye coordination leaves much to be desired. Both the granola bar and the water bottle sail past my head.

Quince cracks open his water bottle, cackling. "Is that the best you got?"

"Yup," I say matter-of-factly. I retrieve the granola bar and water. Scamp, who had been in the water bottle's trajectory and only narrowly missed getting whacked in the head with it, is glaring at the both of us.

"You offended Scamp," I say through a mouthful of chewy raisins and oats.

Scamp shoots me an exasperated look and stalks ahead of us in the direction of the lake Quince thinks is nearby.

Apparently, "nearby" is a matter of perspective. On the map, it doesn't look far, but after an hour of hiking I'm beginning to wonder how close to the lake we really are. Quince has been using his right arm to hold the lantern ever since we left Folsom behind. Maybe flexing the muscles in his left shoulder bothers his broken wing because I've only seen him switch the lantern to his left hand briefly then immediately back to the other hand. It's drooping in his grip a little more than earlier, hovering in front of his torso rather than held high for better light to see the path.

"I know we're looking for a moonstone by a lake," I say to fill the silence, "but how will we know we got the right one?"

"We won't," Quince replies, his eyes narrowing as he looks into the trees to our right. "Do you think that looks like a clearing over there? It could be a sign that we're near the lake."

We pick up the pace, but then Scamp reappears, racing into the circle of light cast by the lantern, meowing exuberantly.

"He's found something!"

Quince and I exchange an excited look. This could be it! We might be minutes away from arriving at the Seelie Court and getting the help we need.

Neither of us tries to be sneaky anymore as we crash through the forest after Scamp, who lets out a constant stream of meows like he's telling us a story.

As suddenly as he appeared, he stops, circling proudly and sitting next to a dead frog, its pale green stomach up to the sky, its eyes closed.

"Oh," Quince says, pausing. "Poor frog." He

leans down to poke at it, but Scamp stands over his kill and nips at Quince's fingers. "Ouch!" Quince pulls his hand back, shaking it.

"I guess he's got a thing against frogs." We watch as Scamp drags his kill out of sight. "Maybe that's why he doesn't like Folsom," I joke.

Quince is watching where Scamp retreated with the frog, a thrilled look on his face making his dark eyes sparkle in the light of the lantern.

"There *is* a lake nearby!" He turns to me, thrusting the lantern high, and I squint my eyes shut, then cover them with my hands.

"You're a menace with that thing!"

"Oops. Sorry."

I crack an eye open and peek out through my fingers. "So there's a lake nearby for sure? How do you know? And how will we know it's the right lake with the right moonstone?"

But Quince is already striding away, taking the lantern with him.

By the time I catch up to him, he's practically bouncing on the balls of his feet with anticipation. I slow down, taking a moment to admire the picturesque scene in front of me.

In the pre-dawn glow, the lake has a mystical quality to it, like someone dreamed it up. Mist rises from the water like smoke, and while I usually think this looks pretty and otherworldly, seeing it now makes me shudder. It reminds me too much of the gwyllyon and the endless fog we were stuck in for a day.

Around the shore of the lake are sandy beaches, and lily pads cover much of the water near the lake's edges. Many of the lily pads are decorated with sunny yellow or moonbeam white flowers. A frog jumps from one of the lily pads and swims over to the reeds. Maybe it's a friend of the one Scamp is currently devouring. I send it a silent warning to stay in the reeds and out of sight.

The frog isn't the only thing in the reeds though. On the beach, Quince is pushing his way into the tall stalks with one hand, mumbling to himself.

"Er–need help?" I ask, hurrying over to him. Some of the reeds slip out of his grip and strike him in the face.

"Yes, please." He shoves the lantern at me. "Can you fly up to give us more light? I'd do it, but…" He jerks his chin backward at his broken wing.

"You're trusting me with the lantern?" I tease as I take it from him.

"Don't let the power go to your head," he warns with a grin.

"Too late!" I crow, launching into the air. "I am the lantern master now. The controller of the light. None shall see at night without my consent. Mwa-ha–"

"Hey, master of the light," Quince cuts in. "Mind staying still?"

Laughter bubbles in me, but I nod and do my best to keep the lantern still, which is not easy since it means I have to hover. Flying is one thing, hovering in one place is another.

We make our way slowly around the lake. Whenever there's a bare spot or a beach, Quince rushes past. I linger over a beautiful, sandy beach, but Quince doesn't even stop. He just heads to the next patch of reeds, gesturing impatiently for me to stick closer to him. "Mom says the moonstone we're looking for is hidden in reeds by a lake." He thrusts aside more stalks and I follow his progress, hovering above him in the air.

"What? That could be any lake," I comment, unable to hide the incredulous tone in my voice.

"A little lower," he calls. I drop five feet and he glances up at me. "Yeah, mom gave me a little more to go on than 'the moonstone is hidden in reeds by a lake in the Seelie Forest,' but I'm not going to shout it for everyone to hear."

I think of Folsom with his buggy eyes and abnormally acute hearing, even for a fae, and I shut up.

Hovering above Quince as he searches through the tall grasses, adjusting my position up, down, or to the side upon request, is dull work, and my mind wanders. What will it be like at the Seelie Court? Thinking of summers in Minnesota, I wonder if the Seelie Court will be in a constant blooming state with flowers and lush trees and bushes ripe with berries, with long days filled with sunshine. The King and Queen of such a court surely have to be kind and benevolent, right? There's no way they won't help us. They'll see how it'll benefit them to help Maeve so Nightglade and his human-hating Court can be overthrown. Quince told me the Seelie King and Queen started an organization of fae who live in the human realm, on Earth, to help humans take care of the planet. Fae like that must want peace between the courts.

A whooping cry from below startles me so much I drop. My wings strain and flap, barely stopping me from crashing on top of Quince. I land ungainly next to him, my feet catching on a rock, then sprawl forward, the lantern tumbling from my hand. My fanny pack pushes painfully into my hip when I hit the spongy ground.

I shove myself up to my knees, feeling the knees of my leggings grow cold with the water seeping into them. Quince grabs my elbow and drags me to my feet.

"I found it!" he whispers in my ear. I pull away, surveying him. His eyes are bright with excitement, and maybe a touch of the fever returning. The sooner we can get him a physician, the better.

He gestures to the ground, and I stoop down to look at the moonstone.

It's so small, I never would've found it on my own. Compared to the Mage Stone, which was large enough for fae to lounge on (though dormant now), this stone is so tiny, even if I had found it, I never would've guessed this was the one of the moonstones that would take me to the Seelie Court. I mean, I could pick it up and hold it in the palm of my hand if I wanted to.

"Shaped like a heart, see?" Quince asks,

nudging the shimmering stone with his foot. "We just need to touch this and we'll be at the Seelie Court."

I look across the lake at the purple sky, with its edges of soft pink. "We'll get there in time for breakfast after all."

Quince takes my hand and leans down to the stone.

"Hold up," I say, yanking him back before he can touch it. I scan our surroundings frantically, then fly into the air again. We hadn't gone far from the path, but no matter where I look, I can't see any dusty-colored fur. "What about Scamp? We can't leave him behind!"

Quince straightens and looks around as well. "I don't know if we'll find him in this forest. He's probably fallen asleep somewhere after having his night time snack."

"Yeah, but…" I hesitate. "It feels wrong to leave him."

"He's a cat," Quince says impatiently. "He'll be fine."

"Maybe." I grab the lantern from where it fell and hold it up, squinting into the distance. "Scamp!" I call. We wait, but not a rustle or a meow reaches our ears.

"If Olearia's sent him, then he'll know how to find us," Quince reassures me. He looks at the moonstone, then up at me pleadingly, and I sigh.

"Fine. Only…" I unzip Quince's fanny pack and pull out a bag of fruit snacks. One by one I drop them on the ground, leading from the moonstone to the path we had been on. I save one for myself and pop it in my mouth as I take to the air and zoom back to Quince, landing much more gracefully than I had the last time.

"Let's go get some royal assistance," I say, sliding my hand into Quince's outstretched one.

He smiles with his whole face and bends down to the small, heart-shaped moonstone.

Berries at the Seelie Court

At first I think it didn't work and the moonstone had gone dormant like the Mage Stone, leached of all its magic. But then it's like my chest is being compressed by a garbage compactor. Our surroundings dissolve, replaced by a sprawling garden bedecked in plants, all in peak levels of bloom. Flowers decorate whole groves of trees, and bushes are dotted with berries of all colors. It must go on for ages, but I can only see what is directly around the small dirt path we're on. I clutch my chest and gasp for breath.

"Still not used to moonstone travel after all the practice you've done?" Quince asks while I continue to fight for air, my heart racing. "And I thought I was the dramatic one."

I shoot him a dirty look. "You are," I manage to wheeze. His grin is both irritating and adorable. I shove him playfully. "Shut up," I say, my voice a little less wheezy this time. I take a breath and feel my heart calming down.

We gaze around us. Or rather, Quince gazes at our surroundings, while I sneak a look at his face, which is full of wonder. "It's beautiful," he whispers, looking like he's trying to drink it all in with his eyes. "Mom used to describe it to me, the gardens and the castle and the forest, but seeing it is…" He trails off, his eyes bright, and I squeeze his hand.

"What castle?" I ask, taking a more scrutinizing look around.

His face goes from wondering to puzzled, and he moves aside some of the branches of the bushes next to us, trying to peer through. "It should be somewhere around here? Mom used to tell me about it. The castle surrounded by the gardens always in bloom…"

"Gardens?" I shrug. "Maybe, yeah. But do you see any clear path through them?"

The air around us shimmers with the haze of summer, even though it's still early morning. Back home in Minnesota, where Cam is probably helping their dad at the brewery at this very moment, the forecast predicted highs of a whopping seven degrees Fahrenheit. A shiver runs through my body at the thought of the cold winds whipping off Lake Superior.

274

I wonder for a moment what humans would do if they knew this was here, if they knew the fairy realm wasn't just stories and, well, fairy tales. If they knew fairies lived among them and had the ability to travel back and forth between the human and fairy realm with visitors. A surge of protectiveness clutches my heart. I've seen the videos online, of huge trash islands in the ocean and smog caking the air of cities. To picture that here…

It's heart-wrenching.

Quince shakes his head, frowning as he surveys our surroundings. "I can't make out a clear path, no. It's almost like it's meant to be difficult to navigate."

"Yeah," I say, rubbing my arms. "Great."

"You're cold?" Quince asks, raising an eyebrow at me. "How? It's the perfect temperature right now." He spreads his arms, keeping his left a little closer to his body, and turns his face up to the sun. "Honestly," he says, his eyes closed, "it's almost a little hot."

I study Quince in his long-sleeved waistcoat, wrapped up in my sweatshirt, and have to agree with him. I'm feeling the sun's warmth, despite my shivering a moment ago, and I'm in a t-shirt.

"You'll probably be sweating soon," I comment. "Should we find the castle? It'll be cooler in there I bet."

He lowers his arms and nods, then stiffens, his eyes narrowing. "Eevee," he hisses, his voice low.

I spin to see where he's pointing. Down one of the paths, in the shadows of a grove of trees, is a darker shadow, moving slowly.

"Someone else is in here," he says, still whispering.

"Maybe they know the way out!"

"Maybe," Quince replies. "But let's be careful."

We exchange a look and hurry over, our pace slackening as we approach the figure.

"H-hello?" I say tentatively, squinting to make out the features of the figure better.

At the sound of my voice, they slow to a stop, their head lifting and cocking to the side questioningly. They're definitely humanoid. I can't tell much about them from the back except that they're thin. I step closer and Quince quickly follows until we're feet away. A ray of sunlight peeks through the canopy and lights up the area around us, and I suck in my breath. They're not just thin, they're skeletal, the vertebrae of their back visible through the thin cotton shirt they wear.

"We've come to seek an audience with King Oakspirit and Queen Hibiscus," Quince says, his voice confident and courteous, a deeper timbre to it than I'm used to hearing. "We hope you can help us?"

Despite his injured wing, he stands erect. I eye him curiously. This must be what he's like in the Unseelie Court. It's like his goofiness has been covered by a mask of gentility and manners. I'm not sure how I feel about this Quince. His expression as he waits for the fae in front of us to respond is polite but distant. It makes him look more mature. As I watch him, I can't help but see similarities between his posture and mannerisms and Nightglade's, from the one time I met him in person (before he got all weirdly insistent about me thanking him for saving me and Quince that night). The comparison unsettles me, makes me feel like I'm looking at an alternate universe Quince.

At Quince's formal request, the fae straightens. Their hair is matted, I realize. I thought it had been styled into a bun on their head, but when they stand taller their hair catches the light. It's a mess, so knotted I wonder why they haven't just cut it off, and is streaked through with gray. The hair that isn't gray is a dingy brown.

They turn to us and I clutch at Quince's arm.

"Do you—is that—?" I whisper, feeling faint.

The figure blinks at us out of hooded brown eyes. They seem to focus on our faces for a moment before their expression slips back into vague, empty contentment.

It was hard to tell from behind, and so I had assumed they were fae. But there is nothing fae-like about them. In Elfaeme, if you don't look fae, you're...

"Human," I breathe. "Quince, they're human." The human gives us a misty smile. It's then I see she—for she's definitely a middle-aged woman—has a basket in her hands, filled with berries.

"Want one?" she asks, popping a berry in her mouth and holding the basket out to us.

Quince gives me a worried look. Food in Elfaeme is fine for fae to eat, but on humans it can have adverse effects, either making them lose interest in human food forever (so they waste away), or unable to leave Elfaeme.

"No, thank you," Quince says, just as politely as he had asked for an audience with the King and Queen. Warmth floods through me. Most fae would drop their formal manners if they realized they were talking to a human, but Quince doesn't. I love his kind heart. Fae are kind to each other (sometimes, when they want to be), but rarely to humans. I had no idea how rare Quince and his family were when I had met them.

"Okay," she says, popping a red berry in her mouth. The juice leaks out over her lips and dribbles down her chin. "They're good," she says, closing her eyes, a beatific smile transforming her overly thin face into an expression of pure delight.

Her vague mannerisms disturb me. They remind me too much of how my parents act any time I bring up fae or the fae realm. I never know what to say to my parents when they're like that, and I'm not sure how to respond to this woman. How many berries has she eaten? Will she ever be able to return to the human realm as herself, or is it too late?

"I'm sure they're delicious," Quince says. She opens her eyes and smiles at him, her teeth red with berry juice. "But before we can enjoy any of that wonderful fruit, we really do need to have an audience with King Oakspirit and Queen Hibiscus."

She stares at him blankly, then pops another berry in her mouth and turns away, humming tunelessly to herself and sashaying off to another part of the gardens and out of sight.

"We should let the King and Queen know there's a human wandering around their gardens," Quince says, gazing in the direction where the woman disappeared. We can't see her anymore, but we can hear her humming. "They'll want to know about it, I'm sure."

"How long do you think she's been in Elfaeme?" I whisper, thinking of Amelia with a sick feeling in my stomach. What if she's offered food by her captors and eats it?

"A while," Quince says, frowning. "She must've wandered here from the human realm through a mushroom circle or something. It happens sometimes. Gotten hungry, and…"

We're silent. I don't know about Quince, but a kind of horror has gripped me. "If Amelia's eaten anything…" I croak.

"We'll deal with that when we come to it," Quince says firmly. "All the more reason to find the King and Queen."

Setting off in a random direction, we make our way through the luscious gardens of the Seelie Court. I've never seen anything quite like it on Earth. The closest would be the pictures of the gardens at the Palace of Versailles in one of my history books. But those are tended, orderly. Everything around us has the touch of the wild to it, like a garden where the gardener had mixed up the seeds and tossed them around to see what would stick. Vines cover the stone walls, and flowers peek out of cracks and crevices in the walls and cobblestone paths, giving the impression that the whole place is covered in colorful confetti. I hear the sound of running water, like from a fountain, but neither Quince nor I can find it.

When I try and fly up to locate the fountain, or find a way to the castle from where we are, I can't get any higher than a few feet off the ground. It isn't quite like hitting a barrier. It's more like my wings grow heavy and I feel suddenly like I would rather be flying low or walking than flying high above the gardens.

After my third attempt, I land next to Quince in a temper.

"It's not you," Quince says soothingly. "Even if I could fly," he looks back at his limp left wing ruefully, "I don't think I'd be able to get any higher."

"What's the point of having wings if you can't fly?" I grumble.

"You *could* fly," he points out.

"A few feet from the ground. Again, what's the point?"

"I bet it's some kind of security measure," he muses. "Unwanted visitors get stuck in a maze and can't easily find their way to the castle. Visitors who know their way have no problem."

The heat and the garden maze are turning my mood sour. "And what about visitors who don't know their way around?"

"They muddle through until they meet someone or find their own way out, I guess."

The cobblestone paths wind among the trees and bushes with no clear pattern either of us can figure out, which, I suppose, is the point. Above us, the sun climbs higher and higher until it's almost midday by the time we take a left turn on a whim and find ourselves facing an immense castle rising out of the greenery like a mountain. It looks ancient, its stone walls covered in climbing ivy, the stone that peeks through weathered and worn. Like a medieval castle frozen in time. But as we get closer, I see it's not as closed off to the world as castles I've seen depicted in movies, with their tiny slits for windows. The castle of the Seelie Court has enormous windows, which I had missed at first because the ivy covers them like curtains. Here and there I can see small shapes in the windows, drawing back the curtains of ivy and peering out at the midday sun, blinking and rubbing the sleep from their eyes.

"Think they partied too late last night?" Quince whispers to me, a laugh in his voice, as some of the figures lean blearily on the windowsills.

It is almost like a scene from a fairytale castle, except the (possibly hungover) people at the windows have skin of every color. Some have horns on their heads, others have wings or, I notice as they turn, tails. A few have all three. There are a couple like me, who have markings on their faces and arms similar to the orange flowers which decorate my temples. A thrill of excitement thrums through me when some of the fae launch themselves from their windows. Apparently the flying restriction is just over the garden, not the castle itself, because now that I'm looking up I see a group of fae zipping and looping around each other through the air, seemingly for the fun of it.

Others dive into the moat surrounding the castle, which sparkles in the sunlight. It's not like the murky moats I'd expect to see. Quince and I continue towards the castle in a daze and I look down into the moat as we cross a wooden bridge. The water is crystal clear. Silver fish dart out from the shade of the bridge, their scales shining as they catch the light. A fae with a fin on his back is chasing the fish. When he does a barrel roll, I see his face for a moment. Bubbles escape his lips, which are open in a laugh, as if chasing fish was the most wonderful thing to be doing.

We cross the bridge and crane our necks to stare up at the castle. Quince looks as amazed as I feel, and I turn in a slow circle to look at it all again—the gardens we've emerged from, the castle, the moat, the laughing fae above and below. But this time, I look at it as if I'm seeing it through Quince's eyes. This is where his mother had lived before she fell in love with Gerald of the Unseelie Court. She had given up this idyllic existence for Gerald and their uncertain future together, and for Quince, though he came later. Turning back to Quince, I notice a strange look in his eyes, a longing tinged with jealousy, but then he blinks and grins crookedly at me.

"Should we go inside, you think?"

I nod, at a loss for words. Hand in hand, we cross beneath the large archway in front of us, and I allow myself to feel the tiniest bit hopeful that everything will turn out okay for all of us: me, Quince, Amelia, and my birth parents.

No Party Like a Seelie Party

Everything after entering the courtyard through the stone archway is a whirlwind. One moment Quince is standing next to me, proclaiming to an official-looking fae wearing spectacles that we're seeking an audience with the King and Queen, and the next we're being separated and shuffled away from each other. Quince had mouthed "I'll find you" to me while a tiny fae murmured and hovered around him, plucking at the bandages and peppering him with questions about his injured wing.

I am deposited unceremoniously in a small room with a discreet suggestion that I should perhaps bathe and ready myself before seeking audience with the King and Queen. Blinking bemusedly at the fae who escorted me to the room, I have two thoughts. One, I wonder if it's customary for the Seelie King and Queen to request visitors bathe before having an audience with them? Two, the bed looks a lot more tempting than the bath. But the way the fae at the door scrunches their nose when they mention the room has a bath which fills itself with warm, soapy water upon command, maybe a bath should happen first. (I think they said their name was Kieran? I for sure remember they said they use they/them pronouns. It made me think of Cam, which is why I was only half-listening when they shared their name– but again, it's been a whirlwind.)

"Any questions?" maybe-named-Kieran asks, blinking back at me.

Shoot, I missed something. "What do I say to make the tub fill again?"

To Kieran's credit, they try to hide their sigh of exasperation.

After they leave, I stand in front of the tub, examining it warily.

It won't work, a small voice in my head tells me. *You're not fae enough, you've been raised by humans for almost two decades, and it'll know and stand there on its clawed monster feet, mocking you with its emptiness.*

I push that voice down and say, "As a guest of the Seelie Court, I'd like a bath, please," and sure enough, water appears as if an invisible person is dumping buckets of hot, soapy liquid into the tub.

Feeling like I should continue being polite, I say "Thank you" once the water stops rising.

I have no idea when someone will fetch me for my audience with the King and Queen, so I scrub myself as quickly as I can and dry off with one of the towels sitting in a pile on a table next to the tub. My arm is reaching through the sleeve of my shirt and I'm relaxing my shoulders like Quince taught me, to turn my wings non-corp (a seriously annoying part about having wings), when I hear a soft tap at the door.

"Just a minute," I call, shoving my arm the rest of the way through and hastily pulling on my leggings. My legs are damp despite toweling off, thanks to the humidity in the room, and it's more of a process than I'd been expecting.

Panting, I crack the door open to see Kieran's face, nose still scrunched. I'm reminded of Trinculo's line in *The Tempest*: "Monster, I do smell all horse piss, at which my nose is in great indignation." Kieran's nose looks like it's in great indignation of something. My lips twitch as I fight a smile. Thinking of Shakespeare always cheers me up.

I'm not successful in hiding my smile, though, because at seeing my lips twitch, Kieran's face scrunches to match their nose.

"Are the King and Queen ready for me and Quince?" I ask, crossing my fingers behind my back. "We're here on kind of urgent business, and—"

"You need to change," they interrupt, thrusting an armful of clothing at me through the crack in the door.

I take the bundle, hardly looking at it. "But I *need* to see the King and Queen," I say again, confused. "As soon as possible. What does it matter what I wear?"

Now Kieran looks at me as if I've truly lost my marbles. "That outfit isn't for an audience with the King and Queen, it's for the soirée this evening," they say sniffily.

I throw the clothes behind me and glare at Kieran. "I'm sure it'll be a lovely party. There's probably no party like a Seelie party, right? But I don't care about the soirée." Heat rises to my face and I clench my fists, thinking of Amelia and my birth parents. How can I attend a party while they're in trouble? "I need to see the King and Queen, as soon as possible. How many times do I have to say that?"

Kieran looks both appalled and offended at my outburst, their nose even un-scrunching in shock.

I run my hands through my hair, which is still damp, and let out a frustrated breath. "Look, I didn't mean to come off as rude—"

"Really." Kieran crosses their arms, revealing scaly green skin on their forearms.

"We're running out of time, we were already delayed coming here, and…" I hear blood pumping in my ears. "And you're not even listening, you're examining your manicure."

Kieran looks up at me slowly. "Whatever you were saying, save it for when you see the King and

Queen," they say in their huffiest voice yet. They turn and stride away.

"Wait!" I skid out into the hall to see Kieran disappearing around a corner. Cupping my hands over my mouth, I bellow, "When will that be?"

Not only do they not reappear, but several heads poke out of rooms along the hall, eyeing me curiously.

Ignoring them all the best I can, I stalk back into my room, fuming, and kick at the pile of clothes Kieran had dropped off.

Kicking clothes does absolutely nothing to relieve stress. I stomp around the room, then lay on the bed and try to fall asleep by taking deep breaths while imagining a calm lake. When that doesn't work, I sit up and conjure my fire fists perfectly the first time just by imagining Kieran's scrunch-nosed face, but none of it takes away the stress rippling through my veins.

I'm laying on the bed again, trying to doze off, when I hear another tap at the door. "I'm not coming out until the King and Queen are ready to see me, Kieran!" I shout, then immediately berate myself.

"You catch more flies with honey than vinegar." It's almost like hearing Amelia say it when I whisper the words. She feels strongly that the best way to get along with people is through kindness, no matter how stuffy or scrunch-faced they may be, and it always irritates me when she says the "honey/vinegar" proverb after I lose my temper. Now I wish she were here to say it rather than me mumbling it to myself. I groan and force myself to sit up.

"That sounded rude again! I'm stressed!" I pause, then add, "I am sure the soirée will be lovely, but I think I should use this time to figure out what to say to the King and Queen, you know, so–"

"It isn't Kieran," says a muffled voice from the other side of the door.

Puzzled, I open the door. Standing in the hall is a young-looking fae (though age is hard to determine, given that Sean and Shannon look barely older than me and they are centuries old) with a mane of red hair. A constellation of freckles forms a dotted pattern across his nose and cheeks, and his eyes are a startling shade of golden yellow. He's dressed in a waistcoat and pants similar to Quince's outfit he wears at the Unseelie Court, but unlike Quince's, his is emerald green with shining gold buttons.

We lock eyes, and I find myself fascinated with the way his catch the late afternoon light coming in from the window behind me. "You're not ready for the soirée," he accuses me as soon as he tears his gaze away from mine and trails it down my body.

I blush, feeling suddenly shy. "Uh–is it time for the soirée already? It's just, I'd told Kieran–"

He chuckles. "We all know what you told Kieran." A corner of his mouth quirks up in the briefest of smiles, drawing my attention from his eyes to his lips, which are pink and look soft. "Didn't get on well with them, from what I understand? Any complaints against my staff can be taken up with me."

"What?" I stammer, forcing myself to look anywhere but at his lips or eyes. "Oh, no. We had a misunderstanding, that's all. I want to see the King and Queen, and they want me wearing that–" I indicate the clothes, in a pile on the floor where I'd kicked them earlier– "to the soirée."

"Oh, Kieran," he says, sighing. "I don't suppose they told you that you'd be seeing the King and Queen at the soirée?"

I freeze. "They left out that detail," I say stiffly, wrangling down the sudden frustration I feel at this announcement.

"I'll wait out in the hall for you while you change, then." He lowers his voice, his eyes smiling kindly at me. "A bit of advice. Change swiftly. King Oakspirit values punctuality."

"Right. Got it. Yes." I step back to close the door, but then open it again. "Wait, what's your name?"

His face lights up with a dazzling smile. "You can call me Dáire." He pronounces it kind of like DI-hray.

"Okay. Dáire, then. I'll be quick." I shut the door tight and, as fast as I'm able, scramble out of my old clothes (which are a bit smelly, I'll admit) and into the requested outfit, a floofy, floor-length dress of some kind of soft white fabric, decorated with pale, embroidered patterns. Looking at my reflection in the mirror, I see the patterns resolve into an image of a tree bedecked with leaves and berries, the roots embroidered into the skirt. It's wrinkled from sitting in a heap on the floor all afternoon. I try to smooth some of the wrinkles out of it, but finally give up and open the door.

"That was fast," Dáire says. "I'm impressed." He offers his arm to me, and his eyes widen slightly when I link mine through it.

"Is this not–not proper courtly manners?" I ask, noticing how he stiffened when my arm linked with his. My cheeks flush. "I'm new here." I gesture vaguely around us. "Here specifically and Elfaeme in general."

"I know about you, Evelyn, daughter of Aspen and Queen Maeve," he says, gently unlinking my arm from his and placing my hand on his forearm instead. "And I wish you luck tonight with King Oakspirit and Queen Hibiscus at the soirée."

He leads me down one hallway after another. The castle is as much a maze as its gardens! The whole way there, he chats with me conversationally, until I feel my body relax. By the time he leads me to where the soirée is being held, which is in a central courtyard decorated with flickering candles and floral arrangements, I'm leaning on him and laughing.

"Quince!" I call, waving to him from across the courtyard. From a distance it looks like his wing has been healed. So why does he have such a pained expression on his face when he looks at me?

Dáire leans down (he's considerably taller than me, which isn't a hard feat to achieve) and whispers in my ear, "Talk to you later this evening, E."

I frown up at him, confused, but he's already

walking away and mingling with a group of fae clustered around a table of hors d'oeuvres. The only fae I've introduced myself to as "E" is Folsom, so why did Dáire just refer to me with that nickname?

Quince sidles up to me, looking grumpy, in a waistcoat similar to the one he had been wearing, but of a deep midnight blue. "Who was that?"

"He said to call him Dáire. I think he might be in charge of the castle staff? He came to escort me to the soirée."

"I could've escorted you if I'd have known you needed an escort," he grumbles.

"You didn't know where I was, it's okay," I say warmly. He still looks put-out, so I hold out a hand. "Escort me now?"

He proffers an arm and I take it correctly this time.

Mis-fae-ken Identity

Quince and I walk through the crowded courtyard. Even the air is swarming with fae flying and swirling together in the air in some kind of beautifully chaotic dance. Music and voices mingle in a pleasant hum, but now that I'm here, my nerves jangle.

"Keep an eye out for the King and Queen," I say, glancing around at all the fae laughing and dancing and eating.

"I would if I knew what they looked like."

We wander around the soirée guests, and despite my worries I find myself completely taken in by the party atmosphere, my spirits lifting. *Remember Amelia*, I admonish myself. *Remember about Maeve's powers*

*waning and the danger Aspen is in. You can have fun after
they're all safe. Right now, you're looking for the King and
Queen.* As we make another round, I catch sight of
Dáire's unmistakable red hair and wave as we pass him
by. He inclines his head, still in conversation with
another fae, and winks at me.

"Shouldn't he be attending to his staff?" Quince
grouses. We sidestep a fae dancing by herself with such
jubilance she is the living embodiment of the "dance
like no one is watching" adage.

"I'm sure he's just on break or something." At
the prickly look on Quince's face, I pull him to a stop
next to a bush which has been magicked so the flowers
all glow with a pearly white light. "Hold on, are you
jealous of Dáire?"

"Should I be?" he counters, folding his arms.

"No!" I say quickly. Heat rises to my cheeks. To
keep Quince from seeing, I crane my neck and look at
the courtyard, which has become even more crowded
since we arrived. "Where are the King and Queen
anyway? You'd think they'd be easy to spot. Won't they
look…I don't know, royal?" I stand on my tiptoes
before remembering I'm a fairy and can fly. The
evening air is warm against my face and arms, as I soar
upward and look down on the guests.

Quince flies up to join me, his magically
repaired wing showing no signs of weakness from being
broken.

"I still can't see them," he says, sounding as
frustrated as I feel.

He flies in a circle, looking back and forth, then freezes, his gaze intent on something.

"Do you see them?" I ask excitedly.

It's like he doesn't hear me. His black-feathered wings beat the air behind him, but the rest of his body is rigid.

"Quince?" My eyes widen. "Look out!" We narrowly escape getting hit mid-air by a group of fae so absorbed in their flighty dance they don't see us as they twirl between me and Quince, forcing us to fly apart. I'm coming to realize these Seelie fae take their dancing and partying seriously.

"Where's Glen, so you can ask him to dance? I bet he'd be super impressed you can fly," I tease Quince once I've righted myself in the air, thinking of the Homecoming Dance and how Quince joked he'd take me only if I let him have one dance with Glen, a troll-like senior at Duluth High.

When he doesn't respond, I turn to where I'd seen him dodging the group of flying fae and feel the laughter die on my lips, replaced quickly by a rising tide of panic. Where is Quince? I need him with me, this afternoon made that abundantly clear. He knows how to act around courtly fae, even if he's never been to the Seelie Court, but me? On my own I devolved into a frustrated mess spewing rude comments and succumbing to stress. I couldn't even sleep, and I love sleep.

I scan the swirling fae in the air, but don't see Quince. He'd stand out in this sea of pastel colors with his dark blue waistcoat. Or at least, I would think he'd stand out. So far, no luck spotting him up here.

Not for the first time, as I descend to the ground next to a fae swaying to the music and drinking what looks like wine, I wonder how the fae know who is affiliated with the Seelie or Unseelie Courts. Tonight, I know they've dressed Quince in a dark waistcoat similar to his own, and most of the fae I see here are dressed in pastels or bright colors, like a field of dancing flowers. But the differences run deeper than fashion choices.

Fae abilities and appearances vary widely. Even Quince, who is related to Sean and Shannon, looks nothing like them and has different abilities. And Folsom, with his froggy appearance, doesn't seem like he'd be an Unseelie fae, given that the Unseelie Court's powers strengthen in the winter and when I think of frogs I think of summer time.

I land with a graceless thump and knock into the wine-drinking fae I'd seen earlier, who splutters, wine dripping down her chin and onto her cream-colored satin shirt. The way the red wine dribbles down her chin reminds me uncomfortably of the woman Quince and I had seen in the gardens. How is she, I wonder? Is she still wandering aimlessly, humming to herself and eating berries? I need to remember to talk to the King and Queen about her, too.

Anger ripples across the fairy woman's face as she wipes her chin on the back of her hand. "Learn how to land properly, oaf." She strides off, nose in the air, probably sniffing around for more wine.

Okay, so my landing lacks finesse, but I had only learned I could fly a few months ago.

"You land just fine for someone who has recently learned to fly," says a voice in my ear, echoing my own thoughts.

Smiling, I turn to Dáire. "I appreciate that. But as one who suffers from natural klutziness, it's not really a surprise it extends to my flying."

"Considering I cannot fly, I must bow to your expertise on the matter," he says.

I snort at his attempt at flattery. "A few months of flying is hardly—"

"A few months of flying is a few months more experience than I've had myself." He gestures to his back, which is wingless. It reminds me of Quince's mom, Myska, who doesn't have wings, either. While wings seem to be in the majority for fae folk, I forget that not everyone has them.

He picks up two glasses from a table and offers one to me. "Here. Drink, eat. Enjoy yourself. My staff work hard to make each soirée exceptional."

"Thanks." I take the proffered glass, but don't drink. "I'm sure you all know what you're doing. But I need to find the King and Queen. Maybe I can enjoy the party after that."

Regarding me with his golden yellow eyes, he raises his to take a sip. "You are certainly singularly-focused," he comments after a brief pause. "Is your companion as well? Where is he? I have not had the pleasure of being introduced." Dáire glances around with an air of mild curiosity.

"I seem to have lost him," I answer, ill at ease.

Dáire chuckles. "Sounds like your friend has gotten into the spirit of the soirée, then." If anything, his words make me feel tetchier. He smiles, then finishes his drink. "Have fun, Eevee. Mingle. The King and Queen always announce themselves when the party is in full swing. They like the heady high of fae drunk on fun."

My hands fly to my hips. "*You* said I had to hurry down here, that King Oakspirit likes punctuality."

"I was not lying," Dáire says quietly. "You should know by now that fae can't lie."

"Of course I know that," I retort. "But you only told me part of the truth, didn't you?"

"I may have, yes. But only to ensure you were where you need to be to seek an audience when the time arrives. And, I must admit, I was curious to meet you." We lock eyes, like earlier, and I find I can't look away, nor do I want to. His eyes aren't a solid golden yellow, now that I can see them up close. They're rimmed with a thin line of green. I step closer, almost in a trance, to see them better. I don't know why, but I want to get a clearer look at them.

He breaks eye contact with me, looking down at the empty glass in his hands, and the sudden disappointment makes me breathless. "You'll know when the King and Queen are announced this evening."

"Oh?" I try to catch his eyes again, but he keeps them firmly looking at his hands. "Until then, enjoy yourself, E."

The use of the nickname I'd told Folsom jolts me out of my disappointment at once. "That's another thing–" I start, but Dáire bows quickly.

"I must see to the refreshments," he murmurs, his mane of red hair bobbing through the crowd.

Enjoy myself. I have family in peril and, inexplicably, have lost Quince, but Dáire wants me to enjoy the party.

Fine. I'll enjoy the party, then. I tip back the glass he gave me, taking a large swig. The drink is sweet and fruity, tasting more like fruit juice than wine, but I feel a warmth spreading through me, even with one sip. If so little of it has this kind of effect on me, it's no wonder so many of the fae around me are dancing and laughing with abandon. I wonder what happens if a human drinks it?

The sweetness stays in my mouth like honey. I continue to sip at it as I meander through the crowd.

It's funny, really, this whole situation. Here I'm at the best party I've been at in ages, possibly ever, and I am bent on not enjoying myself. Why? Because my family and friends are in danger. Well, and what will a little more time do? Like Dáire said, there's not much I can do until it's time to see the King and Queen, so I might as well enjoy myself. It is a little worrisome about Quince, though. Where could he have gone? I place the empty glass on a table and pick up a new one filled to the brim with a new drink, this one with a pleasant, minty taste to it. I giggle when the bubbles tickle my nose, and the fae standing next to me joins in. His eyes are unfocused and he wobbles on unsteady feet, his bulky shoulders tilting ominously backward.

"I got you," I say through laughter–mine? Or his? Both? Setting my drink down, I grip his forearm and tug him forward, then steady him.

"You're stronger than you look, little fairy," he slurs, patting my shoulder and ambling away.

The spot on his arm where I grabbed him catches my eye as he turns to avoid two vigorously gesticulating fae. It looks blurred, discolored, whitish against the rest of his orange skin. I squint down at my hands.

My palms are covered in orange paint.

The buzzing in my head makes it hard to concentrate, and I don't know how long I squint down at my hands, looking at one palm, and then the other. Something is off here. I survey the crowd, but can't find the orange-skinned individual.

What I can't get out of my head is the rule of thumb Quince had told me about Elfaeme. If it doesn't look fae, it's human.

Unless…

I pick up my drink with shaky hands after wiping them on a silky napkin and drain the whole cup. No. It would be crazy to think I just helped a human dressed up to look like a fae.

Wouldn't it?

I take a drink decorated with basil and limes from a fae with baseball-sized eyes and examine the fae around me more closely.

Most, from what I can tell, are actually fae. But here and there, interspersed throughout the bedecked and bejeweled throng, are humans. Humans with smeared paint on their faces and arms and legs, or horns on their heads somewhat askew, or wings which are too stationary and stiff to be functional, let alone real.

My brain is cloudy, but I'm starting to think the human we met in the garden wasn't there by mistake.

What I can't figure out is what the humans are doing here, at a Seelie Court soirée? And all of them are eating or drinking the fae food. Don't they know they're trapped here forever now, or, if they go back home, they won't be able to stomach human food? Or are they too dazzled by the festivities to care? My drink tastes suddenly like vinegar in my mouth. The Seelie obviously know about the humans among them. But they don't seem to care that all these humans are fated to wander the fae realm forever or starve on Earth. I thought that Quince said the Seelie King and Queen cared about humans and Earth? How could they allow this?

Uneasy, but wanting to learn more about why so many humans are here, I seat myself on a bench by a cluster of bushes.

And I listen.

At first, I don't hear anything I can make sense

of. The courtyard lights up with a twinkling glow as the sky above me darkens. I am glued to this bench, unwilling to move until I hear something to help me make sense of this. Eventually, certain snippets of conversation start to stand out.

"Oh, she isn't going to bed on time? You know, you shouldn't feed them so much sugar on an empty stomach, does funny things to their heads…" says a fae woman with a deep voice and a smug, self-righteous expression on her face to her companion, who nods thoughtfully.

"He's looking marvelous, what do you do for exercise?" asks a male fae, gesturing to a human who looks like he lives at the gym. Does the Seelie castle have a gym? If so, I doubt I'd find it in that maze of halls.

"Mine couldn't come tonight, she gets into such fits sometimes. Tears for days. But eventually she comes around and is right as rain. She's usually such a pleasant little thing…" twitters a birdlike fae to her towering friend.

The more I hear, the more my insides twist and tangle.

A thought bubbles to the surface of my brain. And once I've thought it, everything clunks into place.

I can't fathom why, but for some reason, the Seelie fae seem to think it's fashionable to "have a human" to care for.

In fact, the way they talk, it's like pet owners talking about their pets.

And not only are the humans being talked of as if they were pets, the fae carry themselves with pride when they talk of the kindly way they treat "their" humans.

This doesn't connect with what Quince told me about the Seelie fae when we were at the Equinox Celebration. He'd told me, "There's even a group of mostly Seelie fae who live in the human realm full time and try to help the humans take care of the earth." How does having humans as pets at the Seelie Court help humans take care of the earth?

Did Quince know about this? I can't think he did, not based on how he acted when we saw the human woman in the gardens.

Is that why he suddenly disappeared on me? Did he notice something I didn't and go off to investigate?

I take an offered strawberry tart and eat it without tasting it. If he did see something, I bet he was even more horrified than I am. Maybe, seeing the way humans are paraded around the courtyard like prize-winning hogs at a county fair, he couldn't stomach it. I can barely stomach it, and my mother didn't live at the Seelie Court like his used to.

Of course, I know how it feels to learn something about your parents you hadn't expected.

That's right, a voice whispers in my head. *Your birth mother was the Queen of the Unseelie Court, and they're not exactly known for their kindness to humans, are they? Seelie, Unseelie, neither seems to be winning awards for great treatment of humankind.*

But the humans around me aren't being treated un*kindly,* I argue with that nagging voice. *And from what Quince has said, the Unseelie Court doesn't do much at all with humans.*

At court, maybe, the voice answers. *You've heard the stories about what happens outside of court, what Nightglade turns a blind eye to. What Maeve probably turned a blind eye to.*

Fine. Like I said, none of it's great. You happy?

The voice doesn't answer.

There's a hush, and the music grinds to a halt.

"I hope you are all enjoying yourselves," announces a voice I recognize.

I sit in surprise for a moment as if I really have been glued to the bench. Shock quickly gives way to confusion, and, now curious, I fly up to get a better look.

There, on a raised platform, are two regal fae clad in emerald green trimmed with gold. Crowns of golden twigs with leaves of emeralds adorn their heads.

My vision swims and I drop to the ground. Dáire…is King Oakspirit?

26

'Cause a Seelie Party Don't Stop

How can Dáire be King Oakspirit?

The Queen's voice floats out over the crowd. "It is our dearest wish for you all to be merry tonight, like all nights we've gathered in the past and all nights we will gather in the future. However, if any have pressing concerns and wish to seek an audience with us, keep in mind our window is short." She smiles, her face transforming into a mask of gaiety, and the crowd laughs. "You have until midnight. For the rest of you, who are simply here to enjoy yourselves…" She claps her hands and the music resumes.

"We will laugh and be merry 'til the light sends us to our beds!" the whole assembly roars as one.

As if there had been no interruption to the festivities, the crowd returns to talking and dancing and, like they so proclaimed, laughing.

My head spins, trying to make sense of humans at the party and Dáire actually being King Oakspirit. I maneuver away from the bench, my whole body rigid with tension as I walk toward the King and Queen. Where is Quince? He should be doing this with me. And then, as if the thought of him has brought him to me, I see him.

Tumbling out of a hedge with…

Ilinor? My pace, which had initially quickened at the sight of him, slows, and all I hear is my heart drumming a frantic beat in my ears.

He pins her down, and I see him bend close to her face. Not even my fae hearing can pick up what he says to her over the din of music and voices.

Then again, I'm not sure I want to know.

Looking away is impossible. It's like one of those programs on TV where they show all the gory details of a medical procedure. Whenever I flip to a channel with one of those shows, I end up watching the whole thing, like I'm frozen to the couch with a combination of disgust, horror, and fascination.

That's how I feel now, but with distinctly less fascination.

All I can think is that I want to leave, to get away from this party and pretend I never saw Quince and Ilinor with their limbs locked together and his face so intimately close to hers.

Maybe she attacked him, I try to reason with myself.

But then Quince spots me. He doesn't call for help or look like he's in trouble.

He looks horrified to see me.

Like that, my legs unfreeze and I turn, tripping over my own feet. With a snarl of rage and, okay, a fair bit of anguish, I take to the skies instead, flying higher and higher until the air turns frigid around me and the party in the courtyard is the size of a cookie cutter.

Up here, the wind bites my skin and the clouds, which look so fluffy from a distance, float over me and dampen my dress. Up here, I'm far away from Quince and Ilinor, the party, King Oakspirit who's actually Dáire, and the humans dressed up to look like fae. With distance, my mind clears.

It doesn't matter if Dáire is King Oakspirit. It doesn't matter, right now, if there are a bunch of humans being treated like pets by the Seelie fae (but it still gives me a nasty feeling when I think about it). And, though my heart feels like it's been stomped on by that enormous ice troll Quince and I met outside Sean and Shannon's, it doesn't matter that something is going on with Quince and Ilinor that I can't understand and don't want to.

What matters is meeting with the King and Queen and asking them to help, somehow, with our rescue mission planned for the rapidly approaching Winter Solstice Festival. Olearia seemed convinced the Seelie King and Queen were the answer to saving

Aspen, even if it meant helping Maeve, too. And while I don't know enough about Olearia to trust her personally, I trust her feelings for Aspen.

With fresh determination, I hurtle to the ground, my eyes on the raised platform where the King and Queen stand, gesturing a fae toward them.

I increase my speed, like a bird dive-bombing its prey, and pull up out of my dive right before I hit the ground.

The fae who had been walking forward, his back hunched in a semi-bow, gives a shout of surprise and topples backward, falling off the platform into the unsuspecting crowd, who take his fall in stride, lifting him up and parading him around. He sits on their shoulders, looking dazed and disoriented. I land, turning to King Oakspirit and Queen Hibiscus, who are, maddeningly, watching me with identical smiles of amusement on their faces. They look more like brother and sister than husband and wife, with the same golden yellow eyes, and freckles dotting their faces. The Queen's hair is darker than the King's, more auburn than red, but it is a minor difference.

"Right," I say, breathing hard. "You can call me Eevee." I curtsy, thinking it is something Quince would suggest I do. "I'm the daughter of Maeve. And on behalf of myself and all the others who have requested help before me, I ask for your aid in saving Maeve and Aspen from King Nightglade, who has imprisoned them."

"I told you she was quite single-minded, didn't

I?" King Oakspirit says to Queen Hibiscus with a chuckle.

She regards me with the same smile of amusement on her face. "You did indeed, my dear," she replies, eyes still on me as she speaks. "How fascinating. And, correct me if I'm wrong, but I heard Maeve and Aspen chose to have you adopted by humans?"

I nod mutely, unsure what my adoptive parents have to do with anything.

King Oakspirit leans over and whispers something inaudible in Queen Hisbiscus's ear. She murmurs something back, then turns her piercing gaze on me again.

"So you chose to accept your heritage as fae, despite being raised by humans? You saw life in Elfaeme as better suited to you?"

My eyebrows come together. "I don't think I've chosen one over the other."

"You chose to find Maeve, when you discovered her note. When you were too late, you could have turned aside, gone back to your life on Earth and lived among humans. But you chose to come to Elfaeme regularly, planning to save Maeve and Aspen."

"Well, they're my birth parents," I explain defensively. "Yeah, I want them alive so I can get to know them someday." How does she know so much about my life?

Then I see, standing in the shadow of the King and Queen, Quince. If I could shoot daggers with my eyes, I would. He must be able to pick up on some of the venom in my gaze, because he looks down at his feet.

"Every choice you make comes with a price, Eevee," King Oakspirit says solemnly. "Your mother knew this."

"My birth mother," I correct him automatically.

At his side, Queen Hibiscus tilts her head, considering me. Her chin is chisel-sharp, I notice, with a small dimple in it which deepens when she purses her rosebud lips at my pertinence for correcting the Seelie King.

"I wasn't referring to Maeve," King Oakspirit says, a sly gleam in his eyes. "Though, of course, Maeve knew the price she'd pay for her choices, too."

I wasn't referring to Maeve. I stare at them both, my mouth dry. "What–" My voice is raspy. I try clearing my throat. "What do you know about my mom? What do you mean, she knew her choice came with a price? What price?"

"I think you know the answer to that, Eevee. Hearing it from me doesn't change anything."

My mind whirls. I think about the memory issues my parents have been experiencing ever since I started telling them about being fae. How they accepted this new truth about me, at first, and then their brains would empty of all knowledge of Elfaeme like sand from an hourglass. Is this the price they had to pay? Did mom know, when she adopted me, that I wasn't human? I shake my head, trying to clear it. Ever since coming to the Seelie Court, it's been difficult to keep my thoughts from muddling together.

"So…" I say, scrabbling to regain my focus. "Will you consider helping us?"

King Oakspirit is examining a gold pocket watch he's pulled out of his waistcoat. "We will…" My heart leaps. "…think on it and give you our response tomorrow."

"What? But the Winter Solstice Festival is on Friday! It's almost Thursday at this point. Maeve's power is waning," I explain desperately. "Nightglade is doing something to her and Aspen. Tomorrow may be too late if we don't–"

"They will survive until the celebration," Queen Hibiscus cuts in, her tone final.

"How do you know for sure?" I demand, but neither of them answer. King Oakspirit has an expression of polite boredom on his face.

"Her persistence, while amusing to me at first, is starting to wear on me now," I hear him say to Queen Hibiscus. I fume. If I can hear it, it means he doesn't care about me overhearing.

"My sister was taken by *his* fiancée," I push on doggedly, pointing at Quince, who's shaking his head, his face white. "She's here tonight. You could arrest her. Surely kidnapping is a crime in Elfaeme?"

Queen Hibiscus turns to Quince. "You're engaged to both sisters?" she inquires curiously.

"Both…what?"

Quince looks miserable, but says quietly, "No, Your Grace. It is a misunderstanding between me and

Eevee."

"I see." She turns back to face me. "No arrests will happen tonight." King Oakspirit shows his watch to her. "Our time to take audience has concluded for the evening," she announces, her voice carrying above the crowd. No one is listening anyway, everyone outside of this platform is in a state of frenetic enjoyment. Queen Hibiscus steps forward until we are mere feet from each other. "We will give you our answer tomorrow at the soirée."

I laugh maniacally. "Another soirée? Do you do nothing but party here with your pet humans?"

"You are a guest in the Seelie Court, Evelyn, daughter of Maeve," Queen Hibiscus finally says, her voice light and airy, but her expression hardening with each word. "Be sure you do not overstay your welcome."

"It is bold of you, to insult your hosts," King Oakspirit adds. "Stupid, of course. But boldness often is."

Quince steps out from behind the King and Queen, bending in a formal bow.

"I don't need you to help me!" I hiss to him.

Disregarding me, he says, "We look forward to hearing your decision on the matter, Your Majesties."

I bore a hole through his back mentally as he straightens.

At his polite words, the Queen's face returns to an expression of frivolous gaiety. She and the King step off the platform and are immediately surrounded by adoring fae and, I'm sure if I looked closer, some humans, too.

Beneath my feet the platform pops out of existence as if it had never been there, and Quince and I both crash to the ground. He reaches a hand out to help me up but I shove it away and stand, refusing to meet his eyes.

"Eevee, let me explain–"

"Not now," I tell him sharply, even though my heart wants him to take me in a hug and tell me about how it was all, according to his words, a "misunderstanding."

I swivel on my heels and head to the edge of the courtyard. Along the way, I ignore all offers of food and drink and dancing partners. All I want is to get back to my room and stay there until the King and Queen decide to tell us if they'll help or not.

So I've never been great at mazes, even the ones on paper. One time mom and dad took us all, the whole Acker clan, to a corn maze, and thought since I was the oldest kid, they'd put me in charge of directions as a way to "practice my leadership skills." We were there until nightfall and had to have one of the corn maze employees come find us with a flashlight.

The castle hallways look a lot alike in the middle

of the night, which doesn't help. They all bear the same stone walls and softly flickering torches aglow with some kind of magical flame. Eventually, not sure why I didn't think of it sooner, I remove one of the torches from the wall, its flame a pale lavender with streaks of white and blue in it, and continue striding through the castle.

It's eerie in here at night. Everyone is at the soirée, apparently. The soirée which happens every single damn night. Who has the kind of energy for that? I suppose that's why the fae were only waking up when Quince and I made it out of the gardens, yesterday near midday. If you party every night until dawn, you need some time to recharge before the next party.

I can't picture Myska, Quince's mother, in this court at all. She doesn't seem obsessed with being "merry 'til the light sends her to her bed," but I suppose she could have a secret, party-loving side I don't know about.

Not me, though. I'm exhausted. When I finally do find my room, I collapse on my bed, which snarls and meows beneath me.

"Aahh!" Instinctively, my wings act while my brain is sorting out why my bed is meowing at me, and I shoot upward, smashing into the ceiling.

Groaning, I float down to the floor, eyeing the bed. My wings feel bruised, and the back of my head throbs, but in front of me, sitting on the bed looking distinctly rumpled and grumpy, is Scamp.

"You found your way here!" I squeal, my pain

forgotten in my excitement. I move forward to pick him up, but Scamp growls, his whole body quaking. Pausing, I feel for his emotions and–there. Fear pulses from him in waves. "What happened to you?" I whisper.

He can't answer, of course, and my power is limited to feelings, not coherent thoughts. Gingerly, I sit next to him on the bed. When he stops shaking, I reach out a hand and pet his head and back as reassuringly as I can. "It's okay," I say, laying down next to him and wishing he were more cuddly like my cat, Slinky. My eyes are heavy. "We're back together now. I asked…" I yawn. "I asked the King and Queen about helping us with Maeve and Aspen, like Olearia wanted me to do, so…we'll see…"

I fall asleep to the sound of him purring, his warm body beneath my hand.

Help Comes at a Cost

1 Day Until the Winter Solstice

"What is Sir Cornelius doing in your chamber?" asks a highly confused Kieran.

I'm not normally a jump-out-of-bed kind of person, but it's amazing how motivating it can be to hear that an uninvited guest is inside my room.

Kieran watches me jump and flail with dry humor etched across their face.

"Who is he? Where is he? How'd he get in here? I thought I locked the door behind me and—wait. How'd you—?"

Kieran holds up a key. Sidestepping me, they walk crisply to the edge of the bed. "King Oakspirit and

Queen Hibiscus have been concerned about your safety, Sir Cornelius. It has been months since your last visit. They require…updates." They glance suspiciously at me, as if I were not worthy of hearing any updates Sir Cornelius might have.

"Who are you talking to?" I ask exasperatedly. "There's no Sir Cornelius in my bed." I narrow my eyes at Kieran. "Is this your idea of a joke?"

Kieran's whole body exudes long-suffering. "I don't joke, but if I did, I would not joke about Sir Cornelius."

"You're the least fun Seelie fae I've met, you know that?" Oddly, Kieran seems pleased by this statement. I stare at the bed now, where Scamp is stretching, his mouth wide open to reveal his sharp teeth and rough, pink tongue. "Is Sir Cornelius invisible?" I ask Kieran, suddenly nauseated to think I'd been sleeping next to an invisible Sir Cornelius this whole time.

Kieran rolls their eyes. "No." They gesture to Scamp. "*That* is Sir Cornelius."

I look from them to the cat on the bed and burst out laughing. "Oh wow. You do slow-burn jokes, Kieran. You really had me thinking for a moment that Scamp was somehow like a spy for the Seelie King and Queen." I wipe tears of laughter from the corners of my eyes with the back of my hand. "Whew. You got me."

Instead of answering me, Kieran addresses Scamp. "You're letting her call you *Scamp*?" They sound scandalized.

Scamp meows and I can feel his defiance and embarrassment.

Kind of like how he acted when Olearia brought up the name. "Scamp, is it?" she'd said. And when he meowed up at her, she'd added, "Oh, no, we're not going to forget that anytime soon, *Scamp*."

"He really *is* called Sir Cornelius?" I ask, dumbfounded.

Scamp's gaze when he looks at me is haughty and dignified, his emotions clearly indicating he's of course worthy of the knightly title.

I wonder briefly if the Seelie King and Queen know Sir Cornelius is also quite friendly with the matriarch of the wild fae of the Sweetbriar Wood, but then decide I'll let them figure that out on their own.

"Can I come in?"

Quince stands in the doorway looking like he hasn't slept at all. His hair sticks up so wildly in all directions it almost covers the small, black horns on his head, and his clothes are wrinkled.

"Scamp's real name is Sir Cornelius, can you believe that?" I blurt out before I remember I'm mad at him.

His brow furrows. This is clearly not what he'd expected me to say. "Um…really?"

Scamp (I can't bring myself to call him Sir Cornelius yet), leaps lightly to the floor, his tail twitching. Then, to my amazement, he opens his mouth and says in a deep baritone voice, "I appreciate your concern for my safety, Kieran. I'll be off to give my report to the King and Queen, then."

Quince and I both look at each other, our faces resembling stupefied fish.

"You…can talk!" I exclaim. Then, my brow furrowing, "You can talk?!"

Scamp pads toward the door, but turns his head. "Yes. Here in the Seelie Court I can talk."

As he exits the room, I grab at Quince's arm and drag him along with me after Scamp. "We're coming with you. We need to see the King and Queen, too."

Kieran huffs behind us. "The King and Queen said they would let you know when they've reached their decision. Nothing will be gained by–"

Seeing the look on my face, Quince says over his shoulder, "Shut it, Kieran. No one can change Eevee's mind when she's in this mood."

Kieran tuts but stops protesting, instead choosing to follow us as we make our way to the King and Queen. Every now and then they allow themselves to let out a disapproving "Hmm." They probably think they'll have to do damage control.

"If you think getting Kieran to stop talking makes up for whatever I saw last night…" I mutter to Quince.

"I don't. You won't be angry once we have a chance to talk about it."

I snort. "And now you're telling me how I'll feel?" The way his shoulders slump and his face gets a squashed look to it brings out my better nature. "Fine. After we talk to the King and Queen, you and I can have a chat."

Scamp has been to the Seelie castle many times, based on how fluidly he moves through the halls without the slightest hesitation at the many intersections we come across.

Soon he trots through a doorway and we join him in a small room bathed in a greenish light from the sun streaming through the ivy curtains on the windows.

King Oakspirit is intent on the board game in front of him. It looks somewhat similar to chess, with pieces of the deepest purple and a muted sage green lined up across from each other. He moves a piece, then looks up with a smile. "Sir Cornelius! But–" His eyes come to rest on me and Quince, then flick to Kieran, who stands next to me both bowing and shrugging their shoulders apologetically.

At first, anger flashes in his eyes, giving them an uncanny resemblance to gold coins, then the expression fades from his face, leaving it blank for a brief moment. The smile which appears immediately after is dazzlingly charming. "You brought company, I see. The party isn't for another couple hours, you know," he says in a joking, genial tone.

His struggle to remain pleasant is one I can identify with. But why does he bother? Isn't he the king? Shouldn't he be able to express his anger? I watch him as he stands and magnanimously greets Quince, and it dawns on me. He and Queen Hibiscus both play the part of benevolent monarchs, and they take that role to heart. For what purpose, though? I think of the words they've used since I've met them: enjoy, fun, merry. The King and Queen "like the heady high of fae drunk on fun," Dáire had told me, right before I found out he *was* King Oakspirit. "I hope you are all enjoying yourselves," he'd said from the platform. "It is our dearest wish for you all to be merry tonight," the Queen had added right after. So nothing is more important to them than keeping up the façade of being in charge of a jovial court. My mind races. Can I use that somehow to convince them…?

"I require privacy to hear Sir Cornelius's report," King Oakspirit says, bending down to pick up Scamp.

A force like an invisible, magical wall pushes us from the room. The door slams shut and I throw myself at it, jiggling the handle fruitlessly.

"Locked." I swear, then a thought occurs to me. "Hang on. That room had tons of windows. We could fly to one of them! Then we'd be able to hear what Scamp—er, Sir Cornelius," I amend, seeing the affronted look on Kieran's face, "has to say to the King and…what?" I bark at Kieran, who is now shaking their head.

"You don't think the King has thought of that? He has spells surrounding that room. No one can overhear what goes on within, and no one is getting through the ivy curtains on the windows, either."

Quince tries the door, slamming his shoulder

into it. The "I-knew-this-would-happen" look on Kieran's face is enough to make my blood steam.

"Eevee, come on," Quince says, rubbing his shoulder. "We need to talk, anyway."

He pulls me away from the door. I maintain eye contact with Kieran the entire length of the hall, mentally shouting super mature insults at them like "scaly turd" and "insufferable busybody," until we round the bend.

We walk for a few minutes in silence. Next to me, Quince takes steadying breaths, glancing at me out of the corner of his eyes every so often, like I'm a bomb about to go off.

"I'm pretty sure most folks are still asleep," I point out to him after we enter, then leave, three separate rooms. "If you're worried about privacy, that is."

"No." He stops next to a window, pulling the ivy curtains back to peer at the setting sun. How is it that time races ahead so fast during the day here? This whole place is disorienting. Mazes. People and fae not what they seem. I'm not sure how much I like the Seelie Court.

Quince turns back to me, exhaling. "I'm stalling. It's complicated, what I found out last night."

"Which was…?" I prompt him when he falls silent.

"Oh. Well." He rubs the back of his head and scratches at one of his horns. "That wasn't Ilinor you saw me with."

"I gathered as much," I say drily.

"I thought it was Ilinor at first, too," he admits. "After those fae bumped into us midair, I spotted her on the ground, and didn't even stop to think. I just flew down and hid in the bushes nearby. I wanted to spy on her. I thought she'd somehow followed us and was up to something. I tailed her until right before you spotted us. I was getting tired of waiting, so I jumped at her to take her by surprise. But then I saw her up close, and I immediately realized it wasn't Ilinor."

"How'd you know? Did she not have the look of an evil kidnapper?" I ask sarcastically.

"No, she didn't," Quince says, choosing to ignore my sarcasm. "She—they've got a lot of similar features, of course. But her name is Jaila. She's Ilinor's younger sister. Actually, she's about Amelia's age."

A pang of longing to see my cheese-loving, smiley, loyal little sister knocks me sideways. I lean against the wall.

Quince immediately steps closer, his face pinched with worry. "Oh, Eevee. I shouldn't have mentioned Amelia. I know you're worried, and—"

"It's fine," I say, looking away. "We'll hear from the King and Queen soon, right?"

He hesitates. "Right."

"Then there's nothing else we can do for her right now." Quince picks at his waistcoat absentmindedly. "So...Ilinor has a little sister? Is that all?"

"Partly." He leans closer, his expression

unreadable. "They have the same parents, Eevee. The same mother and father."

"Okay?" I say, not sure I'm picking up what he's hinting at. "They're full-blooded siblings. Good for them."

"Nightglade is their father, and their mother was a fae named Viivi."

"Was? Did she die?" I don't want to feel bad for Ilinor, but I feel bad for Ilinor's sister Jaila, anyway.

"No, she…she turned into a gwyllyon."

My eyes widen. "That can happen? You don't think she was the one…?"

"I have no idea," he says. "She could've been the gwyllyon we ran into. Stranger things have happened."

"They have indeed," I say, thinking of the moment I realized my life wasn't what it seemed. I hadn't been willing to believe in fairies or magic, until I took a picture of my birth mother's note, only to realize not even cameras can pick up the blood ink she used. Something bothers me. If Nightglade is her father… "So, why is she *here* if both of her parents are Unseelie?"

"I wish I knew. I asked, but I didn't get a chance to find out. She slunk off during your audience with the King and Queen."

"Shoot." Curiosity burns in me now. What is Jaila's part in this whole thing, and why isn't she with her sister? "If we see her tonight, we should ask."

Quince agrees. "But I don't know if she'll tell

us," he warns.

We meander through the castle, resigning ourselves to the reality that the King and Queen aren't going to share their decision with us before the soirée. Eventually the sun dips its edges into the horizon and I heave a sigh. "We should get ready for tonight, I suppose."

We hug, and, knowing now there was nothing to forgive, I plant a quick kiss on his lips. "I'm sorry for assuming the worst last night," I whisper, avoiding his intense eyes which darken with hunger when I pull away.

"I don't blame you. It's this place, it's so…"

What the place is so like for Quince, I may never know. He draws me in for another kiss, which I think is a better answer than none at all. His lips are hungry for mine, and I feel heat rush through me as he wraps his arms around my waist.

"See you soon," he says in a husky voice when we finally break apart.

Same party, different night. Oh, and different dress. I had returned to my room (after getting lost on a detour which led me to the kitchens—a detour I'm not complaining about, by the way, as I was able to sample some of the desserts ahead of time) to find a silvery satin dress waiting for me on the bed.

Tonight, though, Quince and I stick together and stay on the ground, keeping an eye out for the King and Queen, or Jaila. Under the cover of music and chatter, I point out the humans in the crowd to Quince.

"I didn't notice that yesterday," he whispers, thunderstruck and disgusted. "I was too focused on Jaila. This place, these fae, I…" He balls his fists and jams them into his pants pockets. "I never want to be so removed from the human realm that I think I'm better than humans just because I'm different." He watches the fae and humans around us with acute interest now, a greenish-tinged, nauseated expression on his face. "How did I miss that yesterday?"

"Quince!" I hiss, shaking him and jerking my head to the right, where I see King Oakspirit and Queen Hibiscus mingling with their courtiers.

They turn toward us and I wave emphatically. Next to me, Quince throws both his arms in the air. The fae near us take this as an inspired dance move and we're suddenly surrounded by fae raucously waving their arms in the air.

"It's like sea grass in the ocean," a fae next to me says dreamily, her arms flowing back and forth above her head.

By the time we duck and dodge around the arm-waving throng, the King and Queen have disappeared from view.

"Damn." I flop down on a bench and grab grumpily at a carrot stick on a tray, munching it with vigor.

"They'll let us know eventually," Quince says, sitting next to me and popping a couple grapes in his mouth.

"I suppose." I gnaw on another carrot, then nearly drop it when I feel something bump up against my leg. "What the…?"

Quince raises an eyebrow. "Bad carrot?" he asks through a mouthful of grapes.

Amusement ripples through my mind.

"I believe I startled her," Scamp says, hopping up on the bench and squishing his skinny body between me and Quince. "What?" he asks, blinking up at me, streaks of suspicion shooting through his amusement.

"You talked with King Oakspirit," I begin to say, but he shakes his head.

"I do not betray my confidences, including yours," he says solemnly.

I stare down into his green eyes. "No offense, but how do I know I can trust you?"

His face bears an expression of pity, something I'm not used to seeing on a cat.

"How lonely life must be if you have no one you feel you can fully trust."

For some reason, tears spring to my eyes, and I look down at my hands. "That's not true. I do trust people. But…" I bite my lip.

Out of the corner of my eye, I see him tilt his head. "You lost trust at an early age when Maeve and Aspen chose to have you adopted. The life you had known, the people who you trusted, left you." He pauses, licking at the fur on his chest, then continues. "I was adopted at a young age, like many kittens. I remember feeling like I'd never trust anyone again. Until…" He paws at where his left ear used to be. "Until someone proved to me it was okay to put my trust in others. It was difficult to learn to trust. Cats are solitary creatures by nature. But, Eevee, if you don't make an effort to come to peace with that betrayal of trust so early in your life, you will only become lonelier. You have to trust harder. Not everyone is out to get you, despite what Nightglade may lead you to think."

It's the most I've ever heard Scamp talk since he arrived at the Seelie Court. "Why are you telling me this?" I whisper, my hands clenched so tight in my lap I can feel my nails cutting into my palms.

"I've been telling you this the whole time I've known you, but here at the Seelie Court is the only time I can say it with words."

He bumps his head under my chin and a sob escapes my chest. I wrap him in my arms, my tears dampening his fur. Quince circles his arms around me, enclosing us both in his embrace.

As usual, the passage of time here is like a dream. It goes in fits and bursts, sometimes slowing down, other times racing ahead like a cheetah after its prey.

My tears have all dried, leaving my face feeling stiff. I lean on Quince's shoulder after Scamp leaves.

"I trust you, you know," I say to him. He

doesn't respond, but he rests his head on mine and I know he's listening. "But Scamp's right. I trust to a certain point. I'm going to try and trust you harder from now on, like I should've last night."

"You were acting from a place of insecurity, with a good amount of confusion mixed in," he says into my hair.

"Which doesn't excuse my behavior," I say, pulling away and looking up at him.

"It doesn't excuse mine either," he says. "I should've told you."

"I'll accept that we both messed up," I announce.

He smiles, his sharp features softening in a way that makes me warm all over.

"You're not perfect. But I don't like you because I think you're perfect, Eevee," he says, his voice low. "I love your passion and your loyalty, and your determination to reach your goals. Your obsession with Shakespeare borders on a little weird, but–"

"To thine own self be true?" I interrupt, unable to help myself. It was a perfect opportunity for a *Hamlet* quote.

He laughs, then bends down to kiss me, which I'm okay with because all of the compliments were embarrassing me and kissing is so much better than talking.

"We shouldn't interrupt such a sweet moment," I hear Queen Hibiscus say in a stage whisper. "Look at the dears. Finally enjoying themselves."

Quince and I pull apart. I'm fairly certain if I were to look in a mirror my face would be flaming red. King Oakspirit watches us with a strange intensity. When I meet his eyes, I'm struck by the sadness in them. He blinks and grins, all sadness erased. Did I imagine it?

"Your Majesties," Quince says, recovering much quicker than I, standing and bowing. "We are indeed enjoying ourselves. We hope you are as well."

The Queen nods, her features shimmering. Tonight she's painted her rosebud-shaped lips a shade of lilac to match her dress, which floats around her as if it were made of air. King Oakspirit wears a matching lilac suit. They both have flowers woven into their hair in place of crowns.

"We have reached a decision regarding your request," the Queen says.

I look around us. Surely some of the fae may want to pause their debauchery to hear if the King and Queen plan to help rescue the former Unseelie Queen and others from under the nose of King Nightglade? But none of them seem to be listening. In fact, they all are acting like we don't exist, dancing and moving around our bench and the King and Queen as if there's an invisible bubble around us.

Queen Hibiscus catches the look of bewilderment on my face. "With such an important political decision, the King and I decided we should meet with you before we take audience with our subjects. He's using simple deflection magic to give us some extra privacy. He's quite adept at it."

Quince straightens from his bow and I stand next to him. My hand finds his and he entwines his fingers with mine.

The Queen nods up to King Oakspirit.

"We will help you on one condition," he declares. He's looking at me as if Quince doesn't exist.

I open my mouth to say, "Yes, of course, anything!" but Quince squeezes my hand and, when I turn to look at him, shakes his head imperceptibly.

"What is the condition?" he asks coolly, his calculating expression making him look much older than his seventeen years.

"It is no secret that the Unseelie Court is run…differently than our own," Queen Hibiscus says delicately.

Again, King Oakspirit looks at me, ignoring Quince. "So in exchange for our help to attempt breaking the curse of the revoked crown, not to mention trying to aid you in saving your loved ones from Nightglade's clutches, all we ask in return is to let us advise you when you ascend to the Unseelie throne."

A second passes, and then another. All I can think is that someone from the Unseelie Court has been talking, and I marvel for a moment at how fast rumors spread in Elfaeme as well as on Earth. Thank goodness technology goes wonky in the fae realm. All the fae on social media, causing mischief virtually? The thought is chilling.

I study the fae around us, unsure how to

answer. Outside King Oakspirit's deflection bubble, the woman Quince and I had met in the gardens yesterday keeps walking toward us and getting pushed back. She's giggling, a vapid, vacant expression in her eyes, and I can feel anger burning inside me.

"Ouch!" Quince pulls his hand away from mine, which is crackling with flames. Quince and I both know I'm not actually going to challenge Nightglade for the throne—we just needed the Unseelie Court to think I was—but the thought that King Oakspirit and Queen Hibiscus hoped to make me their puppet on the Unseelie Throne, so they effectively ruled most of Elfaeme, enrages me.

"Eevee…" Quince whispers at my side as the King and Queen watch us patiently, waiting for a reply. "Cool the fire. Like Shannon taught you."

Trust harder, Eevee. I really want to let loose on the King and Queen, informing them with a few choice words—maybe some of Shakespeare's—how I feel about their "condition" for helping us. But it wouldn't help the situation. And Quince actually has experience at court. I take a breath, imagining what it would feel like to douse my hands in a snowbank. *Cool the fire.* The flames flicker, then extinguish. A corner of Quince's mouth turns up in a smile. "I trust you," I mouth to him.

He turns his attention to the King and Queen. "What a generous offer," he begins. My heart thump-clunks. He doesn't mean to accept their proposal? "However, I think I speak for both Eevee and myself when I say that, whoever rules the Unseelie Court after Nightglade, I hope they do so in a way that is both true to the way of the Unseelie fae while being respectful to other fae in Elfaeme as well as humanity."

A single line forms between the Queen's brows. "I do not understand. Yes, the fae have their differences and we have agreed to live separately because of it. But the humans at our court have been rescued from lives of drudgery and pain." She stands defensively, her eyes flashing. "We treat humans *kindly*, we help them. They like their lives here."

"Do they?" I ask. "Or are they enchanted to like it? What about when the enchantment wears off? By that time they've eaten your fairy food and they're either stuck here forever or, if they somehow get back to Earth, they starve. Do you think they like knowing their fate? You imprison them in this charade of kindness!"

King Oakspirit is quiet, but Queen Hibiscus is now so angry she's practically spitting when she says, "So. I take it you do not accept our offer of help?"

"We respectfully decline," Quince answers. The Queen raises her arms, her eyes glowing, and opens her mouth, a strange sound like a foghorn bellowing forth. King Oakspirit touches her shoulder and whispers to her while Quince and I both clap our hands over our ears, doubling over with the pain of the sound.

Whatever he says to her works and the sound stops. Snarling, she rushes away, for once ignoring the adoring courtiers who flock to her as soon as she exits the deflection bubble.

King Oakspirit watches us, a look like he wants to say something on his face. He steps toward us, then his jaw tightens and he hurries away, taking with him any hope we had for the Seelie Court to help us.

Sticking to the Plan

The Day of the Winter Solstice

Going from the nightly partying and the disorienting, dreamlike summertime of the Seelie Court to the frigid temperatures and drudgery of a Duluth winter is jarring.

To add to the disappointment, no one was at my house by the time Quince and I appeared in the morning.

"Lucky your mom sometimes carpools to work," Quince had said from his spot in the passenger seat of my mom's car, where he sat shivering despite the heat pumping from the vents.

I feel trembly myself right now, and not because

of the below-freezing weather outside. Today's the day: the Winter Solstice Festival is this evening. And, despite a great amount of effort on my part *not* to follow Sean and Shannon's advice, I'm now sticking to the plan and not doing anything stupid.

I just wish I knew where Cam and Maggie were.

From our spot in the parking lot, I watch as Quince exits the car and walks in the front doors of Duluth High for the second time. I'd tried going in with him the first time, but whatever Cam and Maggie had said about my absence was effective. As soon as Mr. Jives saw me entering the office with Quince, his eyes bugged out in alarm. "Out!" he barked, in a very non-Mr. Jives fashion. Just as alarmed, I backed out the door while Mr. Jives scurried out from behind the desk, his face buried in the crook of his arm, brandishing a can of disinfectant spray.

Quince leaves the school after a few minutes, shaking his head when I catch his eyes.

I start sweating. Cam and Maggie should be in school. Neither of them have texted me. So where are they?

When I ask Quince this, he lifts his shoulders. "Jeeves said they were gone today, wouldn't give any reason. He also says he hopes you feel better soon."

I rest my head on the steering wheel. "It's not a good sign, is it? That they're gone and they didn't even text me or anything?"

"Well, no," he admits. "It's not a great sign, that's for sure."

"I wish we could go to Sean and Shannon's," I say into the steering wheel. "How are we going to prep for tonight?"

Okay, it may be the least important thing on my list right now, but being able to blend in at the Winter Solstice Festival until we're ready to make our move is a crucial part of ensuring our plan succeeds tonight. We'd been banking on taking advantage of Sean and Shannon's diverse collection of clothes to outfit ourselves.

"Where do you think Sean and Shannon get half their clothes?" Quince asks.

"Probably not from a strip mall in northern Minnesota," I reply pessimistically.

He laughs. "Okay, probably not from here exactly. But a lot of their clothes come from the human realm."

I lift my head from the steering wheel at his comment and stare at him. "Are you suggesting we go shopping together?" I ask, dumbfounded.

"We can't go to Sean and Shannon's anyway, it'll help kill time until tonight, and I don't know if we've gone on a normal date…ever?" He ticks off on his fingers as he speaks. "Lately we've spent all our time together in Elfaeme."

"You know what? Fudge it. Let's go shopping." I shift the car into reverse and back out of the parking space.

It's the Friday before Christmas, so even though school's in session, the mall is bustling, all the shops bedecked in garlands of red, green, and silver. Twinkling lights sparkle from the ceiling and trees, and every store we enter has holiday-themed music blaring from the speakers.

The normalcy of it all–shopping, eating at the food court–is simultaneously nice and strange.

Quince scoops a final spoonful of mac and cheese from the bowl in front of him and leans back in his chair contentedly. "I haven't had mac and cheese in forever."

My lunch, a pesto pasta dish dotted with bright red cherry tomatoes, is delicious, but there's a lot left and I'm more interested in checking my messages and emails in case anything comes in from Cam or Maggie. "Want mine?"

I don't need to ask twice. Quince reaches across the sticky table (the food court is as packed as the rest of the mall and the table we grabbed looks like it hasn't been wiped down all day) and pulls my bowl toward him, wasting no time digging in.

"I should've gotten this!" he exclaims after his first bite.

"Well, the rest of it's yours," I say absently, scrolling through social media. It's been weeks since Cam posted anything–they're more of a lurker online– but Maggie's last post was Wednesday, and she usually posts something daily. My foot taps incessantly on one of the table legs.

"Whassup?" Quince asks, his cheeks stuffed to bursting like a chipmunk's. He chews and swallows.

"You're making the table rattle."

I force my foot to be still. "He's taken them, too," I say, my chest constricting painfully. Tears sting my eyes. "I just know it."

"Did you find something else?" Quince shoves the pasta bowl aside and stands, striding over to my side of the table and sitting in the chair next to me.

"Not exactly." I sniffle and blow my nose on my napkin. "But Maggie always says how important it is for her to post daily to build her future audience as a journalist, and…" I hand him my phone.

He takes it with his right hand and places his left arm across my shoulders. The weight of it is comforting, but not comforting enough to stop the tears falling on my face and into my lap. His expression tightens as he looks at the day and time of Maggie's last post.

"Here." He hands the phone back to me. People walking by our table shoot accusatory looks at Quince, assuming he's the reason I'm crying. But none of them would believe me if I said the real reason I'm bawling my eyes out in a food court is because my two best friends are the latest victims of my birth mother's ex-husband, who happens to be the King of the Unseelie Court in the fae realm.

When my eyes have no more tears to shed, I take in a shaky breath. "Is there anything else we need to get?" We're surrounded by shopping bags.

"If there's anything we've missed, I can't think of it," Quince says, closing his eyes as he thinks. "I've been going over our plan in my head on repeat. Aside from making sure we're at our agreed-upon spots at the Unseelie Court tonight at 7:10, there isn't much we can do, which means we still have…" He checks his phone. "Three hours and forty minutes. Three and a half hours to get to the moonstone we're using to take us there."

"We better bring the car back to my house before mom gets home," I say, suddenly panicky. "She should be back by four, she usually tries to finish work early on days she carpools."

Gathering up our plethora of shopping bags, we head to the car. I want to drive straight home, but Quince convinces me it'd be a good idea to refill the gas tank first.

The house is empty, and the only sound that breaks the silence as we enter from the garage is the garage door closing. The emptiness and quiet sets my nerves on edge.

"I can't stay here," I say right after Quince plops down on the couch.

He clambers back up. "Why not?" he asks, flustered at the note of agitation in my voice.

"Because…" I pause. How do I explain this? "Because it'll be easier for me to pretend they all came home after we left, rather than–if they don't–" My voice cracks. "All but Amelia, that is."

"Hey." Quince places his hands on my shoulders, looking into my eyes. "It's okay. We can go."

My laugh is more of a sob. "Where?"

"Gimme a sec." Tapping on his phone, a grin

spreads across his face.

"What?" I ask, suspicious.

"Jim's online." He types something. "And…yes! He can pick us up. He doesn't live far from here, maybe five minutes tops?"

"Jim for the win!"

We stow our fanny packs, which we've carried with us since leaving Cam's (except for when we were at the soirées), in my room, and gather up our shopping bags.

I chew at a spot on my lower lip that's drier than the rest as we wait at the end of the driveway for Jim to show up. "What if he asks about Cam or Maggie?"

"We'll tell him the truth. We don't know where they are."

Jim's beat-up silver car ambles toward us. As soon as he slows to a stop we toss our bags in his trunk and scramble in, Quince taking the front seat while I sit in the back.

"Where to?" Jim asks. He's bundled up in a white, puffy jacket, which makes him look like a big marshmallow with brown, feathery hair.

Quince shows him his phone.

"On it."

The entire drive, he looks at Quince a lot, his head tilting to the right so much it's like he has a twitch. I catch him glancing in the rearview mirror at me a few times as well. But he doesn't ask any questions, thank goodness.

He brings the car to a stop and I look up from my phone to see that we've parked in the movie theater parking lot.

"A movie?" I ask, nonplussed for the second time today. "That's your brilliant idea?"

Quince's grin is impish. "Yes, Evelyn Gray Acker. I'm taking you to a movie. You got a problem with that?"

"No." I unbuckle. Jim is looking between the two of us like he's trying to figure out the answer to a particularly tricky riddle.

"So, do you guys need me to pick you up, too? Because my family's got this thing tonight, but I could leave for a bit."

"Jim, my dude, you're too good a friend," Quince says, clapping him on his poofy, white shoulder. "But, no. It was just getting here we needed help with."

"We wouldn't want to take you away from your family." My voice is higher-pitched than usual, and Jim swivels in his seat to give me a quizzical look.

"You okay?"

"No." I laugh and wipe my eyes. "But that'll change soon, I hope."

We retrieve our bags from the trunks and thank Jim again for all his help.

"He really is too good a friend for you, you know," I comment lightly to Quince.

"I know," he says, his eyes on Jim's car as it drives away.

"Here, let me take some of the bags." I wrestle

a couple from him and we head inside the theater. As the doors open I'm hit with the smell of popcorn.

"I want to do this movie date thing right," Quince says once we've bought our tickets and are in line for snacks. I haven't heard of the movie Quince selects, but it looks like a comedy. We stare at the rows of movie theater candy while the employee behind the counter stares at us with our assortment of shopping bags in our arms. "What do you want?"

"None of it," I tell him. My stomach is churning and high quantities of sugar won't help the situation. I check my phone for the time. "How long is the movie again?"

Quince finishes paying for his popcorn and drink, then checks our tickets. "About an hour and forty-five minutes."

"How long *exactly*?" I ask, tugging one of the tickets out of his fingers and scanning it. "One hour and forty-eight minutes," I comment. "With previews, that'll bring us to about 6:45."

He nods, slurping his drink. "Plenty of time to get ready before we leave."

I'm not sure about that, but I figure I can always duck out of the movie early if I need to.

As we wait for the movie to begin, chatting and holding hands, I'm reminded of my last movie date. It had been my last date ever with Damian, and we had spent most of the movie making out since we didn't have much to talk about. The vibe between me and Damian that night was so different from the one between me and Quince right now. With Damian, I always felt like I had to work to please him or keep him happy. But here with Quince, hours before our rescue attempt begins, I don't feel like I have to pretend I'm anything other than an exhausted bundle of nerves. It's not like what we have is easy (we still have his fiancée situation to deal with), but with Damian, I often felt uncertain in our relationship. With Quince, I feel safe. And I know we're young and this may not be forever, but for this moment, right now, I can't help but feel stupidly in love with Quince "eats-popcorn-way-too-loudly" Florentz.

"What?" he asks, finally noticing I've been staring at him.

"Nothing." I lean on Quince's shoulder and he kisses the top of my head. Amazingly, I'm more at peace with Quince, a few hours away from possible impending doom, than I ever was with Damian.

As ridiculous as the movie's plot was, it made me laugh, and for a brief period of time I was engrossed with a fictional character's troubles rather than my own. I forgot all about leaving early to get ready, however, so when the credits start rolling, I pop out of my seat like a jack-in-the-box.

"Crud! I'm sorry, Quince."

He picks up the upturned popcorn bucket. "It's okay, I was done with it."

At the end of the aisle, a movie theater employee wearing a black vest adorned with battery-operated Christmas lights glowers at us.

We exit hurriedly and sit on a bench outside the restrooms, sorting through the shopping bags. Once sorted, I grab all of mine and dash to the women's room to change.

Unfortunately, wearing a mask to the Winter Solstice Festival to hide my face, which bears a striking resemblance to Maeve's, would be too conspicuous. I'd already done that once, and tonight I need to blend in, not stand out. I step out of one of the bathroom stalls to see the effect of my outfit in the mirror. Over a velvety gown of forest green, I drape a hooded gray cloak, then pull the hood down over my eyes to cover most of my face. The cloak is lined with soft, faux fur the color of snow. It'll do the trick, I think, tilting my head to see my appearance from different angles. With the hood pulled down low, it's hard to get a good look at my features. I pull concealer out of my purse and slather it on my temples. Right now my face has nothing on it except makeup, but in Elfaeme, the orange flower markings on both of my temples would be a giveaway of my identity. I can't do anything about my wings, but it's my face that's more of a problem.

I stuff my other clothes in one of the shopping bags, dispose of the rest, and hurry out to meet Quince.

He's already dressed and reading one of the movie posters as he waits. We had found a cloak for him, too, but his is black and doesn't have any fur on it, faux or otherwise.

"What are we going to do with our clothes?" I ask, holding up the bag.

He turns and lowers his hood. "Leave them here."

I raise an eyebrow.

"Someone will report them to the staff and they'll put the clothes in the lost and found. We can come and get them when this is all done."

I have very little confidence in this plan, but leave my shopping bag next to Quince's under the bench. "How do you know someone won't just take them?" I ask, casting a look back at the bags.

"I don't."

We find a quiet spot outside, away from security cameras.

"Almost time," Quince says, his jaw tense as he pockets his phone.

"No going back from here," I whisper to myself, steeling my nerves for what is to come. We both lift our hoods over our faces and embrace.

I take one more look around at the back parking lot of the Duluth movie theater. It's starting to snow, and the snowflakes sparkle in the gleam from the streetlights in the parking lot.

Then, together, we travel to the place where, if the first part of the plan has gone off without a hitch, we should see the moonstone that will take us to the Unseelie Court in time for the Winter Solstice Festival.

At the Winter Solstice Festival

The snow around the moonstone in front of us is trampled. To me, it looks as if more than two people had been walking around it, but I'm not skilled in tracking, so I could be wrong. Maybe Sean and Shannon did a lot of pacing before they traveled to the Winter Solstice Festival.

Quince takes heart at seeing all the footprints in the snow. "They were here," he whispers, his breath puffing out in clouds of mist. "Step one, done. Now, for us to join them."

The next part of the plan is also the least predictable. We know Nightglade intends to bring out Maeve and Aspen for their public execution, but we don't know when he will do it, so we intend to arrive early in case he decides to start the festival with bloodshed.

"Have you been practicing your fire fists?" Quince asks, turning to me. He's obviously thinking ahead to step three.

"We've been together for days and you're only asking me that now?"

His smile is sheepish. "I didn't want you to feel pressured any more than you already were."

"I think I've mostly got the hang of it now," I tell him, thinking of Kieran's face with its permanent "better than thou" expression. "New inspiration has helped."

"Oh–good." He looks only a fraction relieved. "Let's head to the Unseelie Court, then. You first."

Right. I've been trying to forget this part of the plan. I've never traveled by moonstone on my own to somewhere I've never been before. Sean and Shannon had me practice using the moonstone behind their house almost every week since October, but I'd only ever traveled to places I was familiar with in Elfaeme. We couldn't exactly have me popping into the Unseelie Court on a regular basis.

"You can do this, Eevee," Quince says, noticing my hesitation as I stare at the moonstone shimmering in front of me. "I'll follow you as soon as I can."

"Yeah." I can barely breathe but I force a smile on my facc.

"Just picture the court exactly how we've

described it to you. The moonstone will take care of the rest. You've got to trust it to do what it's made to do."

"Are you telling me I need to trust inanimate objects harder?" I ask, thinking of Scamp's advice.

Quince chuckles. "Maybe? How about you trust yourself while you're at it?" He kisses my temple, then adjusts the hood of my cloak.

"Now that we're here, I'm not sure I'm ready," I say to him, ashamed and glad of the privacy the hood gives me. Heat floods my cheeks.

"Eevee."

"I don't want to mess this up. There's a real chance none of us will get out of this alive."

My whole body shakes uncontrollably.

"You don't have to do this, you know," Quince says, enveloping me in his arms so my body quivers against his. Had he heard what I said to myself before we left the movie theater parking lot? "I thought we made it clear when we were planning for tonight. If at any point any of us can't continue with the plan or choose not to, we will adjust."

"Sean does like all his contingency plans," I say in a muffled voice, my face buried in his chest.

"Yeah, he does. So if you can't go on or choose not to, Sean already has a plan for that. It's okay."

"I don't really have a choice, though, do I?" I ask bitterly, pulling away. "Nightglade took that from me when he kidnapped my birth parents and Amelia. And now Cam and Maggie."

"No," Quince replies, his voice firm. "No,

Eevee. He's taken a lot from you, but he didn't take your power of choice. Only you can choose whether you want to do something about the game he's playing."

"The dangerous game."

"Yes, it's dangerous. The stakes are high, not just for those he kidnapped. But it doesn't all fall on you."

I can't meet his eyes. "I know. Or, at least, part of me knows. It's just…I want to do this for you and other fae who are children of both courts. My family's lives are not the only ones on the line. I don't–don't want to disappoint you."

A tear drops into the snow at my feet.

"Oh, Eevee." Quince moves to hug me again, but I back away. "Don't you know? Whether you go to the festival tonight or not, I won't hold it against you. That's too much pressure to put on anyone."

My limbs lighten, as if they've been released from invisible chains I didn't know I'd been carrying these last few months.

"Really?"

"Really really."

I raise my chin and straighten my shoulders, then wipe the tears from my cheeks. "Thank you for saying that." I hold my breath, then let it out slowly. "But I'm doing this." I quickly kiss his cheek.

Marching forward, I picture the Unseelie Court how Sean, Shannon, and Quince had described it to me, holding the image securely in my mind as I bend down to touch the moonstone.

I know immediately, with a sense of accomplishment blooming in my heart, that I've done it. The Unseelie Court appears around me, and a feathery fae nods at me as I materialize next to the moonstone. I'm underground, inside a spacious cavern in the snow-topped mountains, and despite all the bodies in here, the air is cool. As I walk away from the moonstone, trying my best to stand upright and not gasp like a fish out of water, my senses are bombarded by all the noise and smells. The spicy scent of cinnamon mingles with the odor of pine. Everywhere, on every surface, are candles. The trees, which seem to be growing out of the cave floor even with the lack of sunlight, are laden with food that fae grab at and eat.

It has the air of a festival. Except for the cages.

From the stone ceiling, among the stalactites, hang wooden cages, each large enough for a person to fit inside. And most of them are occupied. My insides turn icy at the sight of them. Some of the prisoners are shaking the bars, shouting down at the crowd below, their pleas lost in the cacophony of the crowd.

Most of the prisoners, though, are barely visible from the ground, their bodies curled tight on the floor of their cages, their backs pressed against the bars.

I resist the urge to fly up there and find Amelia, Cam, and Maggie.

Tugging my hood down further, I wander around the cavern, keeping an eye out for Sean and Shannon, when a thought occurs to me. They'll also be in disguise, now that their connection to me has been revealed to Abscons. Crap. What do I do now? How will I know they're in position and ready for stage three of the plan?

I spot Quince's black cloak among the crowd, but I don't dare make any sign that I know or recognize him. I watch as he tilts his head up to gaze at the cages like I did. He must see something he doesn't like, because he sways on the spot and stumbles over to a chair.

Looking up in the direction Quince had been gazing, I clap my hands to my mouth.

Myksa and Jerry are imprisoned together in one of the cages, but theirs has bars of what I'm assuming is iron. Not a trace of Myska's usual cheerfulness is left on her face. Nor does she seem to have any of her anxious energy. She looks small and pale, slumped in Jerry's arms. Jerry's condition is even worse. He has a black eye, and dried blood is crusted on his face and neck. His wings, nearly identical to Quince's, are missing many feathers, like someone had plucked them, and the few feathers that remain are bent and ruffled. Below them, fae jeer up at their cage, their faces filled with malice.

So they've paid the price for helping their son escape. Whatever Nightglade had told the court about them is effective. I don't see anyone, aside from myself and Quince, who is upset to see Jerry and Myska caged above us. Oh, Quince. I can only imagine the guilt he's feeling for leaving them.

"How are we expected to get up there?" I overhear someone whisper. "This plan has so many holes it could be Swiss cheese." Interesting. There are others who have plots afoot tonight? Something about the voice is familiar to me, but I can't place it. I strain to hear more.

"I dunno," someone replies, a different voice. Now I know who they are, but I can't believe it. "Wait," the second voice says. "Is that freaky-looking guy with the goat eyes looking at us again? Yeesh, those eyes creep me out."

I whirl around, taking a risk and lifting my hood to study the fae milling around me. My heart is beating fast. It couldn't be. And yet...

There! Walking away from me are two figures, one tall and slouching to seem smaller than they are, and the other stylishly dressed with barrettes in her hair that match her outfit.

Cam and Maggie are *here*, and not as prisoners, but dressed to look like fae! Resting on Cam's back is a pair of bright red wings that look like a dragon's, all shimmery in the candlelight, and Maggie has a fox tail, with matching fox ears poking out of her Afro.

I skirt through the crowd, holding my breath, and draw up next to them.

"What are you guys doing here?" I hiss out of the corner of my mouth, equal parts relieved to see them and scared for the danger they're in.

Cam jumps as if they've seen a ghost and Maggie clasps a hand to her heart.

"Don't scare us like that, E!" she says, pulling me and Cam over to the shadows of a large pine tree.

"Don't scare *you*? How about don't scare *me*! Do you know how worried I was when I got back to Duluth today to find out you guys were MIA? Couldn't you have at least sent a message?"

"Sean and Shannon didn't think any message we sent would be safe. Anything we said would have had some revealing information in it, and they didn't want to risk 'any more than Eevee and Quince already have,' as Sean put it," Cam says, drawing air quotes around Sean's words.

I have an overwhelming urge to throttle Sean and Shannon. "Stick to the plan," they'd told me in their letter. "Don't do anything stupid." Apparently they decided not to follow their own advice. "Where are they?" I ask, lifting the edge of my hood again to look around.

"To your left, over by the tree with the pink cakes on it," Cam whispers. "That's Shannon."

I steal a glance over at the tree. Next to it, pink cakes in each hand, is a fae I never would have picked out as Shannon, even with the batlike wings. He must be wearing a wig because his silvery blonde hair is hidden. Instead, he sports short, spiky hair with blue tips. He smiles widely at something a fae next to him says and stuffs one of the cakes in his mouth.

"And Sean?" I ask quietly.

"Straight ahead," Maggie answers. "The one in–er–well, you'll see."

I look, then lower my hood. "No way," I say, grinning. "Sean's in drag?"

"And rocking it, honestly," Cam says approvingly. "I think the feather boa is a nice touch."

I want to look again, but turn toward Cam and Maggie instead. "So they brought you guys here? Why?"

"Amelia," Maggie whispers. "They wanted our help freeing her and getting her out of here. Only we didn't know she'd be one of many. I wish we could save them all!"

"Nor did we know the cage would be attached to the ceiling," Cam says, fiddling with the edge of their shirt.

"No offense, I love you both, but what can you two do to save Amelia that Sean, Shannon, Quince, or I couldn't?"

Maggie leans forward, opening the vest she was wearing to reveal the pockets in it, all stuffed with three daisy chain bracelets. "As soon as they give us the signal, we're supposed to break out Amelia, then put these on her and ourselves and run. If they don't meet us after a certain amount of time, then we're supposed to all turn one article of clothing inside out."

"Uh. What?"

Cam shrugs. "They said it's a crude way to leave Elfaeme but that it'll do in a pinch. But they can't promise we'll end up back where we came from."

"And you guys agreed to do this?" I ask, amazed especially at Cam.

"We weren't aware of how shaky the plan was

when we agreed to it," Cam admits, looking briefly up at the cages.

The only way they're getting up there is by flying. I have my part of the plan to put in motion as soon as Maeve and Aspen are brought out, but Quince...

"Quince might be able to help you guys," I whisper. "I'll tell him you're here. He's wearing a black cloak. Then I need to go there." I point to Nightglade's throne, which is hewn from stone and looks almost like it grew out of the cave floor fully formed.

Nightglade sits, erect, on the seat of his throne, an ornate silver crown on his head, quite different from the simple circlet he had worn when I first met him. His steely eyes are cold as he surveys the jam-packed cavern.

I pass by Quince, pausing briefly to tell him about Cam and Maggie, then continue winding my way around the cave, keeping a careful eye on the throne.

Is Nightglade carved from stone as well? He hardly moves. Only his eyes show signs of life, flicking back and forth as if looking for something. A shiver trickles down my back. Or someone.

My palms break out in a cold sweat when those eyes flick toward where I stand and—maybe I'm being paranoid—but it feels like they linger on me for a fraction of a second.

I turn away, wiping my palms on my cloak.

Then someone claps, and gasps ripple through the crowd. The candlelight throughout the whole cavern dims and I swivel back to face the throne.

Illuminated by magic in two circles of cool, blue light, are Maeve and Aspen. My birth parents. My eyesight goes blurry with tears.

They both look awful. But now that I'm looking at Maeve from a distance, I can see why some fae react strongly when they see me. She and I have the same face; the only difference is the markings on our temples. Mine are orange flowers and hers are red roses the color of blood. Her face is hollowed out, though, gaunt, and pale. Despite how frail she looks, she stands proud, shivering in the torn rags they've clothed her in.

Next to her, Aspen lies prone on the ground. For a second I'm frozen in fear, worried he is dead and we're too late, but then, with wobbly arms, he pushes himself to his knees and sits hunched forward, his blonde hair falling limply over his eyes. It's caked with something. Dirt, or dried blood. Maybe both. He looks close to death, trembling there on the ground.

Between them stands Nightglade, joined by Ilinor. Nightglade slowly claps his gloved hands and the festival-goers lapse into captivated silence, all eyes on their former queen and her lover.

"I have promised retribution," Nightglade says in a voice like a winter's night. He speaks quietly, but his words carry through the underground chamber. "Retribution for crimes committed against myself, and against the Unseelie Court."

This should be when I run up to him and raise my fist of fire. But I'm rooted to the spot.

"My father wants a clean slate," Ilinor calls out, her spidery fingers splayed out as she gestures with open arms. If she's going for a welcoming appearance, she's failing. She can't keep the predatory pride from her face.

Nightglade nods to her. "Until the past wrongdoings have been wiped away, my *true* daughter Ilinor cannot be the heir to the throne."

He knows, then, that I'm not his daughter. I wonder when he found out?

Nightglade looks out at the crowd, as if weighing their loyalty. "I want an heir of mine to take the throne after me, don't you?"

The crowd murmurs, then roars its approval. He waits for them to quiet down.

"Her ties to the throne must be erased." One of his arms moves in a regal fashion to indicate Maeve, who refuses to look at him.

"His ways are not the only way," Maeve calls out in a voice that sounds like it hurts her to talk.

"The curse of the revoked crown has been invoked," Nightglade intones over Maeve. "Her power is waning. Now we as a court will finally be able to embrace our future, a future where the Unseelie can show their strength."

"No!" My limbs unfreeze and I fly above the crowd, landing in front of Nightglade and Ilinor and pulling off my hood. Nightglade looks unsurprised at my appearance, but Ilinor's eyes widen and she moves forward as if to grab me.

I stare at Nightglade and raise my fist in the air.

"It's her," I hear someone whisper. "The one who wants to steal the throne from Nightglade."

Out of the corner of my eye, I can see Maeve watching me.

Then my fist bursts into flame.

Nightglade and Ilinor freeze, just like we'd planned. I see Shannon in the crowd, his wig askew, with a white light emanating from him just like it had in the wyvern tunnels beneath Crystal Lake.

"We have thirty seconds at most!" Sean calls. He stands behind Shannon, guarding him with knives of ice in both hands, looking fierce in high heels.

I turn to Maeve. "You heard him. We need to get you and Aspen out of here. Now."

Why isn't she meeting my eyes?

"Maeve, please, we don't have time–"

"I can't come with you," she says.

In my peripheral vision I can see Quince flying Maggie up to one of the cages.

"Shannon's power only affects Nightglade and Ilinor, but it won't last much longer. We need to move before it wears off."

"My beautiful, brave daughter," she whispers.

"Stay back!" Sean says, and I hear grunts and scuffles.

Behind them, the crowd parts to let Maggie and Cam through. They're each holding one of Amelia's arms. All fae who try and approach them start scratching at their bodies vehemently.

"Please," I say, turning my attention back to Maeve, weeping in relief for Amelia's safety and because I can't understand why Maeve is resisting my help. I move closer to her. "This is the only way we can save you. I want to get to know you, to be a—"

"Don't," she says, meeting my eyes for the first time. Her are full of torment. "Don't say it."

"—family," I finish.

"I can't hold it any longer!" Shannon shouts. The white light emanating from him fades and he slumps to the ground.

Then multiple things happen at once.

Nightglade and Ilinor unfreeze. To them, it will have seemed like only a second has passed, rather than thirty. But they recover quickly. Nightglade reaches for Maeve, sparks of ice flying from his fingertips, his expression manic.

Sean kneels next to Shannon and whistles. From some hidden nook of the cavern I hear the same keening cry I had heard at Sean and Shannon's place. A young wyvern swoops down out of the darkness and lands next to the twins. Sean helps his brother onto its back. Shannon is barely conscious, but Sean sits behind him, adjusts his skirt, and whispers something to the wyvern. It takes off and zooms away before anyone can do anything to prevent it.

On the ground, Aspen lets out an anguished moan. "Maeve, no!"

I turn to see Nightglade's hands on her shoulders, her body immobile.

No, not immobile.

Stone.

"You!" I move toward Nightglade, but Ilinor steps between us. Nightglade sneers at me, his features twisted with hatred.

"It's time we sorted out the Quince situation," she says, raising her hands. In Elfaeme, she doesn't have nails, she has claws.

"Like hell it is," I growl.

"Maeve," Aspen whimpers. He's crawling toward where she stands, frozen in stone, her face downcast. He's shoved out of the way by Folsom, who throws himself at her feet, sobbing. I should probably be surprised that he's here and crying on Maeve's stone feet, but I can't feel anything right now.

I have less than a second to make a decision. I find Quince in the crowd. He's standing beneath his parents' cage. When he sees me staring at him, he shakes his head.

He's staying with them.

My heart breaking into a million pieces, I dive for Aspen and think of home.

On the Run

"Unless we manage to remove Nightglade as Unseelie King, he'll always use his power and influence to track us down and kill us, Eevee. Just like your mom feared."

"My birth mom," I remind Aspen automatically, my whole body numb. "For now, we're safe. That's enough."

We've been driving non-stop, staying at various hotels under different aliases. This is a common discussion for us. It's like Aspen and I, after years apart, are unsure or unwilling to talk about anything else. We have our hatred of Nightglade that unites us.

He frowns at me. "We're not safe, we're on the

run. You should be in school, finishing up the last half of your senior year, preparing to go to college so you can become a vet tech."

I laugh, but it has no humor in it. "You remained hidden for nearly two decades," I tell him, my voice cold, distant. This harsh, unforgiving person, it isn't me. I regret the tone of my words as soon as I see him flinch and look out the passenger side window.

"It's not living," I hear him murmur. I don't know if he meant for me to hear. His voice is weary. "It's not life. It's survival."

Fine, I think to myself as we pass a car on the freeway. A "Welcome to Iowa" sign stands on the side of the road. *Then we'll survive.* The memory of seeing Maeve transform into a stone statue, a month ago already, of Nightglade's face sneering at me from behind Ilinor, threatens to overtake me. My hands tremble, and I grip the steering wheel, my lips pressing together in a hard line.

He's not going to do that to anyone else. Not me, not my friends, not any more of my family. I glance at the man next to me in the car, my birth father who I still know so little about, despite our near-constant time together lately. No, not even him.

I will survive, I think grimly. I will survive, and I will someday make Nightglade regret that I got away.

Someday soon.

A Note from the Author

I'm a child of adoption. It is as much a part of who I am as my hair color, my allergies, and my propensity for telling bad jokes when tired.

Like Eevee, my adoptive family was and is warm, welcoming, and wonderful. In that sense, I am lucky.

Not everyone who is adopted has the same experience, though. If you know someone who is adopted, be kind. Help them trust harder in humanity.

There are many resources available online about adoption if you want to learn more about the experiences and trauma children of adoption go through.

Scamp
(Chapter 1)

Eevee and Olearia Talk
(Chapter 6)

Sean and Shannon Dress "Like Humans"
(Chapter 12)

Quince Answers Eevee's Message
(Chapter 15)

Acknowledgments

I never start my acknowledgements without mentioning my editor, Laura Cossette. Laura, your ability to tear apart my writing to make it better never ceases to amaze me. Thank you.

I also want to thank my husband, Ty, and my kids, Gavyn and Chase. Maybe I would have finished this book earlier without you, but without you, my life would not be as rich and wonderful as it is. I love you all half an infinity plus one.

Like with *Finding Fae*, I must thank the real Sean and Shannon for letting me steal your names (and little bits and pieces of your personalities) so I could make intriguing characters for Quince's cousins. It was so fun including them more in this book.

To all the friends and family I'm so lucky to have in this crazy thing we call life: thank you for your enthusiasm and your support of my writing.

About the Author

El Holly loves to write, especially books full of adventure and whimsy. When she isn't writing, teaching, or "mom-ing," you can find her sipping on coffee or taking her dog, Mack, on walks in Minnesota. Like Eevee, she is adopted. Unlike Eevee, her birth parents are not fae (that she knows of).

Follow the author for updates on new releases

Facebook:
http://www.facebook.com/elhollywrites

Website:
http://elhollywrites.com

Amazon Author Page:
http://www.amazon.com/author/elholly

Instagram:
http://www.instagram.com/elhollywrites

I'd love to hear from you!
eholly42@gmail.com